Endorse

The Mescalero Pro[ject has a] dense, intricate plot; characters you believe in and care about passionately; language that is vivid and fresh - a sustained pleasure to read. But this page-turner does much more than entertain: it teases you into thought, planting questions that stay with you long after you've put the book down. What hidden resources in the human spirit can change us in unexpected ways? What forces can threaten to turn a society into a mob? What can cause the opposite? His first novel, Mr. Buchs writes with the grace and confidence of a man who's been writing all his life.

--Rhina P. Espaillat
Dominican-born poet, author of: Lapsing to Grace; Where Horizons Go (1998 T. S. Eliot Prize winner); Rehearsing Absence (2001 Richard Wilbur Award winner); Playing at Stillness (2003 National Poetry Book Award winner), and numerous other publications and awards.

Doug Buchs has constructed an intricately imagined world that is self-contained in every sense. Under the great dome, with its own micro-climate, a society based at first on vengeance and horror undergoes an astonishing, but utterly convincing, transformation. Mr. Buchs has written a page-turning story of considerable moral and psychological complexity. The pivotal character of James Stryker is as mysterious and compelling for the reader as for his fellow inmates in the sinister prison known as the Mescalero Project.

--Janette Turner Hospital
Australian-born novelist and author of more than a dozen books, including: The Last Magician (Publishers' Weekly Best 50 Books of 1992), Oyster (NY Times' Editors' Choice and Notable Books List 1998), and most recently, Due preparations For The Plague (Queensland Premiere's Literary Award for Fiction 2003). Janette Turner Hospital is the Carolina Distinguished Professor of English at the University of South Carolina.

The Mescalero Project

by
Doug Buchs

Behler
PUBLICATIONS
California

Behler Publications
California

The Mescalero Project
A Behler Publications Book

Copyright by Doug Buchs 2000
Author photograph courtesy of Lynn Fitzgerald
Cover design by Sun Son – www.sunsondesigns.com

All rights reserved. No part of this book may be reproduced or transmitted in any form or by any means, electronic or mechanical, including photocopying, recording, or by any information storage and retrieval system, without the written permission of the publisher, except where permitted by law.

> This is a work of fiction. Names, characters, places, and incidents either are the product of the author's imagination or are used fictitiously. Any resemblance to actual persons, living or dead, events, or locales is entirely coincidental.

Library of Congress Cataloging-in-Publication Data is available
Control Number: 2004094874

FIRST EDITION

ISBN 1-933016-05-1
Published by Behler Publications, LLC
Lake Forest, California
www.behlerpublications.com

Manufactured in the United States of America

To the two most important women in my life:

My beloved, Merrily, the greatest expression of God's Grace in my life,

For Virginia, who broke my heart by leaving this world before she could see this story she always believed in, in print.

Acknowledgements:

My heartfelt gratitude goes to my wife and first editor, Merrily, and my mentor, Rhina Espaillat, for their honest and tough editing and unwavering support.

Thanks go to the editorial and production staff at Behler, who made the entire process from the author's perspective a joy.

Finally, my thanks to numerous readers for their important insights – particularly Gail, Rob, and Beth of the Hamilton Writer's Group, to Janette Turner Hospital, whose excitement at the premise of the story has sustained me from the beginning, and to Rae Francoeur, who first urged me to write *this* story.

Overhead View of the Mescalero Prison Facility

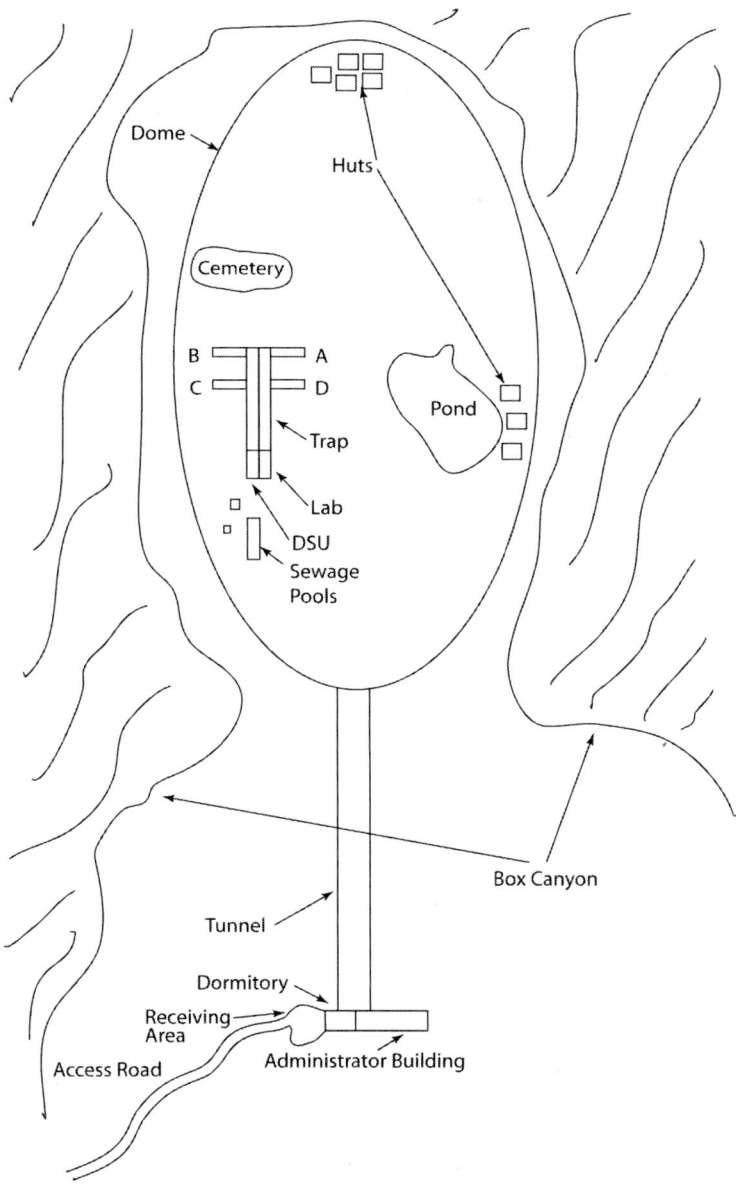

The Mescalero Building Layout

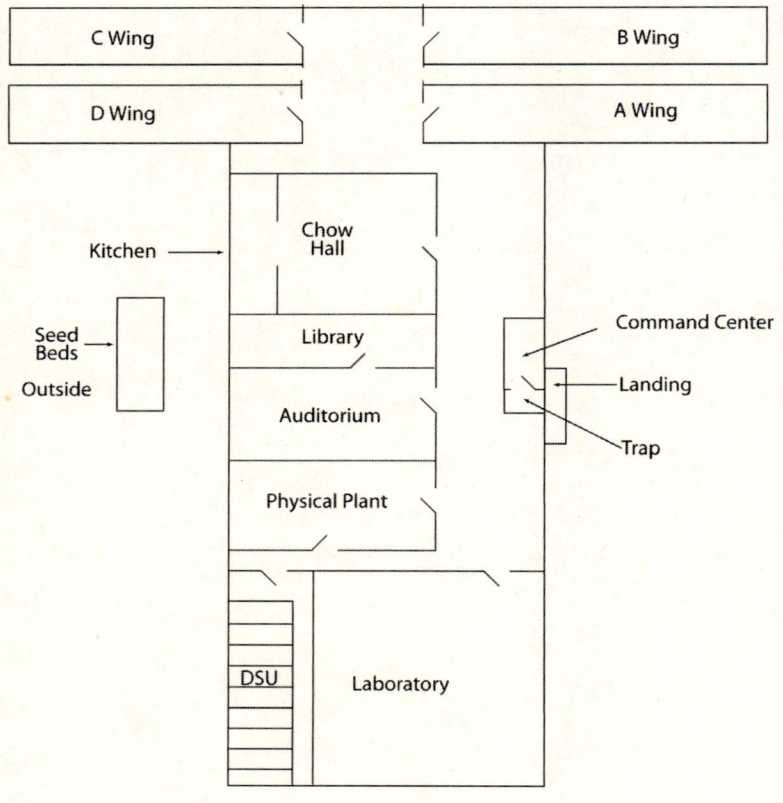

The Trap

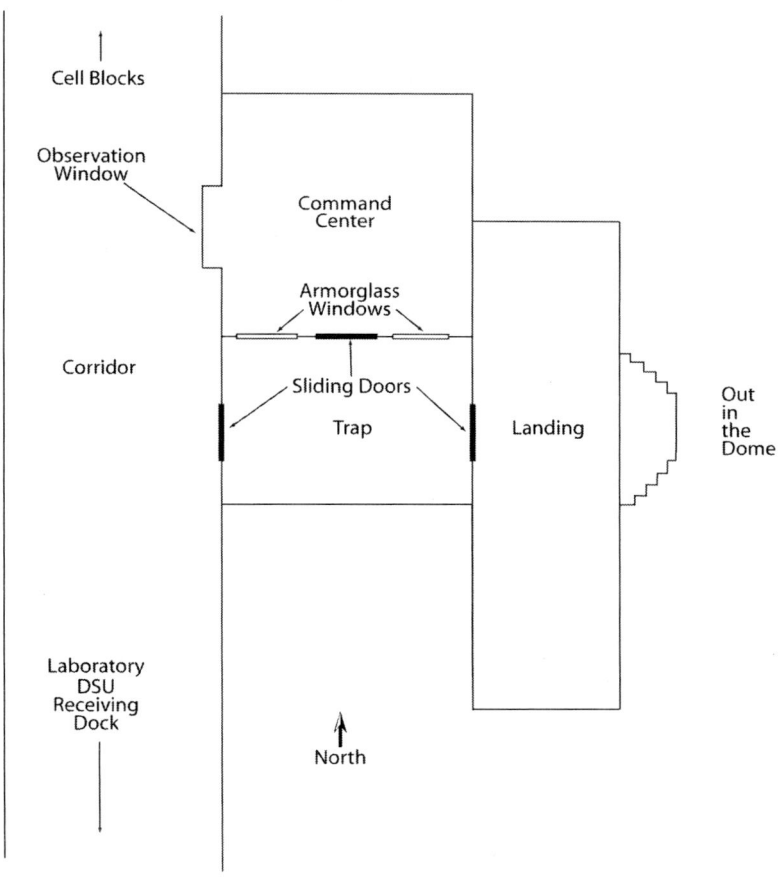

Prologue

After universal adoption of the *Three Strikes, You're Out* policy of 2009, the number of inmates sentenced to life without the possibility of parole increased dramatically. The government, beleaguered by expanding costs threatening to bankrupt the national budget and no sign of the policy losing political popularity, necessitated the development of a radical new prison paradigm by the Ministry of Prisons.

With the advent of inorganic molecular design technology, it had become possible to create *Armorglass* enclosures that spanned a considerable area without losing tensile integrity. A practically indestructible crystal dome could be grown quickly and at a fraction of the cost of traditional construction methods and materials.

In June 2021, the Ministry of Prisons initiated a clandestine experiment, *The Mescalero Project,* a self-sustaining biosphere hidden in a remote area of the desert. The dome at the facility encompassed one hundred fifty acres of reclaimed desert, most of which was reserved for cultivation. An underground passage tube connected the dome to the administrative offices, staff dormitory, and physical plant, five hundred meters away. The latest technology in electronic monitoring systems allowed almost total management of the facility, including its security, with far fewer personnel than previously required.

Two hundred convicted felons, serving life sentences without possibility of parole, had been secretly transferred to the facility, their records at the Ministry having been expunged. They would be the labor raising the livestock and crops, producing the food for the prison.

One of the crops would be *Pax*, a plant discovered in tropical habitat along the equator a century earlier. Promising new research with extracts from the plant was to be accelerated in clinical trials conducted on inmates. The hoped for result: to neutralize the proclivity toward criminal behavior in individuals.

By the end of the first six months of operation, the project appeared as though it would be a model for future prisons everywhere. Then, on January 12, 2022, an intense solar disturbance—geomagnetic solar winds of a greater magnitude than ever before recorded known as *Solares*—occurred, disrupting satellite and landline communications as well as power grids around the globe. Links to the national center disintegrated and vast amounts of data were erased, bringing government agencies in many parts of the world to near chaos.

By 2071, even though communications and power grids had long since been restored, the Ministry of Prisons was unaware that some files had never been retrieved, and The Mescalero Project had been forgotten....

CHAPTER ONE

Moss wasn't more than thirty meters from the entrance but didn't realize it. He stood looking out from the shade of the red rock escarpment that breached the flat desert landscape, arching its spine toward the east. The only irregularity in the smooth sweep of terrain out in front of him was a sandy knoll to the southeast.

He had walked a grid pattern back and forth through the sagebrush and mescal and ocotillo since noon without success. His clothes and the bandana tied about his head were soggy with sweat, and his eyes ached from the scorching sun despite the expensive sun shields he had bought for the trip. There had at least been spots along the access road in from the two-lane, visible now and then, where the wind had bared the shoulder enough to keep him from driving off into the soft sand. But right where his comsat compass confirmed the coordinates shown on the blueprints, there was no sign anything had ever existed here but sand drifts and mesquite, cholla and tumbleweed and saguaro.

In the suffocating late afternoon heat, he busied himself setting up camp, determined to keep doubt from staining his hopes. He rigged a shade break with a tarp off the side of the pickup to two tent poles and set his camp chair and table under it. He had decided not to bother with the tent this first night. He would sleep in the open in his bivouac bag.

The shadows cast by the saguaro stretched farther and farther as the sun slipped lower in the desert sky. He put a pot of water on the camp stove he'd set on the tailgate, and when it came to a boil emptied a pouch of dehydrated beef and vegetables into it. While it simmered and the water thickened to a more or less satisfying broth, he went looking for firewood. It was cold at night in the desert even in June.

When he returned the stew was ready. With a small campfire under way just beyond the shade break, he opened a tube of saltine crackers and sat eating at the table under the tarp.

The landscape was in deepening shadow, the sky turning from sanguine to purple as the sun dropped behind a butte off in the distance to the northwest. He threw a piece of mesquite on the fire now and then, watching the flames dance higher again, casting swirls of sparks up into the rapidly chilling night air. As he dipped saltines into the stew, he was aware of how odd the smell was, the aroma of stew mingled with the odor of a sweat-soaked man and the bone-bleached scent of the desert sand.

This was the first time since starting out that he'd taken a break of any duration. All at once he realized how weary he was after a weeklong drive and merciless heat, then crisscrossing acres of spiny desert underbrush on foot and finding nothing. He wondered if he had come on a fool's errand.

He awoke before daylight. The cold desert air had settled on his face and on his ears exposed as they were to the night. Lying there in his bivouac bag, staring up at the glory of the heavens, he became aware of a weight on his hips, like when his cat, Charlemagne, slept on the covers.

He started to get up, but the instant he moved he heard the unmistakable sound of a rattlesnake. Moss became as still as a stone, feeling the movement of the snake on top of him, as it wound itself into a new coil. His heart was pounding and he could hardly take a breath, terrified the snake would strike his face or throat from where it was coiled over his groin. He waited, taking the shortest of breaths, trying not to move, though he was starving for air. He realized it probably crawled up there to stay warm during the night, as he tried to think what to do. Coming daylight began to reveal the shapes around him. Moss slowly lifted his head high enough to see down the length of the bivouac bag. The snake, with a girth as thick as his forearm, was coiled two feet away, staring at him.

He slid his forearms slowly up to his shoulders. If he felt the snake move, he froze and waited. Once he could reach the zippers, he began undoing them, on one side then the other, trying to keep his pelvis as level and still as possible. When they were undone enough to throw up a block with the upper half of the bivouac bag, he took a deep breath and made his move. The thump of the rattler striking at the thick insulated flap sounded like a fighter's jab hitting a heavy bag. Moss scrambled out of the jumble of material and sprinted a half-dozen meters away. He looked back and saw the big rattler slither off in the opposite direction, disappearing into the sagebrush. He rekindled the fire and stood warming himself, breathing in the sharp scent of mesquite, aware that his quivering stomach and the shaking in his hands had little to do with the cold.

As the sun edged above the horizon to the northeast, he noticed something unusual: A dozen or more saguaro cacti stood in a line—much too straight a line to be natural—and they were spaced evenly apart. He walked to the nearest one and began to grin. It wasn't a cactus at all, but a ventilator made to look like one. It had to be one of the ventilators for the underground office complex of The Mescalero Project.

Moss ran back to the pickup and grabbed the building plans to see where the entrance was in relation to the ventilators. It would be just about where the sandy knoll was. He hurried over to it and worked his way up the loose, sloughing sand to the top, where something caught his attention. He knelt down, brushing and sweeping the sand away with his hands, exposing what he guessed was the corner of a roof. It had to be the roof of the stairwell to the complex. Grinning more broadly, as he turned to climb down off the knoll, he spotted a flash of light to the northeast. He squinted, looking in that direction. There, hardly visible, its crystal surface camouflaged by fifty years of sand dust build-up, was the dome, hidden in a box canyon that ran north and south, only the southern tip of the biosphere evident. If he hadn't been standing there just then to catch the reflected sunlight, he would not have noticed it. With renewed enthusiasm, he headed back to the pickup to secure the camp and grab something to eat, eager to get started excavating the door to the stairwell.

He ate quickly and as soon as he finished and had taken a long drink from his canteen, he grabbed his shovel and went back over to the knoll. He shoveled all morning, in the stifling heat, cursing the blisters blossoming in the palms of his hands.

By the time the sun was directly overhead, the doorway was uncovered enough to try the latch. It was locked and the solid steel door was too much to pry open with any tools he had, but he saw that it opened outward. So, in the middle of the afternoon, with all wheel drive set on the pickup and a chain hooked to the door handle, Moss put the pickup in gear and wrenched the door open. Then, he grabbed the prism lantern and the calcion torch he'd bought, locked the rest of his gear in the pickup, and stepped across the threshold. The feeling of butterflies in his belly was identical to the day he began his first archaeological dig his junior year in undergraduate school.

He set the beam of the torch to broad configuration and started down the stairs. It was wonderfully cool as he descended. Cobwebs hung thick from the ceiling, like dirty lace, swaying with his every move. He wouldn't have been able to see his hand just inches from his face without the panoramic illuminating flood of the torch in the thick darkness of the chamber.

At the bottom of the stairwell to his right was the door to the offices, and to his great relief, it wasn't locked. He crossed the threshold cautiously. The first, most obvious thing was the musty odor. He set the lantern on a desk covered in a layer of dust and lit it, scanning the room quickly in the brilliant light. Monitor screens at the workstations stared back at him blankly.

Torch in hand, he moved around the room. At one point he glanced down and noticed the tracks he was leaving in the dust. He hadn't considered this before and wondered, then walked back to the door and shined his torch out into the tunnel. No prints but his. This put him more at ease. He resumed his exploration of the room, rummaging through desk drawers, flipping through documents and manuals. It was clear the computer system monitored and managed the security and life support in the complex, and he was impressed by the sophistication of the electronic technology back in the '20s.

At the back corner of the room, to the left, a door opened into a restroom equipped with an archaic cremative commode like the ones he remembered using in grade school. He needed to piss and set the torch down on the sink. When he had finished, he pushed the flush button and the drum in the bottom of the toilet made a half rotation enclosing the fluid inside, and he heard the incinerator ignite. A moment later the drum turned open again, empty and dry, ready for the next use. He turned on a faucet in the sink. It still worked, though the water ran black. He left it running to see if it would clear. As he moved about, he kept thinking he had missed something, overlooked something obvious, but in his excitement he sloughed it off.

At the opposite side of the room a hallway led to a door marked, Warden Samuel Smalley. The door complained with unnerving squeals as Moss pushed it open. Right then, what had been gnawing at him came clear: The toilet could not have worked unless there was electrical power. He quickly aimed his torch at the wall near the door and found a light switch, pressed it, and the lights came on. He had mistakenly assumed all along that there would be no power at Mescalero after all these years.

He glanced around the room. There had been a fire, and it was deliberate, all the file and desk drawers open; stacks of papers and data storage wafers in a heap on the floor in varying stages of incineration. Moss was certain many of his questions would be answered examining those files or what was left of them, but that could wait. His primary goal was to get into the biosphere. Someone might still be alive.

Before leaving, Moss examined the electronics panel adjacent to the desk. It was disconnected. He plugged it in and the panel lit up like a Ferris wheel at a carnival. The lights flickered on and off as though the panel was having an electronic orgasm, then stabilized, and a sultry female voice spoke, identifying herself as *Primary*. Moss gave his name and asked her for a report on the status of the facility's life support and security. Primary stated that she did not recognize his voice and could not comply without a corneal verification. Moss smiled, knowing he would be denied but enjoying the encounter anyway, and complied, first blowing the dust off the scanner, then pressing his eye against the sensor lens. A few seconds passed, and as he expected, Primary explained that she could not provide him with that information, as he was not on the approved access list.

He was eager to get to the dome. Any further attempts to gain entry to the computer would have to wait. As he stepped out of the office and started back out to the main office area, he noticed a black stain on the tile floor that trailed out into the hall. He guessed that whoever lit the fire spilled some of the fuel used to start it. Out in the main office he turned the lights on and shut the prism lantern off. He went back to the sink in the restroom and shut off the faucet, the water running clear now, then went to the entrance to the offices and stepped over the threshold, back into the blackness of the tunnel.

He found the switch for the tunnel lights and pressed it, but they did not come on. And he discovered the power cells on the three electrocarts plugged in just beyond the stairwell were dead, too. There was no power in the tunnel. He traced the conduit from the light switch to a junction box that routed power out to the biosphere. The fuses were missing, and the high voltage wires leading from the junction box to the biosphere had been cut. He went back into the office to get the prism lantern, then started along the tunnel. The question of why the power to the biosphere had been cut faded in his growing excitement as he walked through the dark toward the dome.

The tunnel was constructed of ten-foot diameter sections of reinforced aggregate culvert. A steel grating had been set three feet above the base of the tube, for a flat surface wide enough for an electrocart to travel on. Groundwater seeping from the seams trickled beneath the grating. The echoes of Moss's steps against the grating and the water dripping interrupted each other as he made his way along the tunnel. Each time a cobweb broke across his face in the darkness behind the torchlight, his skin crawled.

The blueprints had indicated that the bulkhead into the dome consisted of two great doors resembling the vault doors in financial depositories, the space between them being a spectral light-cleansing chamber. When he got to the outer door he was surprised to find it wasn't locked. The manual locking mechanism moved freely in and out. But when he tried to open it, it would not budge. He switched the beam on the torch to narrow focus mode so he could inspect the seam of the huge steel door, thinking it might just be corroded. Instead, he found the door had been sealed with a prellenium iodide weld.

Moss cursed under his breath, slapping the door with the palm of his hand. Another delay. This was the only way into the dome. Cutting the seal with a laser wand was no problem; he'd learned how to use one of them before he was twelve on the farm. But he was going to need a couple of canisters of prellenium iodide to do it, and that meant a five-hour drive back to Felicity, the closest town. Then, when he got back, he'd have to lug everything down two flights of stairs and the half-mile up the tunnel. That meant the best part of another day before he could actually enter the biosphere.

He set his torch down to turn the prism lantern on, when all at once he yelped and jumped backwards, tripping over himself, and falling to the grating. The light beam, slicing through the blackness, revealed vacant eye sockets above a gaping, grinning jaw. Moss scrambled to his feet quelling the childish impulse to run. The hair on his neck bristled as he groped for the lantern and lit it. Light filled the tunnel and he now saw a second skeleton, lying next to an electrocart. He backed up to the wall opposite the great bulkhead door and leaned against it, shaking, staring at the scene, trying to collect himself.

When the initial shock of the scene passed, Moss relaxed somewhat and began trying to piece together what had happened there. The skeleton he had first seen was on its back with the hose and laser wand of a welding unit beneath it. The one next to the electrocart lay on its back, too. A few inches away from its right hand there was an automatic pistol. Looking closer, he saw that a good deal of the back of the skull was missing. It appeared to him that the one laying over the welding hose had welded the bulkhead door shut, and the other one killed him when he was done. Why he would've then killed himself, though, he had no idea, and as he looked around, neither the clothing they wore, rotted almost entirely away, nor anything else, offered any clue. He pulled on the hose of the laser wand, slipping it out from under the skeleton, to see if the canisters had any prellenium iodide left, but they were spent.

Reluctant to drive to Felicity but seeing no way around it, he picked up the calcion torch, shut off the prism lantern, and started back down the tunnel.

CHAPTER TWO

When the power goes off, Smalley is sitting on the toilet, reading an old issue of *Prison: Issues and Answers*. As fast as he can in absolute darkness, he cuts short what he's doing, pulls up his pants, and gropes his way back to his office across the hall. Auxiliary power brings the lights back on just as he opens the door. Primary is unaffected by the outage, its separate emergency power cells engaging automatically. Smalley requests an explanation for the power outage from Primary. Information necessary to answer the question is not yet available, she says.

Smalley's clothes are disheveled, after dressing in the dark. He undoes his belt and rearranges his pants and shirt properly, then tightens the belt again. He is about to call Big Red Collier at the Cayuse power plant when Primary reports the alarm in the dome has been activated. Seconds later, it announces it has initiated Lockdown Sequence. The dedicated comlink to the dome is flashing.

"What's goin' on, Jack?" Smalley says, knowing it would be Caldwell, his chief of security in the dome.

"We got a problem, Sam," he says in his resonant bass voice. "Some of Briscoe's goons got the drop on one of my men. Got his sidearm and his AR25. Weapons fired. Knowing those guys, I'm guessing he's dead."

"Christ, Jack, lock down! Lock—"

"Already in progress, Sam."

"How the hell did that happen, Jack? Who screwed up?"

"Hey, Sam, give us a break, huh? It was pitch dark in here."

"Right. Sorry. How many, and where?"

"The infirmary. There's four of them."

Smalley begins a run through camera stations on his terminal with one hand, searching for the laboratory visuals while he talks with Caldwell. As usual, he has difficulty using the icon touch tray, pressing more than one at a time and having to reenter directions, the fingers of his broad, stubby hands are so thick.

"You okay, Jack?"

"Yeah, sure, but Jesus, Sam, they got hostages."

"Who?"

Caldwell hesitates.

"They got Abby, Sam, and the nurse, Maria. Don't know yet if there's anyone else."

A long silence on the comlink before Smalley speaks again.

"Where are you right now, Jack?"

"Command Center."

"Can you see anything on the monitor? I'm still trying to bring it up out here."

"Yeah," he says, "I can."

Smalley is fumbling, frantic to bring the lab visual up on screen.

"What, Jack? What's goin' on? For Chris'sakes, tell me!"

"Sam, they're...uh...they're....Geez, Sam, they're all takin' turns at Abby and Maria."

A longer silence.

"Sam?"

"Yeah." Smalley's voice is barely audible now.

"One of 'em just fired at the camera. I got no more visual, but I don't think.... Aw, Sam, God." Caldwell is choking up, trying to suppress the sobs forcing their way to the surface, "Neither one of them were moving, Sam."

"What about audio, Jack? Can you hear—"

"Tried that, Sam. It's dead."

All Caldwell hears is the click when Smalley disconnects.

Smalley knows Primary is in charge of the dome now. No one can get in or out. First chance to disengage—twenty-four hours away. No point in heading for the dome. Locks on the bulkhead doors will be frozen. He paces, pressing his hands against the sides of his head, trying to let it not be true, to make it not true. Jack's wrong. He must be mistaken. It can't be true. Oh, God, please don't let her be dead.

He locks the door and instructs Primary to notify him ten minutes before releasing the dome back to him tomorrow. He'll stand by in his office until then. He tries to busy himself with paperwork; makes a halfhearted attempt to contact Collier at the power plant only to discover the contax lines are dead. He tells Primary to keep trying to find out why the power went down, why contax lines are down. And all the time he has flashes of Abby in the hands of those filth.

"Oh, Daddy, not that again," she says, feigning annoyance. "How many times have we had this discussion?"

She takes his plate from the table after he spears the last piece of turkey. He watches her at the sink, thinking what a fine and beautiful young woman she's become. Reminds him so much of her mother.

"I don't care, Punkin," the warden says, wiping his broad mouth with his napkin. "No matter how safe it is, there's always the chance. Something can happen." *I don't know what I'd do if anything ever happened to her.*

She's facing him, leaning against the counter, and now her annoyance is genuine.

"I'm not your little girl anymore, Daddy. I'm a woman. And this is a terrific opportunity. This is my specialty and—"

"I know, I know," he says, hands in the air, shrugging his husky shoulders.

"—I don't know if I'll ever have another chance like this."

He gets up and walks into the next room, and slumps his short, thickset frame in the easy chair, knowing what is coming. She moves to where he's sitting and sits on the arm of the chair, stroking the few strands of hair on the crown of his head, her eyes soft and pleading—his little girl asking for just one more ride on the carousel. A broad smile forms over his wide, powerful jaw, and it juts out even further, and he melts like he always has.

"I am so grateful you pulled strings to get me the appointment, Daddy. You know that, don't you…how much it means to me?"

She bends down and kisses him on the cheek, and he smiles again.

He has raised Abby and her little brother, Seth, on his own for the past thirteen years, after losing their mother to cancer. He never remarried, wrapping himself up instead in his work and his children, Seth now in his first year at university, and Abby with a master's degree in biopsychology and working toward her doctorate. When she had asked him to see if he could get her an appointment to Mescalero, he tried to say no. He's never been able to do that well with her, but that time he had tried hard and could not dissuade her. And now....

Smalley stops for a minute, rubbing his burly hands as if he's washing them, then up on his feet, pacing from one end of the room to the other. The image flashes across his mind again: Filthy scum, putting themselves in her. Sons of bitches! He collapses back onto the small leather couch against the wall facing his desk.

"Oh, Abby."

"Where is Mommy now, Daddy?" she asks, a puzzled expression on her face.

He pulls out of the funeral home parking lot into traffic, wondering what he should say.

"She's...in Heaven now, Punkin...with Jesus."

"Oh," she says, sitting there, a perfect little lady, straight up in the seat, hands in white gloves tucked between her knees, above patent leather shoes. She cranes her neck to look out at the stores they pass. He hopes it will be enough of an answer. Seth sits silent and sullen in the backseat.

"Will we ever see her again?"

"Of course we will, Punkin. She's waiting for us there."

She thinks about this for a while. Then, as he turns onto their street, she looks up at him, concerned.

"Will we be good enough to go to Heaven, Daddy? As good as Mommy was?"

"Sure we will, Punkin."

Throughout the day and into the night hours, the torment of worry and grief and guilt is relentless. One moment he is sobbing, slumped in his chair, the next screaming curses and slamming his fist on the desk.

There is no relief. The pictures in his mind of them going into her keep coming back. He pounds his head each time they do, desperate to make them go away. He can't stop them. He buries his face, wet and slick, in the couch cushion, heaving in anguish. Sleep never comes, only surreal, searing, desperate visions through the night. Smalley is unaware of it as his anger sinks to a place in his gut he never knew existed, becoming a smoldering rage, spawning things only Hell could conceive. And in the morning, he knows what he will do.

Jack Caldwell is anxious about Sam. He hasn't heard from him since he told him about Abby. It's not like Sam to leave a situation like this unresolved. On the other hand, since Primary has control, there isn't anything he can do until it's ready to disengage. When the contax in the Command Center rings, he is sure it'll be Sam.

"Anything change, Jack?" Smalley speaks in a slow, deliberate manner, as if he were trying to mask the growing rage boiling in his gut.

"No change, Sam," the big man says, running his free hand through thick graying hair. "They're still holed up in the back of the lab. How're you doing?"

"Fine, Jack."

Caldwell is silent for a moment. If his old friend Sam had said okay or all right, something like that, maybe he wouldn't notice, but fine?

"Listen, Jack, are you sure? I mean, could you be wrong about—?"

"Aw, Sam, I wish I was. I reran the tapes three times. I'm pretty sure.

"I just thought—"

"S'cuse me a sec, Sam, I'm getting something on the tactical band from one of my...." Smalley can hear him talking in the background. "Oh, okay. That's good," he says. "And the others?"

"What is it, Jack? What's going on?" he says, hope gushing wildly into the empty pit in his belly.

"My guys just found the pharmacist and the doc. They're okay. Slipped out through a ventilator hatch. No other hostages. But...they confirm what I thought, Sam...about Abby and Maria, I mean."

"Oh," Smalley says almost in a whisper, the certainty that there is no longer any hope, crushing in on him.

"I'm sorry, Sam."

Smalley is silent for what seems to Caldwell a long time, and when he finally does speak the voice does not sound like anyone he ever knew.

"Then I want the bodies, Jack," the warden growls. "Now!" The patient, deliberate tone of moments ago has evaporated. "I don't care what you have to do to get them."

"Sam, you givin' me authority to—"

"Do it," he says. "Get me my baby, Jack."

Jack Caldwell has been chief of security at Mescalero since it opened. A good man, everyone says. Does his job. Tries to be fair. Doesn't taunt or toy with the inmates, and won't tolerate that behavior from his men, though he's sure they do it from time to time. He's known Sam Smalley for years, long before Mescalero, Abby and Seth, too, since they were born. He knows precisely what the warden is saying. If they don't surrender, terminate them. There aren't going to be any deals.

"But Sam—"

"Like I said, Jack, get me the bodies—Abby's first. And make goddamn sure the crematory is pure, scrubbed clean of every particle of the last sonofabitch we did in there. You got that?"

Caldwell acknowledges the order and hangs up, concerned about his old friend, about the ice in his voice. When he carries out the assault on the infirmary, Eddie the Tin Man is the only one left alive, cowering on the floor in a corner of the room, with his hands in the air.

Caldwell notifies the warden when there is less than an hour before *Primary* will disengage.
"Right," Smalley says, and hangs up. He tries several times to get through to Seth again, to tell him about his sister. He cannot. He tries the power plant. No luck. The Ministry of Prisons in the capital. Nothing. From what he can tell, all communications outside Mescalero are inoperative. He queries Primary again on the situation. It still does not know why this has happened. He has to take care of his baby right now. Seth will have to wait. Work will have to wait. He'll keep her ashes on the shelf in his office until a memorial service can be arranged. Yeah, Seth and me. She'd understand, wouldn't she? You'd understand, wouldn't you, Punkin? Huh? He leans back against the wall next to the door, and settles slowly to the floor, hugging a framed photograph of her to his chest, and begins again to sob. Just then Primary announces the first opportunity to disengage the lockdown sequence is in ten minutes.
At the moment the request to disengage comes up on the screen, Smalley in his office and Caldwell in the Command Center enter an affirmative response at the same time, and lockdown status in the dome is neutralized. Smalley heads for the dome. Caldwell meets him at the trap and leads him to where they have Abby. He tries to help the warden lift the body bag up onto a gurney, but Smalley shakes his head almost violently, motioning with his arms spread out, to back away from the body. Caldwell watches him, moving about oddly, unfocused. He hardly recognizes him. What hair he still has, a band just above his ears and around the back of his head, is wild. His face is drawn and grave, his broad, jutting jaw darkened by more than a day's growth of stubble. His eyes are cold and distant. Smalley turns the gurney around and starts to push it out the door.
"Let me help you Sam. Might be tough getting her in the chamber by yourself."

"No, Jack. I'll manage," he says, holding up one hand signaling Caldwell to stay back. "I want to do this alone."

He looks down at the bag that contains his daughter's body, and speaks softly to it as he guides the gurney out into the hall. "Don't want to embarrass you any more than you already have been, Punkin, being stuffed inside this bag by strangers."

One wheel on the gurney squeaks what seems a soft lament for Abby, as the mournful procession of one steers the cart down the corridor to the crematory.

The furnace is ready just as Caldwell had promised. The chamber is the same height as the gurney. Smalley releases the clamps of the thick steel door and swings it open. He longs to unzip the bag to look at her face just once more, kiss her one last time, but he knows: She will be different, ashen, waxy complexion, a gaping laceration across her neck, and the blood. It would steal the memory of her beautiful smile the previous morning.

Jack was right. It is a struggle. But when he's convinced she is properly inside the chamber, that she is not uncomfortable, twisted in some way on the hard ceramic floor, he closes the door and secures the clamps. When he presses the ignition switch, a roar fills the room. He has it in his mind to pray for her, but then he thinks not. God will not hear. God is deaf. And the murderous, churning bile in his belly is too thick now. No more words from his lips or from his heart.

And so he sits on a wooden chair, sobbing, listening to the bellow of the flames in the furnace consume the love of his life. When it is finished and cool enough inside the crematory, much of the day is gone. He vacuums the chamber with great care, and transfers the contents to a large glass jar from the lab. When he leaves the crematory, he carries his daughter's ashes like a newborn, in the crook of his arm. He whispers to the jar as he goes, unaware that the last vestige of his soul he might still have possessed was incinerated with her in the furnace.

Back in his office, in a lucid moment, Smalley thinks to try calling the power plant again to find out why Mescalero is still on auxiliary power. The recording on the line states that all systems are out of service. He keeps trying. Hours pass. At times it appears he has managed to reach someone, but it turns out what he hears are only comsat ghosts, faint echoes fooling the caller like a mirage in the baking desert heat. Then, toward evening, he gets a static-filled opening.

Big Red Collier, superintendent at the Cayuse substation, tells Smalley it is almost impossible for him to get a hold of anyone, either. Intense solares on the sun have disrupted power grids and communications networks everywhere in the country— probably around the planet as well. At this point, he has no idea when power might be restored, but if it is as bad as he has heard, it could be a long time.

"How long is a long time, Red?"

"Don't know what to tell you, Sam. The power grids oughtta come back on line pretty quick, a month at most. But I got a feelin' it could be a lot longer before communications are straightened out."

As he disconnects the contax, Smalley is tantalized by the realization that this is his chance, and much sooner than he had hoped. He opens a drawer of his desk and thumbs through the tabs to Transfer Authorization Forms.

A month after the insurrection, several more solare events have continued to prevent restoration of power or communications. Smalley spends all his time in his office now, engaging in long conversations with Abby's ashes up on the shelf, only leaving to use the toilet or to get something to eat. Even then, he hurries back to his office with the food. He is careless about washing, shaves infrequently. And he has been unable to reach Seth.

For the time being no one can check up on the personnel reassignments he's made. He hopes the confusion throughout the country continues, though he isn't sure it's even necessary. He has often been witness to the incredible logjams, mix-ups, and pure stupidity bureaucracy can generate, even without a nightmare like solar eruptions.

When the phone rings, he is slow to answer, resentful of being disturbed. He knows it will be Caldwell, who pesters him every day.

"Sam, it's me."

"Yes, Jack, I know. What is it?"

"The roster's getting pretty low, Sam. I mean, all the lab people are gone, the cook here in the dome, and I just called maintenance to see about getting one of the servomules repaired but they've been transferred out, too. But now, you—"

"Look, Jack, it's not your job to keep track of who's here or not. You just keep those murderous scum in check, okay? I'll take care of the rest."

He saw it happen. He's the one who told me. He's the one who put her in the body bag, too. He was the one responsible for her safety, for Chris'sakes. He's the head of security. He's the one responsible. He's the one—

"And that's just what I'm doing, Sam."

Sam is brought back to the moment by the powerful bass voice on the line.

"You just shipped more of my men out. How am I supposed to maintain security without—"

"Never mind, Jack, it's just for a few days. Replacements are on the way."

"Aw, horseshit, Sam!" Caldwell says, and slams the contax down.

Smalley gets up and walks around the room. He doesn't want to get Caldwell on the fight. He's not someone you jerk around, but the man is getting edgy about all the transfers. *And he doesn't believe me about the replacements.* He decides to put all communications on his authorization only. A few minutes after he sets the restricted code in Primary, the sultry voice speaks:

"Security is requesting an outside connection to the Ministry. Will you authorize?"

"No."

Smalley's old friend is becoming worrisome to him.

Santos glances over at Caldwell, surprised by the sound of the contax being slammed down.

"Well, I'll be a sonofabitch," Caldwell yells, the veins at each side of his bull neck gorging. "He's put communications into authorization status."

"Sir?"

"Never mind, never mind," he says to Santos brusquely. "Listen, I'm going to the warden's office. I got some things I gotta straighten out with him, pronto."

"Yes, sir," Santos says, feeling awkward beneath the towering figure of his boss, as well as finding himself in the middle of whatever's going on between him and the warden.

"All right, let's see. You and Strong Knife are pullin' a double tonight, right?"

Santos and Strong Knife both nod.

"Well, I won't be back then, for the rest of the shift. You two will have to do the best you can without me." He crouches and ducks a little stepping out into the trap to avoid hitting his head. "I'll relieve you in the morning."

Caldwell walks toward the tunnel at a pace just short of a jog, powerful shoulders and arms churning, heading for Smalley's office. He's decided to have it out with him. When he gets to the door of Smalley's office, he hears Smalley talking to someone and listens.

"You see why, Punkin, don't you?" Smalley says, walking around the room rocking the jar of ashes in his arms like a mother with a colicky baby. "They must be punished for what they did to you...no, I won't kill them, I promise. I'll let them do that themselves." Grinning at what a clever idea it is, he sets the jar back on the shelf. "I'll just lock the dome so they can't get out, and let them loose inside."

Caldwell doesn't hear anything for a moment, then sobbing. A second later a bloodcurdling scream. He barges in without knocking, to find Smalley standing bent over the desktop, his stocky torso heaving with each sob, his arms struggling to keep him from sinking to the floor.

"Sam?"

No response.

"Sam, it's me, Jack," he says, approaching cautiously.

Smalley slowly turns his head and looks up at Caldwell.

"Jesus, Sam, are you all right?"

Smalley doesn't speak. He just stares at Caldwell.

"Sam, what the hell's goin' on? What's happened to you?"

Caldwell steps up to him, motions to the chair, then gently guides him down into it. He reaches for the jar of ashes, thinking to move them somewhere other than right in front of Smalley.

"Get your hands off that! <u>Don't-you-touch-her,</u>" Smalley growls.

"Okay, Sam, okay. Take it easy."

The anger and frustration that brought him charging over from the dome to confront the warden is blunted now by his concern for the pitiful creature in front of him.

"Sam, you can't keep on like this, spending so much time in here alone. Things are falling apart around here, Sam. I'm worried about you."

Smalley sits there, motionless, looking at the floor.

"Maybe you should let the doctor at Western Region HQ take a look—"

"No!" Smalley says emphatically. "I'm not going anywhere."

"But, Sam, you can't go on like this," Caldwell says, pleading, "you're makin' yourself sick. Please, Sam."

The years they've known each other and the friendship win for just a moment. Smalley lets his guard down, certain he can convince his old friend that his cause is a just one.

Jack will understand. I'll bet he'll even help.

He tells Jack everything. But Caldwell doesn't understand. Instead, he is astonished.

"Sam, are you telling me that you're planning to leave these guys loose inside the dome? With no security? That's crazy, Sam. And how does that exact the best revenge?"

"Ohhhhh, Jack!" Smalley says, quivering with excitement. "Think about it. These guys wake up one morning and discover the doors aren't locked. What's the first thing that's going to happen? Every sorry scumbag in there is going to go looking to settle an old score with somebody. But killing's too good for th—"

"Geez, Sam, I could maybe see wantin' to go after the ones who raped Abby, but they're dead, except for Eddie the Tin Ma—"

"Yeah, and they died too quick and too easy, Jack," Smalley says, getting more animated, disturbed by Caldwell sounding like he's defending that scum. "They should'a—"

"—but to throw them all to the wolves, Sam, it ain't right."

"Jack, wait a minute. I don't want to kill them. This is better than that. Just picture it. No connection with the outside world. Never able to sleep, always watching their backs. No explanation for why they've been left alone. Maybe they figure it was a nuclear attack—Armageddon even. And for the ones who don't get their throat cut right away, the wondering—even just the loneliness—is going to make them slowly lose their minds. Don't you see?"

"Yeah, Sam, like you maybe, huh? I don't want any part of it," he says, standing up and moving toward the Primary terminal.

At hearing this, Smalley is overwhelmed by feelings of contempt as well as fear, as he moves next to him.

"I'm disappointed in you, Jack. I thought you of all people would see the justice in it," he says, looking up at his friend of so many years.

Caldwell pulls a plastic card on a chain around his neck up out of his shirt, and starts to insert it into a slot at the terminal.

"What are you doing, Jack?" Smalley says, starting to panic.

"Sam, you're sick. You need help. I can't let you do this. I'm claiming Article 12 authority to relieve you of command until we get this straightened out."

As Caldwell goes to insert the card into Primary's portal, Smalley moves behind him to his desk. He takes a pistol out of the top drawer and fires twice.

When Smalley awakes, Caldwell is lying in front of him, soaking in his own blood. He is horrified. He glances at the time. After dark. Hours are missing. He hadn't been tired, hadn't wanted to sleep. *What happened, for God's sake?* He sits there staring at Caldwell, remembering nothing, deciding nothing. Quite still.

He glances at Abby's ashes and his mind begins to clear. He looks again at his old friend whose glazed, open eyes are staring at him, kneels down, and closes them. Then, he picks up the contax line to the dome.

"Com Center, Sergeant Santos speaking."

"Santos, Warden Smalley. You working a double tonight, right?"

"Yes sir, me and Corporal Strong Knife. Hardly anyone left to pull a shift, what wi—"

"Yes, I know. Sorry about all the extra hours. New troops arriving day after tomorrow."

"But it's our last one. We leave in the morning, right after work."

"Right," Smalley says in a calm, almost gracious voice. "Reason I called, Santos. I want you people out of there."

"Excuse me, Sir? Who do you want out?"

"You and Strong Knife. I want you to withdraw from the dome during the graveyard shift, say…between three and four AM."

"What about the inmates, Sir?"

"You leave that to me, sergeant," he says in a laconic tone.

"So, how do you want me to do this, sir?" Santos is a little wary, but given all the strange orders he's had over the past weeks, it does not surprise him.

"During the shift you and Strong Knife remove all weapons and ammo out to the tunnel with as little noise or notice as possible. Stagger your trips so you don't arouse suspicion. Then, when you've finished, release the master switch to the cell locks and leave the dome, and secure both bulkhead doors behind you."

Santos confirms the warden's instructions and hangs up the contax.

At half past three, when they are about to leave the biosphere with the last load of ordnance, the phone rings, startling Santos.

"Santos, Smalley again. One more thing."

"What, sir?"

"You know Eddie the Tin Man, the blacksmith?"

"Yes, sir."

"Bring him with you. I'll meet you at the outer bulkhead door."

Santos is uneasy. *What does he want with Eddie at this hour of the night?*

He sends Strong Knife after Eddie, knowing he'll be like a shadow getting him up to the trap without anybody knowing. When his partner returns, Eddie is shackled hands to feet, and just to be sure they aren't given away, Strong Knife has stuffed his tie into Eddie's mouth. Eddie is shaking, eyes bulging, darting wildly back and forth as he steps inside the trap.

Santos makes his last entry in the Command Center Log, making sure to state that their withdrawal from the dome was the direct order of Warden Samuel Smalley, and trips the master lock switch to all the cellblocks.

"C'mon, let's get out of here," he whispers to Strong Knife, "before somebody figures out they're loose."

They open both doors of the trap and slip out of the building into the soft late night rain. They reach the bulkhead carrying the last of the weapons and ammunition, and leading Eddie by the arm, his mouth still stuffed with Strong Knife's tie.

Smalley is waiting in the tunnel with an electrocart from the maintenance shop, loaded with canisters of prellenium iodide and a laser wand.

"Handcuff Eddie to the locking wheel in the cleansing chamber for now, Strong Knife. I've got a little job for him down this end of the tunnel."

As Strong Knife leads him back inside the chamber, Eddie tries to say something to him, but cannot do anything but grunt and moan because of the tie.

"Shut up, Eddie," Smalley growls in a whisper as he closes the great door behind the terrified con. "I'll run you guys back to the dorm so you can load your things in the personnel transport and be on your way."

Again, as Santos hands Smalley the key to Eddie's shackles, he wonders what the warden is up to, but then the prospect of getting away from Mescalero quickly overrides his concern.

"Stow the weapons and ammo in the ordnance vault," Smalley says when they reach the end of the tunnel. "I'll start lifting the bay door while you get your gear loaded."

"Do you know where Captain Caldwell is, Sir?" Santos asks. "Like to say good-bye."

Smalley is surprised by the question and unprepared.

"Oh...he's...uh...he's tied up with something right now, guys," he says, forcing a half-smile. "Can't be disturbed. Sorry. I'll...I'll tell him you were asking for him, though."

As soon as Santos and Strong Knife are gone, Smalley lowers the bay door and returns to the bulkhead. He pulls up next to the other cart and reaches beneath the seat for his pistol, gets out and opens the door to the cleansing chamber.

"We're going to do a little welding job," Smalley says just inches from Eddie's face. He digs the muzzle of the gun up under Eddie's chin as he pulls the tie out of his mouth and unlocks the shackles. The last thing he does is make sure the inner bulkhead door latch is unlocked, then they step out into the tunnel and he closes the outer door.

"Warden," Eddie pleads, "I'm sorry...you know...I mean, what we did—"

"You keep your filthy mouth shut," he hisses at him. "Now, seal the door."

The warden sits in the electrocart, pistol in hand, watching Eddie the Tin Man work. The moment the weld is finished, Eddie realizes he will be finished, too. He figures he's only got one chance and spins around, hoping to blind the warden with the laser beam. Smalley had anticipated this and is not surprised. He fires off three quick rounds into Eddie's chest and he falls to the grating, face down, as the echo reverberates through the tunnel. The warden waits a few seconds, watching for movement. Eddie's still breathing, but it's labored. He kneels down close to the dying man's ear.

"Didn't want you to die so quick, Eddie," he says, breathing rapidly. "I wanted it to be slow, you know, like my Abby, when you cut her throat."

Smalley rolls him over on his back and pulls a knife from his jacket pocket. With one swipe of the blade, Eddie's throat is cut from ear to ear. "Can you feel that, Eddie?" Smalley hisses. "I hope so."

A moment later, the Tin Man stops breathing, and his head sloughs to one side. Smalley stands, his hands slick with blood, kicks hard at Eddie's ribs, then starts toward the other end of the tunnel.

Back at his office, Smalley attends to the last detail. He drags Caldwell's body out to an electrocart in the tunnel and returns to the bulkhead. Once there, he sets the corpse in the seat of the electrocart with the welding equipment in it. After wiping the pistol clean with his shirttail, he places it in Caldwell's stiffened hand, positions the muzzle in the dead man's mouth and forces the trigger finger to pull it. The shot is muffled as the back of Caldwell's skull explodes. Bits of bone and brain matter splatter against the wall behind, and the corpse slumps awkwardly, falling onto the grating.

Smalley looks at the Tin Man, kicks his lifeless flesh hard again, and starts back down the tunnel, the pale light from each luminant he passes under a witness to his bitter tears.

It wasn't enough—not nearly enough.

CHAPTER THREE

Moss left for Felicity in the blazing late afternoon swelter. He had expected it to be easier driving out to the two lane than it had been on the way in, but the wind had all but erased his tracks. The abandoned road was still hard to make out. And as he struggled to keep the pickup on track, he wrestled with whether to notify authorities of the remains he had discovered in the tunnel.

What if he didn't tell them, right away at least? Whoever they are, they've been dead a long time. What difference would a week or two make? If he got the police into it now, Mescalero would be on every telecom monitor in the country, and he'd be road-blocked at every turn trying to gather data to complete research.

And Moss was starting to second-guess himself as well. He had gotten involved in something much bigger than he ever expected, and wondered if the decision not to tell anyone about his rediscovery of Mescalero was a mistake.

A sign at the edge of town read:
WELCOME TO FELICITY
Gateway to the Great Desert
[Population 375]

Moss had paid little attention to it when he first drove through before dawn the day before, heading south. As he scanned the twenty or so buildings on both sides of the road, he found it hard to believe there were even that many people living there. As for its being the gateway to anything, it seemed a ludicrous claim. The only prominent thing about Felicity as far as he could tell was the water tower. It was visible from two or three kilometers out on the two lane, and appeared to sway, looking at it through the heat ripples wafting up off the tarmac.

He passed Ketchum's Welding & Fabricating shop on the east side of the road. They'd have what he needed, he was sure. A little way beyond that was the Range Rider Café. And a short block past that, on the west side of the road, were the Rest Easy

Guest Cabins. He stopped just across from the motel. An arrow on the old sign blinked sporadically, pointing at the word Vacancy. He looked back down the highway to the south, then at the café, then the motel. The heat and the shoveling and the sweat of the past day and a half held sway: Get a room. Take a shower. Get a hot meal and a good night's sleep. Look for the gear he needed in the morning.

Moss pulled across the two lane into the motel parking lot. The rickety screen door of the office slapped closed behind him, as the jingle of harness bells hanging from the handle announced his arrival. A pungent odor of burnt beef fat hung heavy in the room.

"Just a minute," someone yelled from a back room.

He waited.

The woman was short and so fat, she rocked from side to side with each step as she came around the corner and squeezed behind the counter. Great folds of skin hung from the back of her arms like opera drapes, and her hair was done up in curlers wrapped in pink mesh netting. Moss guessed she might not be much older than he was, but her appearance made it hard to gauge. Perfume, lilac water he guessed—splashed on moments ago he was sure—failed to cover her body odor, the sour scent mingling now with the smell of beef fat.

"How many?" she asked with a forced smile.

"Just me," he said, as he tried to avoid staring at a mole on her chin with several thick black hairs curling out of it.

He looked around for the EyeDent lens to register and debit the room to his citizen account, but she handed him a registration form and a pen instead.

"We ain't got one 'a them high tech doodads for ya to look into, Mister, if that's what yer lookin' for. Don't figure we need 'em round here. Pen and paper works fine."

This could turn out to be a break in his favor, he realized, suddenly aware he'd become a bit paranoid since discovering those remains in the tunnel. Paying cash meant he could avoid being traced, and he found himself filling out the registration card with a phony name, address, and tag number. He was sure she wouldn't bother walking outside to check his vehicle tags.

She watched him, eyes squinting with suspicion, as he filled out the form.

"Just traveling through?"

Moss nodded, not wanting to be rude, but he also didn't want to offer more than was asked for, a personality trait that sometimes got him in trouble.

"Is it too late to get something to eat across the street?"

"If ya hurry. Midge is prob'ly gettin' ready to close."

Moss took the antiquated door key she had laid on the counter and left, the screen door slapping shut behind him, bells jingling frantically, as he stepped out of the office.

Midge, the owner of the café, seemed to know he was coming. She was setting a place at a booth in the big window facing the street.

"Good thing Bunny called," she said as Moss walked in the door. "I was fixin' to close up for the night."

He thanked her for the kindness, hanging his straw hat on the hat rack and slipping into the booth.

A young woman in the kitchen stuck her head out the pass-through window, asking if there was anything else to wash before she left. Midge said it was okay to go, she would wash the few dishes after Moss finished his meal. She passed close to Moss on her way out. She was thin, her face fine-featured, and he couldn't help notice she had a high, muscular rear end, like a sprinter's. He caught the teasing look in her face when she glanced back, catching him watching her ass move in her worn denim jeans, and then she disappeared out the door.

Midge brought chicken enchiladas and refried beans, flour tortillas, salsa on the side, and a bottle of beer with a label that read: Paco Paco. She set the plate of food in front of him, then walked across the room and faced the big industrial fan more toward where he sat, and turned up the speed.

They talked while he ate.

"That's my granddaughter," she said, motioning with her head in the direction the young woman had gone.

"Pretty," Moss said.

"Well," she said, pleased at hearing his compliment and slipping into the other side of the booth, "they say she's the spittin' image a' me, ya know…I mean, well, when I was that age. Same ornery little spitfire, too, I might add."

Moss didn't say anything right then, as Midge sat there with her arms folded on the table, remembering her youth with a mischievous grin.

But by the time he finished his meal he had learned that Midge was second generation running the café; that she was hoping her granddaughter would want to take it over one day; that Bunny over at the motel was the biggest gossip in a thousand kilometers; and that Felicity had its dark side, though she didn't go into any detail. Moss, on the other hand, had been careful not to let her know anything about him, keeping a guarded watch over what he said while they talked. And with a full stomach he soon became aware of how tired he was. He paid his bill and left a respectable tip, thanking her for staying open long enough to feed him.

He checked out of the motel early, barely daylight, but decided against going back to the café. Several pickups were already parked in front of the building, and going in for breakfast would draw unwanted attention. He always kept tins of something—sardines or beans, nuts or raisins, tubes of saltines in the pickup, and his canteens were full. He turned south out of the motel and drove the short way beyond the café, to Ketchum's, the welding shop he had passed on the way into town the night before.

When Moss stepped inside, it was noticeably cooler than the already uncomfortable temperature outside. The acrid odor of burnt engine oil hung in the air above the oil-soaked wood plank flooring. Metal slag covered the floor around an anvil strapped to a large concrete block. Worn plowshares were leaned against it, waiting for new cutting edges to be welded on. Hand tools and hardware coated with a thick gray dust were displayed at one end of the shop: barbed wire or chain, nails and staples. Burlap. Rope. Bailing twine. And standing in a crib against one wall, a dozen or more canisters of prellenium iodide.

He immediately recognized the putrid odor welding common steel with prellenium iodide makes. Smoke from spent fuel and scorched steel obscured the form of a man at a workbench with his back to Moss. The man finished his weld and turned the laser wand off. Then, as though sensing Moss's presence, he stood up straight and turned around, shifting his goggles up onto his forehead, and looked across the room at the stranger.

"Whatcha need, Friend?" he said, his pretense of civility punctuated by the look in his small, black button eyes. He was tall and wiry, with close-cropped hair. Moss thought from the expression on his face that he might've just sucked on a lemon. The narrow set eyes above a long nose, and his jaw accentuated by a moustache extending down to the jaw-line, gave him a ferret-like appearance. And with sweat shining on his brow and drenching his shirt, he looked as if he'd just rolled in soot.

"A couple canisters of prellenium iodide," Moss said.

At this, the man's expression tightened, the flinty eyes closing to just a slit, as though this would allow him to penetrate Moss's flesh better and discern who he was and what he was about.

"Well now, that could be a problem, Friend." Moss was already becoming annoyed with the man referring to him that way. "I mean, you cain't buy 'em, you can only rent 'em, and you ain't from around these parts, see? I mean, these tanks is expensive, don't ya know? And how do I know you ain't gonna just not bring 'em back, see what I mean?"

He ran the inside of his hand along under his nose, then wiped it on his pant leg. Then he pulled a rag from his back pocket and wiped his brow and the back and sides of his neck.

"Whatcha gonna do with all that *P.I.*, out here, anyway? Ain't nuthin' south a' here fer hunerds a' miles 'cept desert, an' I know you ain't doin' nuthin' for nobody north a' here. I'd a' awready heard, ya see."

Moss wasn't about to tell him what he wanted the canisters for, and he knew better than to make up a local address. This guy probably knew everybody and everyplace for two hundred kilometers in every direction.

"Well, how much would it cost to replace two full canisters?" Moss said.

The man peered at him, eyes narrowed again with suspicion, curious about Moss's persistence. He looked straight up for several seconds, as if the answer to the question was painted on the ceiling.

"Three hun'erd."

"Well, I give you my word I'm going to bring them back, but what if I give you cash to replace them, in case...like you say, I don't come back. How'd that be?"

The man looked at Moss for a minute, thinking about it.

"Make it five hun'erd. Yeah, five hun'erd an' you can take 'em." He had a grin on his face like a dog Moss had when he was a boy. The dog would bare his teeth and smile, but if someone didn't know better, they'd think he was getting ready to bite.

Moss was pissed having the screws put to him like this, but he couldn't get into it with him. He needed those canisters. There was no way around it. He paid Ketchum and got a receipt, and loaded the prellenium iodide in the pickup.

The sun was well above the horizon now. Before pulling out he adjusted the solar charging panel on the roof of the pickup to the southeast to get maximum reception, and started back south to Mescalero. As he drove, he again thought about notifying authorities about what he'd found at Mescalero while he was in Felicity. He realized that by not contacting them, he *had* made a decision: he wasn't going to, at least not now.

By the time he got the canisters to the end of the tunnel and cut through most of the seal, the day was nearly gone. There would be little or no light in the dome when he got inside. He decided to wait until morning to finish cutting the seal.

Back at the office complex, Moss had become more accustomed to the musty odor. He felt he could sleep with some sense of security since the door to the offices was steel and locked from the inside. Up on the surface, he had thrown the four-man tent over the pickup as camouflage. He wasn't sure why he was so concerned about security. Nobody knew about this place or that he was here. But the mild paranoia that had begun at the motel in Felicity lingered, and he wasn't going to take anything for granted.

He followed the hallway that led from the offices to the staff dormitory and dining room. Four round tables with chairs occupied much of the floor space of the small dining room, with a couch and several easy chairs along the walls. After looking in each sleeping room, he picked the one closest to the showers and set his bivouac bag and knapsack on the bunk. While he let the showers run to clear the turbid water, he sat at a table in the dining room studying the plans of the complex, eating from a tin of baked beans from his knapsack.

The plans showed a vehicle access to an underground receiving dock. It was a hydraulic platform at the surface that opened like a clam. Moss decided the first thing to do in the morning, even before opening the bulkhead door, was to get his pickup underground, out of sight. He checked the water in the showers. It was clear, but ice cold. He was weary, too weary to go looking for the hot water heater. He would forgo the shower and try to get some sleep.

In the morning he ate sardines and crackers, then went up to the surface by the pedestrian stairwell to rub out his tracks. When he got out where the pickup was he discovered the wind had already done that. He retraced his steps down to the receiving area below ground. The electricity was working there, too, so he found the control panel and tried to raise the platform. The servomotors strained under the weight of the sand that had drifted onto the platform at the surface over the years. He didn't know if it could withstand the additional weight, so as soon as there was sufficient clearance for the pickup, he ran up the ramp and drove it down inside to the dock, then lowered the platform to ground level again. Any possibility of being discovered had now been eliminated, he was sure.

Moss loaded a hand truck with the gear he figured he'd need inside the dome, and trudged the gradual incline to the other end of the tunnel, where he set about cutting the last of the seal. Just before noon the door came free. He wedged a pry bar in the hole that the latch tongue seated in, and pulled. The immense door complained loudly as it began to open, then a sucking sound and a rush of air as the vacuum was breached and the thick, vault-like door swung away clear of its threshold.

He stepped into the cleansing chamber (as it was labeled on the plans), a space twelve feet square between the inner and outer bulkhead doors. Its purpose had been to bombard anyone entering the dome with disinfectant alpha rays. With torch and lantern in hand, he went straight across the chamber to see if the inner door had been sealed, too, and was relieved to find that it had not. He went back to close the outer door but the now imperfect edge made it impossible to seal tightly. Moss rigged what he could with the pry bar and a piece of chain to keep the door shut tight, so as not to corrupt the environment inside the dome. He went back over and spun the manual bolt latch of the inner door free, and with his heart beating madly as the huge door swung open, Moss stepped out into the biosphere.

Sweet scents saturated the air. He closed the door and stood gazing out into the dome, marveling at the sheer magnitude of it, the ceiling a hundred meters above him. He felt as though he had stepped into Eden as he breathed in the exotic fragrances, and surveyed the stunning panorama of plant life. And there was a stillness that seemed almost holy. He recalled such a silence once before.

The vast plains of the interior. Three in the morning. Not a sound from a transport or a cricket, or an airfoil overhead. Not a breeze driving the tumbleweed or a railtram whistle in the distance. Nothing. Moss heard the silence that night—felt the stillness—accompanied by the silent glory of the heavens overhead. He had been in awe then, and he was now, too.

His first thought was to yell, *Anybody here?* But it passed quickly as he remembered the pistol and the remains in the tunnel.

He moved out into the expanse. The light was milky, subdued by the sand dust that covered the outside surface of the dome. It was hot, almost tropical, and humid, and wherever he looked the vegetation was lush and thriving.

A gravel pathway overgrown with timothy and clover and vetch led to the main building, a hundred meters or so off to his left. The building was situated in a north-south direction along the west wall of the dome. On the landing at the top of the steps to the entrance stood two large sculptures, an eagle in flight on a pedestal at the railing on one side of the steps, a vulture ready to pounce on the other. Moss stopped and studied them. The craftsmanship was impressive though the symbolism evaded him. He found it, at the least, curious that such fine sculptures would be exhibited in a prison.

He entered the building through what was marked on the plans as *The Trap*, two steel sliding doors at either end of a ten-meter passageway. The security command center was adjacent to the passageway, separated by a large armorglass window. When someone entered the trap, the door in front of them would not be opened until the door behind them was closed. Both doors of the trap were open, and Moss passed through and out into the main corridor that ran the length of the building.

The plans showed four wings that branched off the northern end of the corridor, two on either side. Each wing could accommodate up to sixty men in individual cells, thirty at ground level and thirty on a second tier. He started along the corridor toward the cells. Life-sized portraits adorned the entire east wall, painted on sheets of plasticene and framed with some sort of woven hemp. About halfway between the entrance and the first wing, he came upon a life-sized sculpture, a replica of Rodin's Adam. He was again mystified that such expenditures for artwork could have been justified in the Mescalero budget, even if it was a clandestine project. What would be the point of such expenditures?

He entered the first wing he came to. The cells were small. Moss was nearly able to reach from one wall to the other. The bunk on one side and shelves on the other were formed out of the metal walls of the cell rather than attached to them. At the back there was a combination commode and sink, and at the front steel bars from ceiling to floor with a sliding door. Each cell was decorated with paintings: landscapes, vases of flowers, a cow with her calf at teat, men playing chess. But what struck him most as he moved along tier after tier in each of the wings was that all the cells were open—and empty.

Where are the men? What happened to them?

He walked the corridor back to the trap. Just across from it was a set of double doors. The plans indicated a large room. He opened the doors wide and stepped inside. When his eyes adjusted to the dim light, he realized the room was a library. Tattered hardcover books, numerous dictionaries, an atlas, and old sets of encyclopedias occupied the shelves. Books on the great artists and sculptors from centuries past, as well as novels and plays and poetry stood silently in their place. In one corner, a handsome globe of the world stood on a pedestal. He sensed something about the room, an almost spiritual sensation, one he would not expect to come upon often in life, let alone in a prison. But it was there.

He studied the room. Far more than what was on the shelves, it was what was *not* on the shelves, but around the room, that amazed Moss. What appeared to be a novel manuscript lay at one end of a long table. A musical composition from what he could gather, possibly even a symphony, lay at the other end. On another, smaller table set in a corner of the room, was an essay on the value of cultivating a spirit of thankfulness.

Here of all places. Thankfulness!

Moss came to an easel at the far end of the room and stopped. Staring at the sketch resting on it, he realized he was looking at a moment in the life of the men who had lived here, captured as if a photo had been taken: a man reading, another standing at an easel painting, two men playing a game of chess. He remained transfixed for several minutes, attempting to project with his mind the images of the men from the paper into the room. He imagined them sitting in the chairs, the sound of their breathing, the charcoal moving across the paper, a page turning, or a book closing. Gazing at the drawing, it occurred to him that they did not look like killers.

Moss was thrilled by the discoveries he had already made, their implications and the conclusions they might lead to, a windfall of human behavioral responses to the unique circumstances of Mescalero. But his focus was still whether anyone was left alive inside the dome. He left the building through the trap and headed out to the larger pathway leading out into the dome from the entrance, nearly impassable now because of a stand of banana trees. Working his way through the grove, he broke out into a small clearing where he was startled by an enormous sandstone statue. It was a fierce-looking creature with a lower body like that of a man, its upper body like an eagle. It was as if it had been set there as guardian of the entrance to this paradise.

He walked on, past livestock pens and once-cultivated fields, composting pits and settling ponds for sewage. A short distance beyond the north end of the main building was a granary and several smaller outbuildings. He found beehives from time to time, the white wooden boxes standing out in stark contrast to the colors of the landscape. Off ahead of him a citrus grove, even though in dire need of pruning, was producing a modest crop of oranges and lemons.

The light in the dome began to fade fast once the sun dropped behind the northwest ridge of the canyon outside. Moss had lost track of time. There was too much that needed to be done in daylight before he could stay the night inside the dome. He decided he would have to spend one more night in the dormitory.

Back at the dormitory, he searched the drawers and cupboards in the kitchen to see what might still be usable in the way of staples or dry goods, and came on a bin half-full of dehydrated meals still sealed in original containers, and they looked good as new. He found the water-heating unit, too. It had been split open from sediment accumulation long ago, but he discovered that the gas stove still worked. He filled several large pots with water and set them on the stove to heat. He'd take a bath of sorts in one of the large kitchen sinks before sleeping.

CHAPTER FOUR

Joey the Gimp lies on his bunk, his good foot hanging off the edge, bouncing nervously. Three hours yet until breakfast but he is unable to sleep. He looks again at the calendar, at the date circled: February 13th. He's scheduled to be taken to the lab this morning—"for a procedure" was all they'd tell him.

He throws off the covers and slips into his prison issue orange jumpsuit and begins to pace, limping on his spindly right leg. The foot flops as though it hangs by a thread. He must exaggerate each step, throwing the foot forward so it lands on the sole when he puts his weight on it. He stops at the bars of the cell door and leans against it—and it moves. *It isn't locked!* He looks out into the block, along the tiers on the other side. *No lights on, either.*

He cranes his neck looking toward the entrance to the block. The monitor screen at the guard's station is dark. *Primary's shut down, too.*

He glances up at the catwalks above the upper tiers, straining to see in the meager winter moonlight filtering down through the skylights.

No screw in sight anywhere!

His senses are poised, on edge, heart beating fast, giddy finding his cell door unlocked, but cautious, like a rat before taking the bait on a trap. He takes great pains to be quiet sliding the steel-barred door on its casters, but just far enough so he can see out along the tier.

Watch your ass, Joey, he thinks.

He pokes his head out several times then quickly pulls it back in, gets up the nerve to open the door a little farther, and steps out onto the landing. He scans the block again, leans over the banister to see the tier below. When he's sure no one is around, he shuffles along the landing, down the spiral stairwell, and back along the lower tier cells to the last one on his side of the block—Briscoe's cell.

Briscoe is on his back in the bunk in his boxer shorts, snoring like a bush hog. Joey tries the cell door. It's not locked, either. He steps inside the cell and kicks the end of the bunk. Joey knows better than to wake him if he's within arm's reach. Briscoe comes up off the bunk like a cat, crouches at the back wall of the cell trying to clear his mind, adjust his eyes to the dark, and assesses what's happening. When he realizes who it is, he relaxes and stands up, his brilliant red hair draped over his shoulders.

"How the hell'd you get in here?" Briscoe growls, flipping his head to one side to sweep a shock of hair from his eyes. "What's goin' on?"

"I dunno, Vince, there ain't a screw anywhere in the block. All the cells are unlocked…least I think so."

Briscoe rubs the sleep from his face and shakes his head, then reaches for his jumpsuit.

"You don't know for sure?"

"No."

"Find out."

"Okay, Vince."

Joey shuffles back along the first floor cells on that side of the block, pulling at every door as he passes, careful not to wake anyone. Every cell is unlocked. He makes his way cautiously across the common area to the other side, and does the same thing. All open. He climbs to the second tier. Same thing. He hurries back to report.

"We need to see if this is the only wing like this," Briscoe says in a hoarse whisper as he ties his hair into a ponytail with a piece of shoelace. "Check the other three wings. See if the cells are unlocked. See if there are any screws in the Command Center. Don't make a sound, you hear? Then come back and let me know."

Joey's only gone a short while.

"Nobody in the Command Center, Vince," Joey whispers, "and the cells in the other wings are unlocked, too."

Briscoe has yet to step out of his cell, preoccupied with trying to figure out what's going on. What about the bulkhead doors? he thinks. He grabs Joey again.

"Can you get by the Command Center, Joey, I mean, is the trap open so you can get out into the dome?"

Joey tries to avoid staring at the tic in Briscoe's cheek. The spasms are so pronounced the corner of his upper lip is raised in an ugly snarl.

"Yeah, sure, Vince, the trap's wide open."

"I wanna know if the big door is open, Joey, and I don't want anybody else to know. You got me?"

Joey nods and ambles off in his clumsy way, and while Briscoe waits for him to return, he racks his brain trying to understand what's happening.

Where the hell are the screws?

When Joey gets back, his hair and the shoulders of his jumpsuit wet from the rain out in the dome, Briscoe is pacing the floor.

"So?"

"Here's the deal, Vince. The inner door of the cleansing chamber is open, but the outer one ain't. You can spin the lock on it all the way open, but it won't budge."

Briscoe starts pacing again, wondering why the cells are unlocked, but they can't get out of the dome.

Several minutes pass without a word between them, then Briscoe sets the question aside and starts thinking about survival: What's most important? Food. The kitchen reefers. Pantry and storeroom. The livestock and granary. Drugs. That means the lab and the infirmary. He wonders what else, as he tries to put together a plan before anyone else finds out they're all loose.

"Joey," he whispers, "you take this side of the wing. I'll take the other side. Wake our guys up quietly, you hear? Just our guys. Tell 'em to break out their shivs and get down here quick. Not a sound from anybody."

Besides Joey the Gimp, forty-five of the sixty men in A Wing belong to Briscoe, and all of them are loyal. Briscoe isn't bigger or tougher than they are. He is just under six feet, medium build, not fat but with soft-tissue beneath an almost albino skin covered with freckles. He commands their loyalty because he's clever, a manipulator, he knows how to get them things. A redeemer of favors: More to eat than the others get, for a gargantuan like Necco the Turk, his bodyguard. An easier job out in the fields for Joey the Gimp, his lackey. Arranging payback to anyone who messes with someone under his protection. Everyone knows he is ruthless in this, so no one provokes his people. Protection by association.

When they've all gathered at Briscoe's cell, he begins dispatching them, whispering orders so as not to wake the others in the wing: Eight men down to the infirmary. No one in unless I say so. Nothing out. Twenty guys to the chow hall. Set up a barricade in the entryway. Nobody eats except us until I say. A dozen guys out in the dome. Watch the livestock pens. Check the toolshed for shovels, pitchforks, anything we can use as weapons. Four guys—and Necco—stay here with me to barricade the wing after we kick the others out.

A shout rings out from down the corridor just then.

"Ah, shit!" Briscoe says, "the others know, now, too. All right, all of you, move! Get to where you're supposed to, and do like I said."

Briscoe's soldiers sprint for the door, shivs in hand. He motions to the five who remain to start rousting the other cons out of the block. The noise gets louder as men from the other wings move into the corridor, surprised, confused. Even if it's just a mistake by the screws and they'll all be locked down again, the feeling of being free—even for a few minutes—is intoxicating. Briscoe and his men shove anything they can find for a barricade into the doorway of the wing while the uproar in the corridor escalates.

The euphoria dies down quickly, though, as men begin to grasp the cold reality: If there aren't any screws anywhere, there isn't anyone to stop them from doing whatever they want. Just a few of them at first, those who have had a beef with someone recently, head back to their cell. Others begin to sense the danger, too, and start for their cells. The sounds of wild, reckless celebration turn somber and the cell blocks go quiet, except for an occasional shout, one man to another—a hail, a threat, a promise.

Not even an hour passes since they first realized they were free before chaos breaks out. An inmate from D Wing charges out into the corridor, staggers to the far wall and crumples to the floor, the ends of a shiv made from a piece of refrigeration tubing driven through his brain and protruding from both ears. Three men in B Wing pile onto a man in his bunk, stabbing him repeatedly, his useless screams for help filling the block. A dozen men head for the chow hall but the entryway is blocked, Briscoe's men grinning defiantly out through the wreckage they've piled there.

Men in fear of old enemies no longer kept away by bars and guards try to rig some way of locking their cell so no one can get in. Would-be gang bosses try to stake out territory, their men locked in combat with anything they can use as a weapon. As Briscoe watches the madness with Necco and four of his soldiers, he calls his grunt aside.

"Joey, get down to solitary and check on Stryker," he says, his facial tic almost constant now. "I wanna know where that fucker is, if he's loose, too."

Joey nods, and as anarchy spreads through the building, he makes his way over the flotsam piled in the entrance to A Wing. Like a shadow, he slides along the corridor wall, heading for the Disciplinary Segregation Unit at the other end of the corridor. While Joey goes to look for Stryker, Briscoe sends another man to check out the Command Center, to look for weapons or if there's electrical power to operate the cell locks. He reports back that the Command Center is open, but he found no weapons. No power on there, either. A few minutes later, Joey the Gimp returns.

"Ain't nobody in DSU, Vince. I checked every cell. They're all unlocked, too."

"He was in the last cell, right?"

"Yeah, last I knew."

"He wasn't there, right?"

"No, Bris, I just sai—"

"Well, for Chris'sakes," Briscoe yells in the little man's face, throwing his arms up in frustration, "did you see any sign of him? How long ago does it look like he'd been there, is what I want to know, numb nuts! What I wanna know is: Is the fucker alive!"

Joey cowers under the barrage of Briscoe's expletives.

"He must be, Vince. I figure he's hidin' somewhere."

Briscoe paces the common area of the wing, assessing the situation. No way of locking any cell in the building. No weapons in the Command Center. He knows Bruno and Manning and Carelli will be trying to take control wherever they can. Once he's sure what's going on, he'll deal with them. *But what about Stryker? Shit. It always comes back to him. Where the hell is he?*

James Stryker is an icon to the inmates. He was brought in alone after the others were locked down, in the middle of the night, and taken straight to solitary. Every con in the system knows of him, some personally, but mostly through the grapevine, the stories over the years gradually becoming almost mythical. More than a dozen years in isolation. No one has ever known why. But if his name is mentioned to a screw, especially one of the older ones, they stiffen right up. And any man who can make the screws do that is godlike to the cons.

Stryker sneaks out of the unit just before Joey the Gimp gets there and is hiding in the observation catwalk between the cells of DSU and the infirmary. He had seen Joey coming and waits for him to leave. Out in the main corridor, in the sparse light coming through the skylights overhead, he can make out three men up near the chow hall, chasing someone. He smells smoke but can't tell where it's coming from. Closer to where he is hiding, a lifeless body sits propped like a Raggedy Ann doll, against the corridor wall opposite the doors to the library.

There's a commotion in the chow hall. He slips out of the catwalk, and moves cautiously along the wall of the smoke-filled corridor. He squeezes into a narrow hatchway and up a ladder that leads to one of the guard observation turrets in the wall above the dining area. Briscoe's men are dishing out food to their men only. An angry mob blocked by the stacks of metal tables and other debris at the chow hall door objects violently. Briscoe isn't there. Stryker shakes his head.

That crowd could overrun those guys just by sheer numbers, he thinks, but no one wants to be the first to take a hit.

Stryker straddles the railing of the turret and drops the twelve feet to the floor of the chow hall silently, like a cat. The crowd out in the corridor goes quiet, not knowing who he is. Someone whispers, "Stryker." The sudden silence draws the attention of Briscoe's men back at the serving line as Stryker starts across the room. He looks at the men in the entryway behind him, then back to the kitchen. He doesn't say anything as he steps up to the steam table right behind Joey the Gimp, his gaze locked on the soldiers on the other side, brilliant, penetrating, ice blue eyes, staring them down. Joey turns around to find Stryker next to him and freezes.

"Joey, tell Vince we gotta meet."

He is stunned, staring up at Stryker, glancing quickly over at the men on the other side of the serving line as if to say, you guys gonna let him get away with this? Necco, ain't you gonna do anything?

He swallows hard. "Geez, I...I...I don't know. I...uh, I mean, what for?"

"Tell him to meet me in the trap at the Command Center, alone, after the dome gets dark. Tell him it's just to talk, but it's real important. You tell him, Joey."

"Okay, James, but what for? I gotta tell him something, ya know?"

"Never mind, Joey, you just tell him. Remember...alone."

Necco, a gargantuan Turk, is Briscoe's primary bodyguard. He is on the other side of the steam table dishing oatmeal out of a serving tray with a long metal spoon. He and Joey the Gimp are buddies. They depend on each other, watch out for each other. As Stryker reaches for a soy muffin, Necco swats hard at his hand with the huge spoon, but Stryker is too fast. The spoon hits the muffin instead, sending pieces of it flying everywhere. Joey takes his eyes off the two men for only a split second as he steps back to get out of the way, when Necco bellows. When he looks again, Stryker is holding the spoon and Necco's nose is gushing blood.

Necco pulls his huge carving knife, the most prized weapon in Mescalero, from the sash around his waist. He leans out across the table and swipes at Stryker in a wide sweeping motion. Stryker pulls back like a dancer as the point of the blade passes his abdomen. He strikes the Turk's wrist with the spoon as fast as a lizard catching a moth with its tongue. Another howl of pain as the blade clatters to the floor at Joey's feet.

Necco is bent over, holding his wrist, the hand dangling as though it were broken. Stryker motions to Joey to hand him the knife. The minute he does, Joey turns and ambles off toward the kitchen as fast as his gimp will let him. Stryker turns to Necco who is watching him out of the corner of his eye. He lays the knife across the table in front of him. Necco looks at him, confused, while Stryker helps himself to a soy muffin again, and half a dozen hard-boiled eggs.

As Stryker turns to leave, he motions to the crowd to move in. Like a dam breaking, they scramble over the barrier, pushing the piles of flotsam aside and dash to the line, grabbing what they can carry to eat. Briscoe's men, overwhelmed without the threat of Necco present, retreat further into the kitchen. In all the uproar, Stryker is able to sneak out of the room. Down the corridor near the library, in one of the many niches along the wall, he opens the grate and crawls into a ventilation tube he had picked out earlier for a hiding place. But he is sure that sooner or later, Briscoe will send men to find him. The two of them were at Carbondale prison together. He knows better than to underestimate him. He can be clever. He hopes defying Briscoe's men in the chow hall was enough to piss Vince off, but not to where he loses face with them.

The pale light of dusk has faded, and clouds obscure the night sky above the dome. Smoke remains heavy throughout the building. It is nearly impossible to see anything the dark is so dark. The cellblocks have gone silent. Ironically, the men are in their cells, door lashed or propped shut with whatever they can find, listening, struggling against sleep, keeping watch for their lives.

Stryker feels his way along the corridor walls to the trap at what would normally be suppertime. Briscoe isn't there yet. He waits, out of sight, in the dark of the abandoned Command Center. From this vantage point he should have been able to see anyone approaching from either direction, but it is too dark. He hadn't planned on that. Thirty minutes pass and still no Briscoe. He starts to wonder if he is going to show. Just then he hears a brogan scuff against the polished asphalt tile floor, then a muffled cough. Straining his eyes, he can make out Briscoe almost to the trap, then sees four of his goons coming up behind him.

He moves quickly over to the sliding steel door of the trap, and as Briscoe clears it and steps inside, Stryker shoves it shut before the others get to it. Then, he jams a chair in the track so it can't budge. The only way Briscoe can leave now is by going through him, and he's sure Vince won't try that alone.

"What the fuck's goin' on?" Briscoe demands as his men pound on the door.

"I told you, Vince, alo—"

"I don't go nowhere in this place alone, you sonofabitch!"

Stryker knows Briscoe doesn't like being vulnerable like this, especially with him.

"You hurt the Turk, James, my number one boy. Why'd you do that, James?"

"I was hungry, Vince."

"Well, you know the rules: You mess with me, I mess with you, right?"

"That's right, Vince, so when you see Necco, you remind him of that for me, will you?" Stryker says, smiling, though it's so dark Briscoe can't tell.

"Ah, you're a pain in the ass, James," he says, scared and frustrated and starting to get angry again. "You're always a pain in the ass. Wherever we been in slam together, you was always a pain in the ass. Now, open the fuckin' door!"

"Not just yet, Vince, we gotta talk."

"What're you talkin' about? What do we have to talk about? Open the door!"

"After we talk, I said."

Briscoe catches the change in Stryker's voice as James's patience begins to wear thin, and backs off.

"Like I said, James, talk about what?"

"You gonna listen, Vince?"

Briscoe makes an insulting hand gesture with a guttural grunt, its effect lost in the dark, and agrees reluctantly, though he has no choice.

Stryker, interrupted now and then by Briscoe's men pounding on the door asking if he's all right, wants to make Briscoe understand why the killing has to stop, but Briscoe is not interested. Control is the only thing on his mind.

"Why should I give a shit if these guys kill each other off?" he says.

"Geez, Vince, you gotta be smarter than that. Think about it. There's no power, so we can't recharge the servomules now, *so we can't use them to farm with now*, so everything's going to have to be done by hand now. So, we won't survive in here without manpower, get it? You let these guys kill each other off, and it's just like putting a gun to your own head."

They are both in dark shadows, but Stryker can see Briscoe's face enough to know he's started him thinking.

"So, what you got in mind?" Briscoe says, acting as if he doesn't have to listen to any of this.

"Well, first off, I know the door to the outside is sealed—"

"How the hell do you know that, for Chris'sakes? You ain't been out there."

"Well, there isn't anybody here to stop you, Vince, and you're still here."

Briscoe grins, looking at Stryker and shaking his head. "You about a smart sum'bitch, James," he says laughing with a grunt like a feral pig rooting in the woods.

"And, as I was about to say, we don't know why we were left in here. Maybe there's been a nuclear disaster or a war. We have no way of finding out."

Briscoe moves close enough for Stryker to see his face more clearly. The expression gives him away. "You think?" he says, his brow furrowed.

"Well, doesn't really make any difference now, does it? We're locked in here and we have no idea when or if anyone will ever open the door again. I don't know about you, Vince, but I ain't ready to die yet, and if we don't get everybody together pronto and stop fighting, that's what's going to happen. We'll starve to death after a while."

Briscoe has relaxed. Stryker finally gets him to agree to a strategy, and they decide to do it right away so they won't lose a dozen more men: a meeting in the chow hall in the morning with the two of them standing together, united on the situation.

"This has to work, Vince. If it doesn't, it's just a matter of time."

Stryker pulls the chair out of the track, the door slides open, and Briscoe's men rush in.

"All right, never mind, you dickheads," Briscoe growls. "I'm okay. Back off. Go on, back off!"

They exit the trap and disappear into the dark. Stryker knows it would be a mistake to trust Briscoe, but he also knows he needs Briscoe to make this work. He can only hope he's convinced him, made a believer out of him. And then, they have to get the rest of the men to see the situation. Stryker waits after Briscoe leaves so they won't know where he goes. While he waits, he notices something that might be useful someday. Levers to operate the doors of the trap manually pull down out of recessed slots in the ceiling.

In the morning Stryker waits in the guard turret above the chow hall. And he waits. And he waits some more. No Briscoe. If he doesn't show, neither can I, he decides. Vince would see it as a threat if I start talking to the men without him. He'd feel forced to draw a line in the sand; I know he would.

Something in Stryker's gut tells him he'd better get out of there, and back to his hiding place. Briscoe might already have men looking for him. He slips out of the turret and moves quickly to the ventilation duct where he's been safe until now, and hunkers down for the long hours before dark, wondering where he can hide next.

CHAPTER FIVE

Sunday morning. Moss had been at the site since Wednesday, except for the overnight run to Felicity. Today would be his first full day of investigation inside the dome. He returned to the main building to explore the half south of the trap and library. At the end of the corridor he came to two doors, side-by-side. The one on the left had *Infirmary* stenciled above it. The other door, marked *Disciplinary Segregation Unit*, was open and Moss entered.

There was no natural light source, no skylights, to this cellblock, so he switched on his calcion torch. The heavy steel doors of each cell, with only a slit large enough to slip a food tray through, were open. He walked the corridor to the end, to the last cell. When he shined his torch in, he was startled by a corpse lying on the bunk, a piece of paper under its folded hands. Moss was uneasy coming upon more human remains, though after his fright in the tunnel a few days before, he adapted to the circumstance more readily. The corpse was well preserved, silvery white hair and beard in stark contrast to its blackened, shriveled skin. He slipped the piece of paper out from beneath its clutching, bony fingers. The writing was in large letters, done by an obviously shaky hand:

September 12, 2064 AD—I spent most of my life in this cell and others just like it. Fitting, I suppose, that I should die here. J.S.

Something was protruding from under the pillow. He reached over and pulled out a leather sheath that resembled an ancient aboriginal quiver, meant to carry arrows. Inside were pieces of paper loosely rolled up. Glancing at them he realized that these were journal or diary entries. There were more bundles as well as some hardbound journals, under the bunk. He wasn't sure what to do with the corpse of J.S. just yet, but he was sure the writings would help to explain what had happened here over the past fifty years. He picked up what he could carry and hurried back to the trap, to get out in the dome where the light was better. He sat on the steps of the landing outside the entrance and turned to the entries in the roll that had been under the pillow, assuming these would be the last entries, and began to read:

April 15, 2064—Buried Manning today. Found him dead in his bunk this morning. Looks as though he died peacefully in his sleep. We carried him out to where all the others are, in a wheelbarrow, said some words then covered him up. I'll carve something to make a fitting marker for his grave. He was a nice old man. Best I know, he was eighty-five. Hope I go as peacefully as he did, in my bunk, when I'm asleep....

Then, Moss read the last entry, though the handwriting was almost illegible. As he did, a knot formed in his throat:

September 10, 2064—Today is my eighty-seventh birthday. Been feeling poorly three days now. Too weak to get out to pick something to eat, even. I have a notion my time has come. If anyone finds this, I wish the world to know I've been in prison since I was fifteen and in Mescalero since it opened in 2021. I never meant anyone any harm, but if I did I'm sorry and pray they will forgive me. And I forgive all those who did me harm, especially the officers who lied at my trial, which is why I went to prison in the first place.
None of us over the past forty-two years have ever been able to figure out why we were left alone, free inside the dome but unable to leave it. It doesn't matter now....

He retied the sheath with its leather thong, set it down, and reached for the hardcover journals. They were in sequence, judging from the dates, apparently the first entries J.S. made at Mescalero:

June 13th, 2021—My name is James Stryker. I was born and raised one of nine children. I don't remember much about my father. He was gone a lot, drunk mostly, and then he ran off for good when I was six. My mother had it rough. She tried her damnedest to raise us to be good kids, but the odds were against her. We lived in the projects south of the city. Seven of us went to prison.

I've been incarcerated since I was fifteen except for four hours after my one and only release, when I got into a fight over the price of an ice-cream cone. I'd been in prison so long, I didn't know how much prices had gone up, and I thought the guy was trying to screw me.

I'm forty-four years old now and I have spent nearly thirty years in prison, more than ten of them in solitary confinement.

Two hundred of us have just been shipped into this new maximum security prison they call The Mescalero Project, *as an experiment. Word is wardens all over the country identified who they thought were their most dangerous inmates, and we were lugged and dispatched—in the middle of the night as usual. They brought me in after the others were locked down.*

Came straight to DSU, and I was glad of it. Everything is so much simpler in solitary. Don't have to watch your back all the time. And it's quieter. No loudmouthed cons yelling from one cell to another all the time. It's not a place where you want to piss off a screw, though. They can make your life miserable in here, hurt you real bad if they want to, without getting caught. Not many screws at Mescalero, though. A computer called Primary *does most of the watching. It's not so bad, being in here. In fact, I've been in solitary so many years now, I get uneasy around other people. Long as they feed me and let me have books to read and leave me alone, I do okay. I think I got it better than the others....*

June 14th, 2021—I asked for books to read, but haven't seen any yet. When I first went to prison I couldn't read at all, and I could barely scratch out a signature. At first I was kept in solitary because I was too young to be in the adult population. Later on it was punishment for one thing or another. A volunteer named Tess and a nun from a local church began visiting me. They taught me to read and write, and during all the years in solitary at Carbondale Prison, I read every book in the prison library, including all the law books. Now, I go just about crazy if I don't have something to read....

Moss continued reading Stryker's journals well into the afternoon, with only a good long chew on a piece of jerky for his lunch as he read. It was not until he found himself squinting that he realized how much time had passed. The day had not gone as he had planned. Now, he needed to hurry back out to the tunnel and get his gear before he lost any more daylight.

He opened and closed each of the immense doors in succession, getting his gear inside the dome. As he did, he debated in his mind whether to bury Stryker or not. Document and preserve the scene the way a good scientist is supposed to, or show respect for the poor man and give him a decent burial?

Once Moss had everything he thought he'd need inside, he closed both bulkhead doors and carried his gear to the main building. He was hesitant about sleeping inside the building knowing there was a dead man in there. It was silly, he knew, but he decided to roll out his bivouac bag below the landing, in the soft, overgrown grass that once had been a lawn. He heated a container of reconstituted chicken and vegetables with the prism lantern, and soon after finishing the meal he slipped inside the bivouac bag and fell asleep.

A little after midnight he was awakened. It was raining. He pulled the weather flap of the bivouac bag over his head and watched, realizing he was witnessing a cycle that took place every night. Moisture condensing on the ceiling of the dome as it cooled was falling to the ground as rain. It was thrilling! He was in a mammoth terrarium. But, as the rain became steady, he was forced to move up onto the landing, under the roof overhang at the edge of the building.

Moss awoke early, his bones stiff and sore from lying on the cool concrete surface of the landing. When he stood, he was suddenly overcome by an odd and unsettling sensation. Despite his fascination with such an extraordinary place, a fleeting yet urgent sense of loneliness verging on despair swept over him. He was dismayed by the strong and unexpected emotion. At first, he thought it must be the closeness of the atmosphere in the dust-covered bubble he inhabited, not able to see clear blue sky or feel the heat of uncensored sunlight. But it was more than that, something disturbing about being inside this capsule, disconnected from the rest of the world. When he imagined it as the extent of his world, it produced a sensory paranoia in him. Even though he knew he could leave whenever he wanted to, the sensation persisted. He shook his head, rubbing his face hard to rid himself of the uncomfortable feeling, and wondered how the men who lived here had endured decades of it.

Brown bread from a tin and a piece of beef jerky for breakfast, then he started off on a path he'd noticed the day before, hoping to find where these men were buried. He moved through an area of grassy vegetation nearly as tall as he was. When he broke out of the high grass, he found himself at the edge of a pond he estimated to cover about ten acres. There was a disturbance a ways out from shore. After watching for a minute he realized this was the artesian well shown in the plans, bubbling up out of a well casing just beneath the surface.

The path he'd followed led away from the pond towards a hill about three hundred meters to the west. Before going on he wanted to refill his canteen. As he squatted at the water's edge, he caught a glimpse of movement in the water, just at the deepest point the subdued light from outside the dome penetrated. *The pond is stocked! Perch? Carp, maybe?* He wasn't sure, but the idea of a source of fresh protein was welcome. All he had to do was figure out how to catch them.

He started following the path again, amazed as he walked at the vitality of the plant life and the richness of the soil. When he came to the base of the hill he found what he was looking for. Grave markers made from everything imaginable stuck out all over the hill, as though it were a great, macabre pincushion. He climbed to the top, careful not to step on the graves, and from there he was able to see most everywhere inside the dome. It was apparent why this spot was chosen for a cemetery. It was too rugged and steep to cultivate for crops. And yet, there was ocotillo and tamarisk, agave, and sage, thriving on it, providing the graves with a certain dignity. And standing like a sentinel at the highest point of the hill, a lone Joshua Tree.

Moss went back for Stryker's remains with a wheelbarrow he'd found in a toolshed, and the shovel he'd brought in with his gear the day before. He had resolved his dilemma about Stryker's body: Do a thorough documentation of the cell, with photos, measurements, and a skin sample, then bury him.

He uncovered Stryker's shoulder to cut a piece of flesh from the frontal lobe of the deltoid muscle. The texture and appearance of the tissue sample was so much like the beef jerky he was so fond of, he wondered if he'd be able to put another piece in his mouth now. The flesh of the muscle beneath the skin was gone. It was as though he was cutting through a piece of sun-dried hide. It forced him to drive the point of his survival knife into the bone of the joint, and then saw across the shoulder. The corpse jostled back and forth like a board, its toes erect under the sheet at the foot of the bunk. After wrapping the tissue sample and putting it in his pack, he picked up the body and set it in the wheelbarrow, noting how light and how stiff it was.

As Moss wheeled the remains of Stryker out into the main corridor, he thought he heard something, like a cell door slamming shut, at the other end of the building. The hair on the back of his neck prickled as he stood in the subdued light of the corridor with the corpse. He stayed still for several minutes, listening. He heard nothing more and started for the trap again, accusing his imagination of wanting to make more of the sound than it probably was.

It took Moss the rest of the morning to dig a proper grave for Stryker. And when he finished, he fashioned a marker from a board he'd found in the barn, said some words over the grave, and left.

Back at the main building, he sat out on the steps of the landing and ate more of the brown bread he'd opened for breakfast and a banana he'd picked, while he studied the building plans further. The utilities page indicated a natural gas well served the whole complex.

The whole complex, man. Of course! If the stove works in the dormitory, then the stoves in here should work, too.

Moss got up and headed straight for the kitchen. As he entered the chow hall, a larger-than-life sculpture of a nude female, head and arms lifted toward the heavens, caught his eye standing against the far wall. The figure was exquisite, so much so, he realized after a moment that he was staring at it. Again, he was struck by how odd a work of fine art was in a place like this.

He went behind the serving tables into the kitchen, where pots and pans of all sizes hung from hooks above long metal tables. At one of the four large stoves he lit his incendium and held it to a burner and turned the valve. It ignited with a puff. It was clear now that only the power to the dome had been cut.

Probably just to kill Primary and communications. But why?

He went to one of the sinks and turned on a faucet. The water was turbid as it had been in the office and dormitory. He turned the faucets on in all the sinks in the kitchen to let the water clear. With Stryker buried Moss thought he'd be much more at ease spending the night inside the building, but the noise he heard earlier still troubled him despite his efforts to dismiss it. How to explain it? What could it have been? The wind? A breeze?

There is no such thing in here. And even if there were, it would have to be near hurricane strength to slam a steel-barred door on casters shut.

He had already made up his mind that he would not bunk in a cell. The confining space made him uncomfortable. He wondered how the inmates were ever able to endure it. He headed for the infirmary. It was the logical place. Most likely, it would have hospital beds.

He had expected a clinical atmosphere and appearance as he entered, but instead found a lounge, a large open space. Chessboards were set up on tables—*chessboards for heaven's sake*—and a mural depicting farmers at the different tasks through the seasons of the year, covered the walls. There were small sleeping rooms off the lounge, and he was happy to see he had been right about the beds.

He fetched his gear from out on the landing and picked a room with a bed he thought was the best of them, and that had a small table and chairs. A chessboard with some of the finest carved chess pieces he'd ever seen, was set up on the table just begging him to make a first move. He couldn't resist, and made his usual opening move of the white king's pawn to king four. He decided that each day, while he went about exploring, he could be planning what his countermove would be when he returned that evening.

Settled now, and with his gear organized, he returned to the kitchen. The water was running clear in the sinks, and he began to shut them all off. But when he came to the small lavatory sink at the back of the kitchen, the faucet was off. He was sure he had turned them all on. Did he overlook this one? He was annoyed with himself that he couldn't recall, and now he wasn't so sure.

Moss went from the chow hall out onto the landing where the light was decent, eager to read more of Stryker's journal entries, and became engrossed in them. When the afternoon light began to fade making it difficult to read, he made a mental note: Always explore in the morning. Study the journals and make field notes in the afternoons, so as not to wear out the fuel cell on the prism lantern. He read until it got too dark, trying to piece together what had happened here, at least as much as the journals would reveal:

June 15, 2021–Everybody locked down since we arrived—three days now. The warden came to each cellblock to explain how it's going to work here at Mescalero. We're going to be the grunts. What a surprise. All except me, that is. They will keep me segregated from the others. They're still trying to break me. I get half an hour a day for exercise in something akin to a dog run outside my cell, where I can walk back and forth. It used to bother me a lot—being caged like an animal—but not any more. I do a two-to-three hour calisthenics workout every day that'd put some of these screws in the hospital, and maybe others in the grave.

When the warden came to my cell he made it clear that he was not happy with the warden at Carbondale for sending me. He'd reviewed my file. I was trouble for always getting the population riled up. I might as well get used to this cell, he said. I wouldn't be allowed to be in contact with the other cons. I tried to keep from grinning when he said that, but Br'er Rabbit don' wanna give away how much he like de briar patch, now do he?

He did say something, though, that made me uneasy, something about experiments in the infirmary. This was the first I'd heard of experiments. Need to find out what Chico knows....

June 17, 2021—I find out what's going on from little Chico, the con who brings clean sheets and laundry, and brings me books from the library. He's not allowed to talk to me so he whispers or sings what's going on while he's mopping the hallway near my cell.

Mescalero is an agricultural biosphere, and we're going to raise our own food, so everyone's going to learn how to farm. Chico says the cons aren't happy about any of this. Not like any other place they've been. No visitors. No mail. No telecom or VideoScreen, either. And word is, you don't work, you don't eat....

June 20, 2021—Chico tells me the men will plant and cultivate and harvest with electric servomules, and by hand, too. And they'll be raising cattle and hogs and sheep. Chickens, too. Most of us have never seen an ear of corn on the stalk, let alone a cow....

June 25, 2021—The policy of "no work, no eat" is effective. A lot of the men resisted the policy over the weekend, but by Monday, with nothing to eat all weekend, they became believers. They're out in the fields learning how to hitch up a plow or a hay rake to the servomules, or how to milk a cow, or whatever. Chico says he thinks the guys are enjoying it, planting something then waiting for it to sprout up through the dirt. He's also pretty sure they would never admit that to anyone.

August 11, 2021—No entries for a while. I still get the news from Chico, but I just don't give a shit sometimes. Sometimes, I just shut down. Can't help it. Starting to get some fresh vegetables now, and the kitchen crew butchered their first steer this week. The beef stew wasn't bad. Just not enough salt....

Glancing at entries as he flipped through pages, several things were clear to Moss: These men were learning new skills and, it seemed from what Chico described to Stryker, there was an attitude of pride developing among the men. Most likely, they didn't know much more than how to steal a pickup or a pistol, or how to pull the trigger if they found out who had just shot their brother or sister, before Mescalero. But now they were raising crops and livestock. Not easy to learn, but they were doing it, and that had to be having an impact on them.

Stryker mentioned Chico talking about the gardens along the path to the main building, that they were muy bueno! Roses and dahlias and asters mingling with begonias and geraniums. The fragrance of gardenia hedges lining the path to the entrance, reached even to Stryker's dank, sterile cell sometimes, according to him. And he wrote of hibiscus and hydrangea planted up against the walls of the building itself. The flower gardens, according to Chico, were an "extracurricular" pastime. Interested inmates could work in them before going to work in the fields after breakfast, or in the evening after supper. He heard the warden say gardening was supposed to have a calming influence on the men. Stryker had one regret—other than being free, of course—about being kept to himself, it was not being able to see the flowers or taking part in growing and caring for them.

Chico told Stryker about how, not long after the men began working in the fields, the screws discovered them sneaking contraband they could use to make a weapon into the building. They installed a special magnetic resonance cylinder in the trap. Now, Stryker writes, when they come in from the fields, the men stand in the cylinder first, so Primary can check if they're concealing something.

Stryker also wrote that the greatest strain on all of them was no contact with the outside—especially women. And there weren't going to be any visitations. As far as anyone outside knew, they didn't exist. This had to be demoralizing to all of them, Moss thought, no matter how incorrigible or antisocial they were.

Stryker was becoming clear to Moss. He was bright and observant, and maintained an informed link to what was going on in the rest of the facility, despite his complete separation from the population. It was also clear that he knew the cons looked up to him because the system hadn't succeeded in breaking him, even after all the years in solitary. And something else was obvious in his writings as well. Stryker was not afraid of dying.

August 19, 2021–They try to manipulate me with threats. I laugh at them. What are they going to do? Take away my freedom? Family? Reason for living? Torture me into submission?

The motherfuckers have already stolen my life. What difference does it make what happens now. They use me in these experiments, injecting me with substances that tear my guts to pieces, then leave me lying in a pool of urine in my cell, shivering, waiting for the effects to pass. They watch, hoping for an appeal for mercy—any indication that I give up. And each time I force the laugh and say, "That all you got, suckahs? That the best you can do?"

In the end, it's nothing more than a test—who gives in first, them or me? That's all it's ever been since the beginning—except I win. If I live, I win. They couldn't break me. And if I die, I win, too. They can't get to me anymore....

They'd taken everything away from Stryker that matters to a man, and in doing so lost all leverage with him. If he wasn't afraid of dying, why should he be afraid of anything else?

It wasn't until the muscles in his face became sore around the eyes that Moss realized he was squinting again because daylight was fading. He gathered the bundles of paper and returned to the chow hall. He set a small pot of water on the stove to heat up one of the dehydrated meal packets he'd come upon in the dormitory. Snooping around in the pantry while the water was heating, he came across a cache of what looked to be homemade candles. The still strong scent of honey was immediately noticeable. Moss was impressed by how these men had adapted to their circumstances, as he went about placing them strategically so he wouldn't have to use the prism lantern as much. When he sat down to eat, he was struck by how spare the light was, even with a dozen candles burning close together. This was the extent of light before sunrise and after sunset in the dome, but unlike the ancients, who had never known otherwise, these men had to *learn* to live by candlelight.

When he was through eating, Moss returned to the room he'd picked out in the infirmary. He was again tired. He attributed the weariness he felt at the end of each day to a heightened emotional state, finding himself in such strange, and at the same time, wonderful circumstances.

He lit two candles and set them in their own melting wax on the table, on either side of the chess set. He had decided what his countermove would be over the course of the day. He reached toward the board then stopped, frozen in place, staring at the chessboard in front of him in the flickering light. He felt his scalp tighten. His move had been answered with a matching move of the black king's pawn.

Son of a bitch.

He spun around and slammed the door shut, grabbing one of the chairs to wedge up under the handle. Then he sat down on the bed, taking deep breaths. Instead of taking off his survival knife as he normally would, he kept it strapped to his belt, and set the sturdy, long-handled calcion torch next to him for a club. He lay back on the bed, staring at the chessboard.

Somebody's in here, Jake—and he's been watching you.

He did not fall asleep until weariness finally overcame his fear. When he awoke the morning was well along judging from the light coming through the skylight. Hungry, but anxious, too, about opening the door and walking the long corridor to the chow hall, he rummaged through his knapsack and was glad to find some saltines. He nibbled on crackers and tried to put the shock of the previous night in perspective with a little common sense.

Could've jumped me anytime, if whoever it is wanted to hurt me.

Moss took a swig from his canteen, then stepped to the door and pulled the chair away. With the calcion torch poised in his right hand, his knife in the other, he pulled the door open wide. Everything outside the room appeared the same. No sound or sign of anyone. He lowered the torch and slipped the knife back into its sheath, and stepped back in the room to grab his pack. He glanced over at the chessboard, and for whatever reason— a whimsy perhaps—he decided to answer the black pawn, moving his king's bishop to queen's bishop four, then walked to the trap and out into the dome.

In his haste the previous day to find the cemetery, he hadn't paid attention to much else outside the building and wanted a better look. He hiked to the north end of the dome, but he no longer moved about as casually as he had been doing. Now, he remained watchful all around him as he walked. And he had brought his shovel along, something beside his survival knife he could use as a weapon.

He came upon a cluster of makeshift huts huddled against the wall of the dome, hidden in the overgrowth of a tall, broad-leafed plant he was not familiar with. Some of the roofs had been thatched with it, others were made from pieces of tarpaulin or plasticene. Moss was bewildered about why the huts were there. He found no tools or artifacts in any of them that might offer a clue, and was about to leave the last one when his boot snagged on something in the dirt floor. He poked around with his knife loosening the soil, and tugged at the loop of leather thong. It was part of what appeared to be a rotten leather pouch, breaking open from the weight of its contents, a great many small, flat, rusted pieces of metal. He noted the curious find in his field notepad and took a few with him, then headed back south.

He turned east toward the pond at what he gauged to be the center of the dome. Heading into the dense vegetation surrounding the pond, he came upon another set of huts in an avocado grove at the east end of it. Unlike the others, it had been a fortification of some kind. A berm had been built around the site from a trench dug to the inside, similar to fortifications used by infantry two centuries earlier. Remnants of sharpened stakes still stood where they had been driven into the earth, angled outward on the top of the berm. Here, too, Moss found nothing in the way of tools or weapons or utensils that could explain why the site was there.

It was midday. Full sun overhead, filtered by the coating of sand dust on the outside the dome, gave a pale white glow to everything, and the atmosphere was sultry. Moss's clothes were sopped with perspiration. Keeping with his plan to explore in the mornings, read and record notes in the afternoons, he picked an avocado then made his way back to the building for some lunch, still puzzled by the huts.

He was apprehensive going into the building, but he had left Stryker's journals in the chow hall so he had no choice. He moved down the corridor in a slight crouch, the spade balanced in his hand at his side, watching for anything that moved as his eyes adjusted to the dim light inside. He had spread the bundles of journals out on the tables to organize them into a time line. He gathered the pages he had set aside to read next, and slipped back outside as quickly as he could.

Moss sat on the landing, facing the trap instead of with his back to it as he picked up Stryker's journals again. Throughout the afternoon he felt like a voyeur as he read his confessions of loneliness and sorrow, mixed with a narrative of prideful resolve not to be broken by the *screws* as they were known. Stryker was convinced that was the reason they used him so much more than the others in the lab experiments—because of his stubborn will. Screws, he wrote, always took it personal—a challenge, a badge of honor—to once for all bring him to his knees. They didn't get it, he went on, that when he saw their faces each time they tried to break him, met again by his stare of pure, undiminished defiance, it was like sex for him. Over the years, that's what it had become for James Stryker.

In the last light of evening before darkness took over the dome, he opened to a series of entries that finally began to detail what had happened here:

January 12, 2022–Chico didn't show today. There was some emergency. The power went off just after 0900hrs and Primary declared Lock Down over the PA system just after that. Geez, I love listening to her voice....

Moss recognized the date immediately, the day the solares began disrupting power and communications all over the planet. Then, a few pages further on:

January 29, 2022–Chico says he got the straight stuff on why the lockdown two weeks ago. He overheard Santos and Caldwell talking when he was mopping the floor in the Command Center. Three of Briscoe's morons and Eddie the Tin Man killed Abby, the good-looking woman in the lab, after they all had a piece of her. They did Maria, too. Trouble is no one knew Abby was the warden's daughter....

Then:

February 13, 2022–The screw didn't show with breakfast this morning and all the lights were off. Strong Knife slipped in here in the middle of the night. Didn't know I was awake. I watched him take Eddie the Tin Man out of here, shackled and gagged. Something's up.

A couple hours later, there was a ruckus in the main corridor. Sounded like everybody was loose. When I went to the door of my cell to see if I could see anything with my hand mirror, it swung open....

***

Seth Schilling stepped awkwardly off the treadmill to answer the contax.

"Mr. Schilling, this is Johnny Little Hawk over at the Cayuse substation."

"Oh yes, John. How are things over that way these days? And that big family, how are they?" Schilling did not ask these questions for want of an answer so much as carrying out his responsibility to the age old tradition of noblesse oblige.

"We're doing okay, Sir."

"What can I do for you, John?"

"Well, Sir, you wanted me to let you know if I noticed anything unusual going on out at the old Mescalero site."

"Yes...right," Schilling said cautiously at the mention of Mescalero.

"There's been a couple surges in usage on the meter out there over the last few days, and the static reading is a steady three to four points higher than what it has been for years. Just thought I should let you know, Sir."

"Well, of course, John. Thank you, you did the right thing."

After closing the connection, Schilling buzzed his secretary.

"Ah, Ortega," he said, as a tall, swarthy man entered the room a moment later. "I'd like you to do a couple of things for me. Get a hold of Ketchum and tell him I need him to come by the ranch as soon as he can. And tomorrow, have Jesus pick out a couple fat Charolais calves and haul them over to John Little Hawk's place at Cayuse."

Ortega acknowledged he understood with a nod and left as silently as he had entered, and Schilling climbed back on the treadmill.

That evening, as the summer sun dropped below the horizon turning the desert sky from pale pink to blood red, Ortega greeted arriving guests under the portico at the front door of the great hacienda. Impeccably dressed in tails and standing with his always perfect posture, his presence ensured that the boys in their black slacks and starched white shirts would open the doors of each limousine promptly, offering a hand to the women as he had shown them.

At a grand party, just after Ortega first came to work at the ranch, he had stood inside the door announcing the names of the guests as they entered with great fanfare, having been brought up in service to Mexican aristocracy and taught to do so. Schilling had to take him aside and explain that he wanted a bit less formality and fanfare at Sunburst Hacienda. With that and a few other adjustments, such as not serving his employer beer in a glass and not driving him because he enjoyed driving himself, he adapted well to the more casual ostentation of wealth Schilling preferred to display. But the qualities Seth Schilling had come to appreciate most in Fernando Ortega over the past twenty years were his discretion and his unerring loyalty.

The Lieutenant Governor came up to Schilling at the bar, apologizing for the Governor: He had wanted to be there, but was unavoidably detained. Schilling was at that moment pretending to listen—and care—to the whining of the woman who ran the National Infectious Disease Tracking Center. He had agreed to host this fundraiser for her organization, but he had not agreed to endure her incessant prattle. Ortega, as if on cue, approached and whispered that there was someone to see him. He asked Ortega to introduce the woman to the Lieutenant Governor and excused himself.

Schilling slipped out the kitchen door, heading for the barn. He recognized Ketchum's pickup parked under the prism lamp next to it. Perhaps the most noticeable aspect of Schilling's appearance was his gait. He was profoundly pigeon-toed. Each buttock would flex to the extreme with every step. And he walked with head and shoulders slouched forward, his hands swinging loosely at his sides. This, with his being a stocky, rather hairy man, made him look like a dolt.

He entered the barn through the tack room and pressed on the light. A couple of the horses nickered in their stalls, expecting it must be feeding time again. Delbert Ketchum was leaning his tall, wiry frame against the tractor parked in the cobblestoned alley between the stalls. He smelled of axle grease and engine oil.

"Sorry, Mister Schilling, about interruptin' yer shindig I mean. Ortega said, 'as soon as ya can,' so I dropped ever'thin' an' come right away."

"Anybody see you...any of the guests?"

Ketchum shook his head.

"Listen, Delbert, I've only got a minute. I'd like you to drive down to the old Mescalero prison site and take a look around. I want to know if anything's been disturbed, if anything's changed."

Ketchum nodded, rubbing a grease-blackened hand along the engine cowling of the tractor.

"And keep this to yourself, Delbert. Let me know what you find. Use the contax number Ortega gave you."

"Yessir, I sure will," he replied with a squinty, puckered-up look. As he started to leave Schilling handed him an envelope and told him to drive out the back way, out the stock road.

Back in the grand living room that his father had always called "the Great Room" when he was alive, Schilling mingled again. He'd learned the importance of this as a young man by watching his father at functions like these. The message was clear: Charm or cajole those you want something from as you move around the room, and threaten, in the subtlest of ways, those who need reminding where the real power lies.

There was never a shortage of women hoping to impress or gain an edge on his attention at these affairs with Schilling still a bachelor. He would humor their transparent flirtations until something more important such as exercising his considerable influence was required, or until he found them tiresome. When he spotted his attorney, Max Amadoux, he waved, deftly slipping to one side of the woman who had hoped to corner him at the French doors that opened out onto the veranda.

"Greetings, Max, you old reprobate," Seth chided, "I didn't see you arrive. How is everything on the island?"

Maximilian Amadoux was twelfth generation Grenadine aristocracy, a tall and elegant black man with hair and teeth white as sun-bleached coral. He overlooked the vulgar greeting with the grace and bearing of island royalty, not only because of his upbringing, but because Seth Schilling was his only client and he was used to it.

"Good evening, young Seth. Lovely party. Life is fine in the islands, thank you. Of course, hurricane season will be upon us shortly, so who knows? And how are you faring?"

"Fine, Max, fine. When did you arrive?" he asked as a waiter offered them canapés from an ornate silver tray. Schilling leaned closer to Amadoux, lowering his voice to little more than a mutter. "And what is it you want to talk about that we couldn't discuss on the conny, that you had to travel all this way?"

"Please, young Seth, do you have a moment when we could talk, in your study perhaps?" he said, trying to speak above the strumming of the guitar quartet strolling by.

Schilling knew the look on Amadoux's face: Something pressing needed to be addressed. He motioned to Ortega across the room, indicating that he and Amadoux were going to his study, and to see to the guests' needs while he was busy. Ortega nodded and the two men disappeared down the long hallway.

Schilling closed the door to his office and walked to the dry sink where he poured scotch whiskey from a lead crystal decanter in two glasses, handing one to Amadoux.

"Now, Max, what's going on?"

"Someone knows who you are, knows about your father changing your names, your birth records, school and bank records and such. I have received a letter. They want money…a lot of money."

Schilling sipped his drink, then walked to his rather modest ebony wood desk, and sat down in the plush leather wing chair. He looked at the framed photo set on the desk, of him as a young man standing at the helm of the two-masted schooner with his father. They were waving at the camera out off the stern. The name of the vessel in gold lettering across the transom: Abby's Dream, Grenada.

"Know who it is?" Schilling asked, sweeping a lock of his thick gray hair back off his forehead.

"Not yet. The postmark was local, though that may not mean anything."

"Well, Max," he said, feigning a lack of concern for the gravity of the situation as Amadoux saw it. "Can't have that going on, now can we? What shall we do?"

Amadoux did not reply, knowing after thirty years of working for Seth and twenty for his father before him, that he would be told precisely what to do. He sipped his drink standing in front of the fireplace, admiring the antique revolver mounted on the wall above the mantle, and waited for the next words, words he'd heard many times before.

"Take care of it, Max. Do whatever you have to, but be sure to find out who all of them are first."

Amadoux nodded, continuing to inspect the display of weapons mounted above the fireplace.

"Play along with them, know what I mean?"

Amadoux nodded again.

"Tell them you can only give them half what they want, so you'll have to have another meet. When you're sure you know who all of them are—"

"I think you should be prepared to leave here on a moment's notice, young Seth, in the event something goes wrong and the truth gets out."

"My dear Max, why do you think that AeroFoil is parked in the hangar out at the runway?" Schilling said with a shrewd look on his face. "Always got a bag and passport ready."

"Your papa taught you well, young sir."

"Yes, he did, Max. I do not intend to have anything go wrong."

"Nor did your father, young Se—"

"Max, will you please stop calling me young Seth? I'm sixty four years old, for Chris'sakes."

"I beg your pardon, Seth, old habits...slow to die," he said, overlooking Schilling's manners again. "As I was saying, your father didn't plan on getting caught. He just knew it was always a possibility, so he was always ready as I see he taught you. And, I would remind you, he never was found out, the money just stopped being funded. Remember?"

"Why do you bring this up, Max, being ready to leave quickly? What's changed?" Schilling removed his glasses and massaged the bridge of his broad, flat nose.

"My sources in the capital tell me the finance committee is about to start reviewing the efficacy of funding in the Office of Clandestine Affairs. They may go back decades as a foundation to illustrate their findings. An independent firm has been hired to do the audit. I cannot imagine them going back fifty years, or making the connection with the Ministry of Prisons and...Mescalero, but as your father would say, 'You never know. They could. Don't take chances.'"

Schilling got up out of his chair and walked to the window. The last vestiges of bloodred sky had given way to night and a sickle-shaped moon. He turned and looked at Amadoux. Were it not for the white hair, he'd never guess Max was an eighty-year old man.

"Max, I want whoever it is that knows about us," he said in a way that could not be misconstrued. "Where is L'oiseau these days?"

"Ah, yes, that was who I had in mind, also. I can find him, I'm sure."

"Yes, put him on it if he's free. Keep me informed."

Amadoux set his glass, the drink hardly touched, on the dry sink, thinking their business was finished, and started for the door, but Schilling hesitated.

"You know, Max, it's funny," he said, gulping what was left in his glass. "Just today I got a call about Mescalero, something about the power usage being up."

"I would be hard-pressed to think it anything more than a coincidence, Sir," Amadoux offered by way of reassurance.

"Perhaps," Schilling said, not as sure.

The two men returned to the party just as everyone was being seated for the dinner auction.

"The new impetus toward global parochialism is necessary," the speaker said with confidence, "if we are to survive. The notion that we are a global community, and therefore must not cut ourselves off from one another, is precisely the reason the National Infectious Disease Center came into being. The world has become so intertwined, so mobile that, without exaggeration, the outbreak of an infectious disease on one side of the globe can be detected within a day or two on the other. This is why we...."

Schilling wasn't interested. He'd heard it all before. Countries around the globe closing their borders to stem the deadly tide of a dozen different killers: A virus, B virus, C virus. In fact, Schilling was rarely interested in any of these big affairs he hosted. They were only a way to maintain his position of influence, to keep his reputation as one of the movers and shakers, the one you went to if you wanted to get somewhere, whatever your purpose was.

He maintained his façade of concerned and committed philanthropist through the coq au vin, followed by the bananas flambé. Smiling always, never knowing when the photographer might be focused on him, he engaged in the shallow chitchat bantered back and forth at the head table. Occasionally, at precisely the right moment, he feigned a convincing laugh at someone's absurd little joke. So the evening went, like so many others, but all the while thinking of Amadoux's disturbing report. He tried to imagine what it might be like if the truth came out, to be brought low, humiliated, to be imprisoned, even. He dismissed the thought as absurd, assured in his own mind that his resources and his influence were beyond threat. Couldn't happen, he thought.

As the evening came to a close and he had taken a properly unpretentious bow for the proceeds the event had generated for the Center, he bid his guests good night at the door, like a priest at church on Sunday morning. A few stayed: The lieutenant Governor and his accommodating young assistant, the whiny little chairman of the Center and her husband, an architect and his wife, there to discuss their host's hope of carving an amphitheater for the performing arts out of the rim rock out beyond the airfield.

Amadoux was to leave within the hour in the executive aerofoil he arrived in. Schilling had a few last words with him about mundane matters at the island compound, then retired to his bedroom. Ortega would see to everything else.

CHAPTER SIX

In the beginning of March, two weeks since the chaos and carnage broke out in the cellblocks, Stryker hides up in the rafters of the pump house at the sewage settling pools. Because of the stench no one thinks to look for him there.

He can see the entrance to the main building through the soffit vent in the eaves. A body is still being brought out to bury almost every day. By his count, twenty-three men have been killed since the middle of February. With the three snuffed by the guards back in January and Eddie the Tin Man missing, it leaves a hundred seventy-three men out of the original two hundred.

"They have to stop the killing," he whispers under his breath, sweating in the heat and foul air of the loft, "or we're all going to die."

Each night, long after dark, he makes his way into the building through a skylight at the south end, near the loading dock. He can't get in through the trap. Briscoe has men on guard there. He paints or scrawls or scribbles messages on walls, on the floors—anywhere he thinks the men might see them. Many of the men can't read or read only a little, so he asks the ones who can to pass the message on. This is risky. It takes more time, and Briscoe's goons are always on the prowl.

One night, as close to the trap as he's ever dared to come, he paints huge letters on the corridor wall with quasi-resin gum he's found in the pump house:

WE NEED EVERY MAN TO GET THE WORK DONE!

A couple nights later, on the chow hall steam table:
CUT A MAN'S THROAT AND
YOU'RE CUTTING YOUR OWN!

The night after that, on the floor at the entrance to C Wing:
IF YOU WANT TO LIVE, WE ALL

HAVE TO GO BACK TO WORK!

The stench in the pump house is much stronger during the hot hours of the day, especially up in the rafters, but Stryker has no choice. He has to stay out of sight during the day. But Briscoe's soldiers are not looking for him as often now, since Bruno and Manning set up camps out in the dome with their gangs. Late at night, when Stryker slips inside the building to paint another message, he spots a note scrawled in small letters at the end of one of his earlier ones:

James, we got no beef with you. Briscoe is the problum.

Stryker is encouraged, but knowing Briscoe as well as he does, he also knows it could be one of his tricks.

Two days and one more body later he hears a commotion inside the building. It's just daylight—usually still quiet at that hour. He takes a chance and sneaks up onto the landing. For some reason, there are no guards in the Command Center or the trap, so he slips inside and makes his way to the guard turret above the chow hall without being seen. Briscoe's soldiers are struggling to hold a crowd of about fifty men at bay, and more are gathering fast. They're hungry.

The reefers and freezers were emptied soon after the power went off, and now the last of the dehydrated foods have been used up. There are no more stored provisions. No one has been working in the fields, or picking any produce. The livestock have been let loose into the dome by Bruno's men. Cows haven't been milked or eggs picked. No steers or hogs butchered.

When it becomes clear there's nothing left in the kitchen pantries, some of the men head for the trap. Others follow. Soon, everyone is moving out into the dome. He stays put, watching, until he sees the last man pass through the trap. The building is empty.

With everyone out in the dome, Stryker makes a dash for the Command Center and looks out through the trap. The men are off in the groves and fields and vegetable gardens, eating as they pick, everything from tomatoes to onions to oranges to eggplant. He steps back into the Command Center, reaches up for the lever to the outer door of the trap and pulls. It slides shut and he places the pin through the hasp that holds it in locked position, then sits back and waits.

An hour passes and Stryker steps over to the window. Men have started back toward the building, carrying what produce they can. Just then, he hears a noise behind him and spins around. Briscoe is standing there with a long, wide-blade chopping knife in his hand, a twin to the one Necco carries. Stryker is pissed at himself for not having been more careful.

"Where ya been, James? I been lookin' for you." Briscoe has a cocky grin on his face.

Stryker doesn't say anything, just keeps his eyes locked on Briscoe's.

"You're becomin' a liability, James. You're interfering with my plans. Can't have that, James," he says waving the blade back and forth. "Unh, unh."

"Like I told you Vince, I'm not ready to die yet."

"Well, we seem to have us a Mexican standoff, don't we? 'Cept, a'course, I got the advantage here in my hand. What do you think we should do, James?" The grin seems almost painted on Briscoe's face at this point.

Stryker keeps staring into his eyes, then moves a step toward him. Briscoe quickly takes a half step back, a giveaway look on his face of surprise and fear. In that instant, Stryker knows he has him.

No good without his goons.

"Watch it, James! I'll cut ya."

Briscoe is looking around, trying to think, and Stryker takes another step toward him. He takes another quick step back, waving the knife out in front of him, at Stryker's face.

"I'm warnin' ya, James."

Briscoe can't seem to think and act at the same time. His eyes pan around the room, the knife pointing wherever he looks. Stryker takes another step toward him. Briscoe retreats again and is out of the trap except for his arm holding the knife. Stryker springs to the lever for the inner door and pulls hard. The door jams into Briscoe's forearm near the wrist and the knife falls from his hand. He bellows at the pain of the impact and wrenches his arm clear. Stryker pulls the lever again, and the door shuts the rest of the way.

Briscoe crumples to the floor moaning and clutching his arm, then gets up and throws himself at the door in a rage.

"You sonuvabitch, James! Next time, I'll—"

"There isn't going to be a next time, Vince," he says, as he secures the lever lock.

"What the fuck you talkin' about?"

"Well, figure it out. You're locked in with nothing to eat, and everybody else is locked out, and that's the way it's going to be until we understand and agree about what we have to do."

"Yeah? Well, you ain't got nuthin' to eat either, asshole!"

Stryker brings his face right to the bars in the door with frightening deliberateness, and stares into Briscoe's eyes. His expression is so intense it makes Briscoe uneasy even though he's safely beyond Stryker's reach.

"I've fasted for thirty days or more, Vince. You?"

Briscoe kicks the door hard several times, then starts back down the corridor toward the cellblocks cursing him. Stryker watches him go, wondering if he will be able to understand what they are really up against.

For the next three days, Stryker keeps to his routine. Meditation, a three-hour workout, sleep, and waiting. He is counting on no one finding the skylight or managing to get the loading dock doors unlocked, or finding some other way into or out of the building. The men out in the dome aren't hungry anymore, but they are more and more agitated struggling to find cover from the rain every night. Briscoe has not been back to the trap. He keeps looking for a way out of the building, and in the kitchen tries to make something edible out of the last of the flour in the pantry.

Day four and Stryker still waits. When there's room at the door because Briscoe's soldiers have tired for the moment from casting useless threats at him, others approach imploring him to open the door. He ignores them, and continues his memorization exercises, reciting passages from the Psalms.

Late in the night, lying on the concrete floor with his bones and his belly aching, he continues to struggle with how to bring everyone together. As the hours pass, he finally slips into fitful sleep:

"Who's there?" Stryker asks, thinking someone is standing in the shadows at the back corner of the Command Center. He tries but can't move to get up off the floor.
"How'd you get in here?"
No reply.
The room is moving strangely. His legs and arms feel as if they've fallen asleep.

Somewhere else now: A sandy beach stretching to the horizon. He yearns to run, to lift off the ground, to fly, but can't, struggling, stuck like a rat in a glue trap.

Then: A bedroom. A little boy lying on a bed, face buried in a pillow, crying. Who is that? he wonders. Another room. Larger. A man in a casket. People milling about. A haggard woman sits in a rocker, staring at the floor. The little boy lifts his face out of the pillow. Why is he dead? Like cathedral bells, the question rings in his mind: Why Daddy? Why dead? They echo. The boy looks again. Not his father, but his little brother.
Now the woman in the rocker holds a basin in her hands, a towel draped over her arm. The basin is full of blood. She beckons to the boy to take it. Briscoe is standing next to the coffin.
"Here, little Jamesey, take it," she says. "Wash his feet."

Then: Command Center again. Blinding light. Stryker is standing at the counter, next to where he had been sleeping.

Day five. Stryker strains to recall his night dreams. It seems important to try but the images only shimmer at the edge of recollection, fading in and out. The shape in the shadows. A dream? His strength is sapped for want of something more than water, and he forgoes his workout. During his meditations, he finds himself thinking about Briscoe, about something he should do for him? To him. What? He cannot remember.

He wonders how long he should keep up this standoff with the men. What does he want to happen? What's the best he can hope for? Gradually, through the day, it becomes clear: He wants their undivided attention. He wants them all to listen—all of them—at one time. He finds the guard's log and rips out a blank sheet of paper, and begins to write what he thinks will make sense to them. As he writes, an image forms in his mind of his little brother, Billy, lying in a casket, and he is trying to wash his feet. He shakes his head. Too weird. Too strange. When it is finally night and the rain has begun again, sleep comes easier than the night before. He is grateful for it as his eyelids grow heavy.

Day six. Stryker can hear one of the roosters crowing out beyond the north end of the building. He is surprised there is even a rooster still alive. The rain has just stopped. For the first time in weeks, though he can't account for it, he feels invigorated. He steps into the trap from the Command Center and after a few moments realizes that Briscoe is at the inner door, and Manning, Bruno, and a few of the other would-be gang bosses in the population are at the outer door—at the same time. And it looks to Stryker as if all of them have had enough.

Stryker hands a sheet of paper to Bruno through the bars and tells him to read it to the men gathered at the bottom of the steps behind him. He hands a copy to Briscoe, too. Bruno looks at it, then the men, then back at Stryker. He whispers to Stryker through the barred window, asks if Joey the Gimp who is sitting next to him can read it instead. Stryker nods and Bruno leans down near Joey.

"Read it for me, Joey," he whispers, "I don't know how."

The little man whose jaw reaches barely above Bruno's belt looks up at him, surprised, takes the paper. Flushed with embarrassment at being the center of attention, he begins to read:

You can't be like you've always been; do things the way you have since you were kids. Think about it. Think. We got no power, right? So that means the servomules and electrocarts are useless because we can't charge the batteries. We're locked in here, maybe for good, no one knows. Feeding everyone is going to take manpower now—a lot of it—so we can't afford to lose any more men.

Stryker tells Joey to stop for a minute to let it sink in. Then he nods, and Joey continues:

If you want to eat—if you want to live—we've got to work together. Whether you like it or not, you don't have a choice.

Joey turns and walks back to the door of the trap. Everyone is quiet. He looks up at Stryker.

"What about Vince, James?"

"What about him?"

"Well, I mean, he's hungry, ya know? How 'bout lettin' him out?"

Stryker thinks about this for a moment then agrees to let him through the trap, but first he has something else to say to the men gathered out on the landing.

"You guys gotta start using your heads," he shouts through the bars. "You outnumber Briscoe, for God's sake. And it isn't like he's got any better weapons. All they have are shivs, just like you. That goes for Manning and Bruno, too. Use your heads, for Chris'sakes. There's five of you to any one of them. Don't let them push you around anymore."

The men are quiet and still, looking at each other, at Bruno, then Manning, for more than a minute. Stryker turns and moves to the inner door and looks hard at Briscoe through the bars. Briscoe is furious, the tic in his face quivering wildly.

"Now, I'm going to open this door, Vince, and you're going to step inside and move right over to the other door, understand? Then I'm going to open that door and you're going to step out quick, got me? If you don't, if you try anything, I'll open you up with this knife you pulled on me the other day. Savvy?"

Briscoe's so hungry he doesn't quibble. He moves quickly through the trap, out onto the landing, and heads straight for the banana groves, running at first, then catching himself and walking with deliberate steps. Some of his soldiers start to follow, but Stryker notices that a dozen or more are slow to get up and go with him.

In the excitement of the moment when Briscoe had first stepped out onto the landing, his men greeting and consoling and praising him, Stryker had slipped down the corridor, leaving the trap wide open. He sees no choice for the rest of the day but to hunker down up on the roof, outside the skylight above the loading dock, and hope what was said has the desired effect.

Well after dark, after the rain begins, he makes his way down off the roof and sneaks back to the pump house. The first thing he does when he gets up in the loft is devour the cluster of bananas he'd stashed there a week ago, undeterred by how blackened and soft they have become.

When it's light, I'll watch from the rafters. See what's what. See if Briscoe still has his men looking for me.

Except for the stench at all hours and the heat during the day, the loft in the pump house is a welcome change for sleeping than the concrete floor of the Command Center. Rolls of plasticene polytarp used to repair the sewage pool levees are stored there and make a decent enough mattress. With something in his stomach and a vague sense of hope he can't explain, he falls easily to sleep.

"Ma?" he calls to her. She's a long way off. "What is it? What do you want?" She's holding the basin and towel again. She's reaching, trying to give it to him.

"Fill it up with Billy's blood," she says. "Go ahead. It's all right, little Jamesey, go ahead." She's looking at Briscoe, and James bristles that he is near her and tries to run to get between them.

"No, Jamesey," she says, "wash his—"

Light floods the pump house.

So bright. Can't open my eyes. Eyelids on fire. And wind. Want to run. Legs won't work. A voice within the light saying something. Can't understand. Can't make it out.

The light and the wind and the voice stop. Stryker is awake, lying there sweating cold sweat, heart pounding, trembling.

A dream? Nightmare? So real, just like in the Command Center. What was it saying?

Stryker watches through the soffit vent as the rain stops and the ever pale sunlight begins to fill the dome. He notices that men are leaving and entering the building unopposed. Climbing down to the ground floor, he's light-headed, unsteady moving around the room. He sees men heading out into the fields with hand tools through the east window.

Chico is walking in his direction pulling a wagon. He figures he's heading for the compost pile, fertilizer for Chico's flower gardens. When Chico is between the pump house and the toolshed on the path, where he is out of the view of most of the others, Stryker calls to him from the north window, motioning him to come to the door.

"Amigo, it's James! Come here."

Chico stops, seeing the hand beckoning from the darkened window, nods, and heads casually for the pump house so as not to draw attention to himself. He parks the wagon at the door, looking around to be sure no one is watching, and calls to Stryker.

"Hey, Amigo, come on out. Ayyy, caramba, it must stink in there!"

"Briscoe still looking to snuff me, Chico?"

"Negatory, James. He's got other problems since your speech yesterday. You can come out, Bro," he says as he looks down, and sees one of his shoelaces is undone.

The door swings open and Stryker steps out into the light.

"Hey, James," he says, kneeling with his head down, tying the lace. "I was wondering where you—"

He stops when he looks up at Stryker, scrambles to his feet, stumbling as he jumps backwards.

"Wha? What's the matter, Chico?"

Chico doesn't say anything, his jaw hanging open, still moving backwards until he trips and falls over the wagon behind him.

Stryker runs over to him.

"What's wrong, Amigo?" he asks again, helping Chico to his feet.

"Mother of God, James! What happened to you?"

"What do you mean?"

"Jesus, James, your hair. Shit, your eyebrows, your beard, too."

"What d'you mea—"

"It's all white, James!" he yells, stepping back again and turning to run. "White as fuckin' snow!"

Stryker watches his friend running as though a puma was chasing him. He can't see his hair or his beard, but he rolls up the sleeve on his jumpsuit. His arm hair is white—not blonde—white. He lifts the leg of his pants. Same thing. He opens his jumpsuit at the crotch and pulls down his under shorts.

"My God," he whispers, as he stares at the pure white pubic hair.

He leaves the pump house, relieved that Briscoe has called off his men, and glad to get away from the stench. But he is troubled by Chico's reaction to him. He heads for the pond where he can see his reflection in the water.

Sweet, earthy scents replace the foul odor of the pump house as he walks at nearly a jog. Approaching the south end of the pond, hidden by a stand of Pax, Stryker hears a splash. He clears the thicket and sees Manning and three of his gang with their backs to him. Something sinks just then, out away from the shore, and he sees the end of a rope slipping slowly off the bank into the water. He moves closer. Manning spins around first, then the others. They don't seem to be able to move—or speak—at first.

"Sonuvabitch!" Manning finally stammers.

James realizes it's a body that just sank and runs toward them.

"Stryker!" the man next to Manning shouts. The two men farthest from Stryker break for the underbrush. When Manning sees them sprinting up over the bank, he glances at Stryker, motions to his last man, and they both take off right behind the others.

Stryker dives for the rope as the end is going under. He spots a blade one of the men dropped, grabs it and a deep breath and goes under, following the rope to the end. The body is wrapped in polytarp and weighted down with a boulder. Stryker cuts the man's feet free of the weight, and as they rise to the surface he kicks with all his strength to get them to shore.

The moment Stryker's feet touch bottom, he holds the man's head above water, cuts the rope wrapped around his neck, and rips a hole in the polytarp. The man is still alive, gasping for air. He wasn't drowning—he was suffocating. Stryker drags him up on the bank, cuts the rope at his waist, then at his ankles and feet which are cut and bleeding.

The man's chest thrusts up and down, wheezing, still gasping for air as Stryker hurries to unwrap the plasticene tarp around him. He pulls the last wrap free from the man's head. It's Briscoe looking up at the man bending over him, and screams in terror.

He rolls away from Stryker, trying to get up and run, but he stumbles in the soft earth of the bank. Stryker leaps and lands on Briscoe's back, holding his arms in a hammerlock until he stops struggling, his face stuffed into the ground. Briscoe tries to speak but starts coughing from breathing in the dirt. Stryker lets go of his arms and turns him on his side and Briscoe lies there staring at him, trying to catch his breath.

"Your feet are cut and bleeding from the rope," Stryker says softly. "The wounds are caked with dirt. Sit at the edge of the water so I can wash them."

Briscoe watches, awestruck by Stryker standing in the water, with his pure white hair and beard looking like a wild man, dabbing and rinsing the wounds on his feet with a square of cloth he's torn from his own jumpsuit.

"What the fuck happened to you, James?"

"I don't know."

"Christ, you look like you seen a ghost."

He nods, thinking about this. "Maybe I did."

Neither of them says anything for what seems a long time, while Stryker flushes the dirt from the lacerations to his ankles and feet.

Then Briscoe speaks. "What now?" he says, unsettled by Stryker's steely gaze.

"I'll have to carry you."

They do not speak, either, after Stryker hefts Briscoe up on his back and carries him piggyback along the path back to the cellblocks. As the unlikely pair passes, the men in the fields stare, drop what they're doing and begin to follow.

Others near the entrance to the building, who saw them coming, gather on the landing as Stryker climbs the steps. Getting a closer look as he approaches the trap carrying Briscoe, they all step back in amazement. Joey the Gimp is at the door. Stryker asks him to get bandages and antiseptic from the infirmary. He is stunned looking at Stryker, and glances at Briscoe who nods his approval. They duck their heads to clear the doorjamb of the trap and disappear into the cool darkness inside.

When they reach Briscoe's cell, Stryker lowers him to the bunk. A few minutes later, Joey the Gimp stumbles in from the infirmary and hands Stryker the things he asked for. Necco and some of Briscoe's best soldiers show up and take up positions around him, fear and confusion in their faces. Briscoe grimaces with a loud groan as Stryker swabs the wounds at his ankles with antiseptic, then wraps Briscoe's feet. And Joey the Gimp stands there paralyzed by what is taking place before his eyes.

When he is through, Stryker gets up to leave, but Briscoe grabs his arm. His soldiers come to alert. Joey the Gimp steps back.

"James, I uh…."

"Yes?"

"You saved my life. I owe you one…a big one," Briscoe says, looking around, uneasy with his soldiers and Joey watching. "Name it…anything."

James looks at Briscoe, then at each man there, then back at Briscoe, with the same steely look so unsettling to Briscoe at the pond.

"Don't go after Manning and his men, Vince."

CHAPTER SEVEN

When it became too dark out on the landing to read any longer, Moss gathered Stryker's journals and took them back to the chow hall. From there, he walked the darkened corridor to his room in the infirmary, afraid someone might jump him at any moment. Once he had closed the door and braced the chair against it, the butterflies in his gut subsided. He fumbled through his pockets for his incendium, lit the prism lantern, and leaned his spade against the wall next to the bed within arm's reach.

He looked at the chessboard. It had happened again—a countermove: black king's bishop to queen's bishop four. Noticing another move had been made was far less jolting than it had been the night before, but he still felt a shiver along his spine. He lit all the candles he'd set up around the room and shut off the lantern, then sat at the little table studying the move. Moss was intrigued, even excited in a way, playing chess with this mystery opponent. As he matched the move with the white king's bishop to queen's bishop four, he realized that he was not as scared either.

Wednesday morning, the start of his fourth full day inside the biosphere, Moss awoke feeling genuinely refreshed for the first time in days. He planned to hike the perimeter of the dome, and to devise a way to catch some of those fish in the pond. On his way out of the building after breakfast, he glanced into the Command Center and saw something on the counter next to the security console. He couldn't believe it. He'd gone through the place three times. How could he possibly have missed it lying out in the open on the counter? It was the Command Center Duty Log. He took it out onto the landing for the better light, and sat down on the steps. He opened to a bookmark to Caldwell's Watch/Day Shift/1/12/2022.

Here it is again, he thought, the date of the solares event.

0800hrs—Relieved officers Santos and Strong Knife. Briefed on their report for graveyard shift: Conditions normal. No incidents. No issues.

0805hrs—Performed standard Primary checks. All results normal.

0830hrs—Made inventory/readiness check on Command Center small arms cache. One AR25 assault rifle appears to have a faulty energy cell. Made out a Request For Replacement form to submit to warden at the end of shift.

0845hrs—Dispatched officer Daemon to escort four inmates to infirmary laboratory for subject studies.

0911hrs—Power outage occurred. No information available as to why.

0912hrs—Primary initiated auxiliary power. All systems indicate normal function. Primary supervising all life support and security systems.

0921hrs—Received intercom message from infirmary. Shots fired. Officer Daemon down. Inmates armed. Instituted Lockdown Sequence and notified warden immediately. Primary in control of the dome. Several civilian personnel unaccounted for. Two female casualties (seen on video) possibly fatalities.

Moss scanned the next few pages describing the steps taken to quell the insurrection. He was surprised at the warden's response. It appeared from some log entries that he had no intention of negotiating with the inmates. It ended with the two females confirmed fatalities, two male hostages escaping, and three of the four inmates being killed in an armed assault ordered by the warden.

What appeared to be fairly routine entries followed for a month, until the last entry, which Moss found to be highly unusual:

Santos's Watch/Graveyard Shift/2/13/2022

0000hrs—Santos and Strong Knife relieved officers Pendergast and Sturns. Primary still in modified manual mode due to the insurrection of 1/12.

0030hrs–Performed modified manual tests on Primary. All functions respond as programmed. Performed standard inspection of weaponry. Weapons and ordnance in ready mode.

0109hrs–Received intercom communication from Warden Smalley with <u>special</u> instructions to be carried out during shift.

0115hrs–Contacted warden in his office. Performed verification sequence on <u>special</u> instructions authorization.

0329hrs–Following specific orders of Warden Samuel Smalley, officers Santos and Strong Knife vacating biosphere with one inmate, Edward Pierce, aka Eddie the Tin Man. All weapons and ordnance removed from the dome. All cells unlocked at withdrawal. Locking outer door of bulkhead upon exit.

Moss set the duty log down next to him and stared out into the dome. He wasn't sure whether this information shed more light on his discoveries to date, or created more questions. He recalled Stryker's reference to Strong Knife taking Eddie the Tin Man out of DSU, though he still didn't know why. And why would the guards be instructed to leave the dome and leave all the cells unlocked? And the biggest mystery still: Why had the bulkhead been sealed?

At times like this, he'd learned the best thing to do was occupy himself with something else, and let the questions on his mind sort themselves out in their own way. He left the duty log on the landing, and headed out to the bulkhead to begin inspecting the integrity of the dome's foundation.

He hadn't walked far when it came clear to him: *Of course. The chess player set that logbook there. He wanted me to find it. That had to be it. I would never have missed it. Hell, I didn't miss it. It wasn't there until this morning.*

He spun around and ran back to the building, and stepping out into the main corridor, shouted as loud as he could, "Who are you? Show yourself."

He waited. Not unexpected, there was no reply and he walked back out to the bulkhead.

He found no indication of structural breakdown anywhere along the foundation. Armorglass had indeed lived up to its half-century claim of being practically indestructible. At the northeast corner of the biosphere, where an outcropping of sandstone jutted up, he came to an excavation site, where timbers supported the entrance to a crude, nearly vertical tunnel. He couldn't see anything down inside, but threw a stone into the darkness and heard a splash. Groundwater. It was obvious they had tried to tunnel under the foundation.

At midmorning, Moss was wrestling his way through another dense stand of the tall, broad-leafed plant he'd come upon the day before at the huts. When he broke out of the thicket he was at the edge of an olive grove. A few meters out in front of him, in a lovely flowering garden, a figure in a monk's cowl knelt with his back to him, at what appeared to be a shrine. Moss was stunned. The person turned and looked up at him, and slipped his hood off.

"Are you my opponent?" Moss asked, as the man stood and faced him.

"In the chess game, yes," he said softly, "but I am not your opponent...I mean, I have no wish to harm you."

Any fear Moss had been courting had dissolved when the man stood up, as he not only towered over the person, but he could see that he was old.

"Are you the only one left?" Moss asked.

"Yes. I am Vincent," he said, "the last of *The Assembly*. And you, are you the only one left?"

"Excuse me?" Moss said, confused by the question.

"Out there, in the world, is there anyone left?"

"Oh, I see what you mean. Yes, the world is still very much populated," he said, extending his hand. "I'm Jacob Moss." He was astonished by the power in the old man's grip, given his advanced age and his gnarled and swollen knuckles. "What do you mean by the assembly?"

"Our community here at Mescalero...all of us...the inmates."

"Oh, sure, of course. They're all up on the hill?"

"They are now thanks to you, may they rest in peace."

"Why didn't you show yourself, Vincent, when I first came inside?"

"I had to see what sort of person you were, young man, friend or foe."

"And you decided I was all right? Why?"

"I watched how you treated James…when you buried him…said words over him. I knew then."

"Yes, James…but why didn't you—"

"Bury him? If you had not found a corpse, you would've known someone was still alive, wouldn't you?"

"Very clever," Moss said, smiling at the mischievous look on Vincent's face.

"Yes. Long ago, I was known for that."

"Then, this morning when I called for you in the corridor why didn't you come out?"

"That's simple," he said, grinning. "Couldn't hear you. Wasn't there. Morning devotions…here, at the shrine of *James the Wise*."

Moss looked about the simple edifice, the garden and surrounding olive grove, immersed for a moment in the bucolic setting. Then he turned to Vincent again.

"I have so many questions, Vincent, I don't know where to begin. Tell me, you put the guard log where I could find it, didn't you?"

"Yes."

Vincent turned and began to walk eastward. Moss followed, embarrassed to find he was having difficulty keeping up with the old man, who seemed to glide effortlessly through the undergrowth beyond the grove. He found Vincent waiting where the thicket and underbrush fell away, near the northern bank of the pond.

"This plant is everywhere. What is it called?" Moss asked when he broke into the open. He was sweating and breathing harder than he wanted the old man to see.

"It is called Pax. Take one of the tender little leaves from the top of the stem and put it under your tongue. It will calm your heart and your breathing, and bring back your saliva."

Moss bent a Pax stem over and picked a succulent leaf from the top. He did not like the sour, lemony taste at first, but soon changed his mind as a subtle tingling began in his mouth. Shortly, his breathing slowed and he felt refreshed. Meanwhile, Vincent was sitting on the bank of the pond, having picked a spot in the shade of a mango tree, and invited him to sit with him.

Moss had been trying to guess his age, but couldn't come to any conclusion about it.

"How old are you, Vincent, if you don't mind my asking?"

"I don't mind. What year is it?"

"2071...June, 2071."

"Ah," he said in a thoughtful tone, "it's as I thought, then. I've often wondered if I'd lost track of the years and months. That makes me ninety-four, young man. I will be ninety-five next month."

Moss was astonished.

"Please, Vincent, call me Jake."

"Jake, then." the old man said, smiling. He seemed pleased by the request.

"I was going to try to catch one or two of those carp today," Moss said as he motioned toward the water with his chin.

"Gourami."

"Excuse me?"

"Not carp. They are gourami. Delicious. Shall we have some for our supper?"

"How do you catch them?"

"I will show you when it is time."

At midday they picked mangoes to eat, then spent the afternoon in the shade of the great tree, answering each other's questions.

Vincent explained they had concluded long ago that abandoning them in the dome was Warden Smalley's doing, though they could never figure out what he had hoped to accomplish. Moss spoke of the two skeletons in the tunnel and the welding gear. Vincent suggested one of them was probably Eddie the Tin Man, who had disappeared the same time the guards did. He had been a fine welder. Moss talked about what the world outside was like now, a bit bewildered though when Vincent showed little interest.

"How did you find the place?" Vincent said. "Mescalero was supposed to be secret, wasn't it?"

Moss nodded. "I found it by chance, Vincent, changing a luminant."

***

It was unlike Moss not to notice the fragrance of just mown grass in the median of the boulevard, such scents always having delighted him working on the farm. But he did overlook it. He sat in his little *Champion*, tolerating the usual snarl of traffic on his way to work at the National Library looking like a salmon stuffed in a sardine can. He was too big a man to drive such a little transport, but Moss didn't mind. The electropod was part of his government stipend. Why use his own vehicle when the DRP provided him with a free transport? The traffic began to move again. He made his way to the central parking garage, plugged the transport in, and made it to the ground level just in time for the shuttle over to the library.

In front of the ancient guardian of the nation's cultural heritage and history, he ducked his head and stepped down out of the shuttle, ascended the great marble steps of the building two at a time, and slipped through one of the heavy revolving doors. The clack of his boot heels against the marble floor echoed like the ticks and tocks of a metronome as he crossed the great domed rotunda of the revered edifice, and disappeared through a hidden door cut into the rich oak paneling behind a large potted fern.

The old wood stairs to the archives groaned under his solid weight as he descended. The dusty, dry smell of ancient cardboard filing cartons changed to a musty odor starting down a second set of stairs to the sub-basement. At the bottom of the steps he activated the light switch with a soft swipe and walked to an alcove at the end of the hall, his head tucked down to clear plumbing and ventilation conduits overhead.

The alcove, stacked high with files in boxes waiting to be examined, was his office, a marshaling yard to begin from each day. His task: Reorganize, repair, and restore the ancient print and long obsolete digital data files used after the chaos of 2022 to reestablish the government databases erased by the solares. A daunting number of cartons and containers had just been tossed back onto the file storage shelves with no regard for their condition or order once the data they held had been transcribed back into the national databanks.

As if we might never need them again, Moss thought. *As if there would never be magnetic storms on the sun again. Short-sighted. Naïve.*

Moss believed this work was important and had been progressing well with it, having a quick mind and considerable intellect. Over time, though, he had become preoccupied, nearly to the point of obsession, with identifying something he had come across, known only as *M.P.*

He settled down at his makeshift desk, an old closet door set upon sawhorses, to check his last point of reference. It had been more than three years since he first came upon an electronic memo referring to M.P., on a fifty-year-old digital disk. He was unable to determine what it was, and thus how to categorize it. He'd found other references to it in print memos and old transcription tapes since then, but they were always vague, sometimes even contradictory. In all his searches of the national data banks as well as the reams of information he sat buried in every day, he had never found anything that described or defined it. Whatever it was—a place, a concept, a weapon system—it had energized him and his curiosity, and when that happened Jake Moss could not rest until the answer to the puzzle was found.

He placed a wafer in the laser stand and selected Handel. The furnace in the next room fired just then, a subtle, deep rumble. The chorus was singing of Zadok the priest anointing Solomon king as he left his desk, weaving through the rows of shelves to the far end of the storage room. He carried a new luminant to replace the one that had been burned out for so long, the one the custodian was supposed to change weeks ago.

Cumbersome, these old files, he thought. *So much space needed to store information back then. So much time involved in retrieving data. Still, what would they have done without them after the solares event?*

With the ladder secured to the top shelf, he climbed up and put in the new bulb. Now that he could see what was up there he reached for a large blue carton at the back of the shelf. He descended with it cradled on his shoulder just the way he would a sack of feed or a bale of hay when he was a young man on the farm.

It was near noon when Moss finished tagging and filing all the documents in the carton. As with so many others, there was nothing in it that might help him solve the mystery of M.P. He carried it back and up the ladder, twelve feet above the floor. When his shoulders were high enough to set the carton down, something caught his attention, wedged behind a heating duct that ran along the wall at the back of the shelf. Cartons and boxes of documents he had already inspected rested against much of it. He climbed back down with the carton on his shoulder and set it on the floor, then climbed up again. He crawled onto the shelf, sliding back far enough to reach behind the duct, and dislodged an antiquated cardboard tube. It was sealed, and in the now much improved light there was no mistaking the label: M.P.

He climbed down and took the tube to his desk. His heart raced as he held it up to the study lamp above his desk and looked again at the label.

It is M.P.

It occurred to him just then that if he hadn't changed that luminant, he might never have noticed it. As he rotated the tube a bit to open it, he noticed a faded stamp below the label:

SENSITIVE MATERIAL – CLASSIFIED/SECRET

Moss was not exceeding his authority opening the tube. He had been cleared all the way to *Top Secret* before he was accepted for the job, because of the broad, encompassing nature of the assignment. He cut the seal on one end with his pocketknife, popped the top off, and rolled what he immediately recognized as a stack of blueprints out on the desk. The

Mescalero Project/Experimental Prison Model, was inscribed in the legend at the top.

"Well, I'll be damned. A prison, for God's sake," he said out loud, throwing his head back and his hands in the air.

He opened the blueprints the rest of the way to the status/location block in the lower right corner: Occupancy date–June 1, 2021. Geo-coordinates of the location were inscribed beneath the date.

He spent the weekend at the library initiating a new search of the national data banks, because now he had a name. All responses were still negative, even after cross-referencing with more than a dozen combinations of systematic search schemes. According to whatever method he tried throughout the national systems the project did not exist.

But the plans say it does.

For the remaining weeks of the semester Jake Moss said nothing about his discovery to anyone, and when exams were over he went to find The Mescalero Project for himself.

***

Moss lay back in the shade, resting his head on his knapsack. Vincent sat with his back against the trunk of the tree.

"Why didn't you just leave the first night, when I was asleep, Vincent? Isn't that what you've thought about or dreamt of all these years?"

"At first, yes, that's all any of us thought about, that…and women. Once we understood—and accepted—the possibility that the dome might be the extent of our world for the rest of our lives, though, we began to occupy ourselves with new things James showed us. Truth is, the last thirty years have been good here, better than anything we'd ever have known outside—except of course for our carnal appetites. I daresay most of us would have been dead long ago out there."

"So, you no longer had any desire to leave, to escape." Moss said.

"No, and we had tried for years. A tunnel. As for the other night, I could have left but I remember the landscape, what I could see of it in the pitch dark the night we arrived here. A man wouldn't have a chance out there on foot."

"And James had a lot to do with these new worlds you discovered, so to speak?"

"Oh, yes," he said, raising his arms and dropping the hood of his mantle to his shoulders again. "He was the one who taught many of us to read and write."

Vincent's hair was long and silver, though sparse, tied in a ponytail that reached down between his shoulder blades. His beard was short and ragged. His eyes, one hazel, one black, were deep set beneath bushy white eyebrows. They interfered with his vision and he would sweep them with his fingers, like a man shaping a moustache. And they looked as though they'd been privy to secrets of Heaven and Hell.

"And Chess, too. After the *Time of Terror*, in the period we called the *Time of the Person,* many of us became interested in the game. As the Time of the Assembly evolved, we started having tournaments."

The light in the dome was beginning to dim. Vincent stood up and went behind the tree, returning a moment later carrying a long, slender pole resembling a javelin with a barbed tip.

"This is how I catch them Jake," he said, grinning.

He stood the spear against the tree, lifted his cloak at the hem and tucked it about his waist, slipped out of his sandals, and proceeded out into the water. Moss was fascinated watching how he moved—strong, confident, agile—as he waded about two meters out, to where the water reached his knees. With arm raised and spear poised, he stood still as a stork, waiting. A moment later, with the speed and grace of a Masai warrior, he thrust the spear into the water and hoisted out a large gourami, thrashing at the end of it.

"See?" he said, turning toward shore.

"Is one enough?" Moss shouted.

"I suppose that depends," Vincent said as he made his way back. "Will you eat more than a pound of fillet?"

Moss understood what he meant as soon as Vincent handed him the spear with the fish, so he could work his way up the slippery edge of the bank. The fish had to weigh at least five pounds, maybe more.

Once up on the bank, Vincent let loose the cloak from around his waist, clutching the fabric about his legs to dry them, and slipped his sandals back on. He unscrewed the barbed tip of the spear and slid the fish off the shaft, then screwed the tip back on and returned the spear to where he kept it, behind the tree.

"Shall we adjourn to the kitchen, Jake, and prepare a feast fit for a king?"

He nodded enthusiastically and they started back to the building, Moss still feeling compelled to ask so many questions.

"Wasn't it hard to leave James there in his bunk?"

"Yes, very hard, but we had talked about that before he died. We agreed, whoever was left, that's what they'd do. Still, it saddened my spirit to leave him there like that. Thank you for giving him a proper burial. That was kind."

Vincent led him across a fallow field where, he explained, they used to grow large crops of soybeans, a hybrid he and some of the others had developed for a tropical climate. It had been successful, he said with obvious pride. As they walked, Moss asked how long ago James had died. Vincent seemed surprised by the question, stammering as though unprepared for how to respond.

"Well, let me think. It was...in '64. Yes, '64. He was eighty-seven."

"What happened?"

"Don't know," Vincent said in an almost insistent tone. "One morning, uh, he didn't come to devotions. I went to his cell and there he was, lying peacefully, just as you found him."

Moss tried to imagine Vincent losing his friend knowing in all likelihood he would be alone for the rest of his life.

"It must've been hard for you, Vincent."

Vincent didn't speak, but nodded, looking at the ground, as they walked along.

Back at the building, after he had cleaned the fish, Vincent filleted it and pan-fried them in olive oil with scallions from his vegetable garden he tended on the west side of the building. While they cooked, Vincent disappeared. When he returned a few minutes later, the fillets were nearly ready. He stepped to the stove and poured a clear liquid over them that steamed and spattered, filling the air with a heavenly aroma.

"What's that?" Moss asked, as the liquid reduced and thickened in the pan.

"Mango liqueur, a specialty of the house," he said with an impish grin.

They feasted on gourami with avocado wedges and mead to drink, and talked late into the night, Vincent starting new candles each time the ones burning were used up.

He told of how they learned to make the candles from beeswax and soap from beef tallow. How they learned to tan leather. And how they pressed olives for oil, feeding the pulp to the cattle and hogs. When James got everyone started playing chess, one of the men, a skillful carver, whittled chess pieces out of what he could find, even bone from cattle carcasses. And with fruits like bananas and mangoes available, many of the men were fermenting honey and all sorts of other concoctions.

The emotional impact of meeting Vincent, along with the honey mead and a delightful meal, had produced a sweet exhaustion for Moss.

"Vincent, I need to go to bed."

"Yes, young ma—Jake, I, too, am tired."

"Where do you stay, Vincent?"

"Until you came, in my cell, the one I've always been in. For the last several days, though, I fixed myself a place in the granary. Tonight I will sleep in my cell again."

"See you in the morning, then. Perhaps you'd care to venture out to the offices with me tomorrow." Moss said in an inviting way, as he turned to walk to the infirmary.

"Perhaps."

Moss started down the long corridor by candlelight.

"Jacob Moss!" Vincent shouted, now some distance from him.

Moss turned around. Vincent was just a silhouette in the candlelight behind him.

"Yes, Vincent?"

"I am glad it was you who found this place, and I am glad you are here. Oh, and when you get to your room, please move my queen to king's bishop three."

Moss smiled, and continued down the corridor. Above him he could hear the rain falling each time he passed beneath a skylight. When he got to his room, he made the move Vincent asked him to make, impressed by the strategy. The man was indeed clever. He countered, moving queen's knight to queen's bishop three, then picked up where he'd left off in Stryker's journals the day before, until he fell asleep. It was clear right away as he read, that he was reading about the period Vincent had referred to as the Time of Terror:

February 16, 2022—Two gangs split from the population today. They've gone out into the dome. One of them is Bruno's, ten guys, I think. The other is Manning's, maybe a dozen. This gives Briscoe control on the inside. I reconned during the early hours when everyone was asleep, and found a new place to hide. Have to make sure I always have one or two back-up places, too, just in case....

A picture of what it was like here after these men were left to themselves was beginning to emerge from Stryker's entries. He recorded the power struggles that began just a few days after they discovered they were free:

February 17, 2022–Bruno's gang raided the kitchen. They were after the meat. Vince must have gotten a little cocky. Hadn't figured on a raid. Only had four guys guarding the place. Not sure how Bruno's men got in. One of Briscoe's goons killed. Two hurt pretty bad. Only a few minor injuries with Bruno's men, far as I know. They got into the reefers, but all the meat had started to spoil. No power since the 14th. They took as much as they could carry, anyway.

Out in the dome, Manning's gang ransacked the equipment sheds, and ripped off siding to get at the studs. Took as much polytarp as they could carry, too. Two of his guys grabbed a ewe from the sheep pens and slit its throat. Not long after that I could smell it cooking from all the way the other side of the dome.

If these assholes keep killing each other and polluting the air in the dome and cutting trees down for firewood, we'll all be dead in a few months.

Then:

February 24, 2022 - Things have settled down some since Manning and Bruno set up camps out in the dome. Things still not good, though. They continue to raid the livestock pens for meat, and cut tree limbs off for firewood. Should've known Briscoe wasn't going to be any help, either. He just doesn't get it. Have to try to get the word to the men somehow. Got to make them understand. Not sure how yet, but can't trust Briscoe. Have to watch my back with him....

In the morning, Moss waited out on the landing for Vincent to return from devotions. He spotted him a ways off, crossing the fields just north and east of the building, impressed by how the crooked little man moved with such vitality. His mantle swept the ground as he walked, which made it seem as though he hovered just above it.

"Good morning, Jake," he said. "It's been a long time since I've said that to someone. May the day go well for us both."

"Good morning, Vincent, same to you. Have you eaten?"

"Oh, yes. The dates are just ripe now," he said. "I ate a dozen of them after *Matins*. Lovely."

"Dates?" Moss asked, bewildered. "From those palm trees along the pond? How did you get them down?"

"I climbed the tree, of course." Vincent said matter-of-factly.

Moss shook his head as he had many times since meeting Vincent, at the idea of a ninety-four year old man climbing up a date palm to pick fruit.

"I will accompany you to the offices if you like, Jake."

Moss was pleased at that, and as they headed for the bulkhead, he began to query Vincent on some of the other questions he'd been wondering about.

"What about the note I found in James's hands, Vincent? The handwriting didn't—"

"I confess, I wrote it. It was necessary to make the deception believable."

"Yes," Moss said, shaking his head and grinning at Vincent. "Again, very clever."

"As I said, I used to be known for that."

"I was reading from his journal last night, from the time you call the days of terror."

"*Time* of terror," he corrected.

"Would you be the 'Vince' he often refers to, Vince Briscoe?"

"The same, I am ashamed to say."

"You and James were not always close, then, were you?"

"No. Even before coming here, when we were at Carbondale, we were enemies, or I should say, I was *his* enemy. I was not a nice person, Jake."

"How did that change…your relationship with James, I mean?"

"He saved my life…twice."

"Really? What happened?"

"In time, Jake. All in good time."

They moved along the path, neither of them spoke for a ways, Moss lost in thought, wondering about these two men and Vincent reminded again of what James had done for him.

"What did you counter my move with, Jake, if I may ask?"

Moss was relieved at the question, wanting to move away from what appeared to be an awkward subject for Vincent.

"Queen's knight to queen's bishop three," he said, grinning at Vincent as though he'd made the quintessential chess move.

"Ah," Vincent said, lifting his head then nodding. "An interesting move, Jake, but I must inform you, my next move will be check and mate."

"*Wha*? How so?" Jake asked, as they came upon the great statue, half man, half eagle, that had given him a fright the first day in the dome.

"I will show you when we return."

Moss looked at Briscoe in disbelief, but he could see in the old man's face that he had every confidence he was right.

"Tell me about this creature, Vincent," he said, pointing and swinging his arm in an arc. "Is it supposed to represent someone in particular?"

"It is *The Visitor, Melchior*," Briscoe said in a soft and reverent tone, bowing as they passed."

"Who was he?"

"An angel."

"Really? How do you know?"

"James told us. *We* never saw him, though Bruno and others reported seeing brilliant light, bright as the sun, coming from James's cell on occasion. James said his name was Melchior, and believed he was an angel, and we came to believe James was right."

"Why did James think he visited here—visited him?"

"I don't know. We never knew. James, either."

"The sculpture is terrifying, and yet…wonderful at the same time."

"That was just how James described him."

"Who was the sculptor?"

"Carelli, the same man who whittled the chess pieces. Necco the Turk broke the piece out of the limestone ledge on the far side of the cemetery and hauled it here with a team, and Carelli sculpted it according to the description James gave. We were all excited—and in awe—when it was finished."

This, of course, was fodder for a host of new questions, Moss realized, but they had come to the bulkhead, and those would have to wait.

He spun the locking wheel of the inner door of the bulkhead and waited for the rush of air to fill the cleansing chamber, and pulled the door open. Vincent stepped back, his face screwed up in apprehension.

"It's all right, Vincent...really," he said, noticing Briscoe's left cheek quivering. "I came here alone. I'm certain no one knows I'm here."

Vincent was shaking his head.

"It's not that, Jake. Imagine for a moment the world is flat," Briscoe said with a grave expression, "and that you are standing at the edge. If I ask you to take one more step, wouldn't you be afraid?" Moss didn't try to reply to the question. "For me, that is what it is like after all these years, stepping into that tunnel."

Moss nodded. He hadn't thought about that, and understood.

When they were both in the cleansing chamber, Moss turned his torch on wide beam and they closed the inner door behind them. Before opening the door to the tunnel, he lit the prism lantern with his incendium and handed it to Briscoe. He warned him that the first thing they'd see would be the remains of the two he had told him about. Briscoe nodded.

Moss released the makeshift lock he'd made from the pry bar and chain to keep the door closed as tight as possible, and they pushed together. It opened slowly, squealing at its hinges, and as the light of the lantern flooded the tunnel, Vincent Briscoe took his first steps out of the only universe he had known for half a century.

CHAPTER EIGHT

James prefers the solitude of his cell when he is not working in the fields. Since the visitations he has worn a hooded mantle fashioned from bed sheets whenever he leaves DSU, to avert the disruptions and discomfort his appearance causes the men. And he has begun memorizing passages of scripture, particularly Proverbs and Psalms, but portions of the New Testament as well. Not only is this uplifting for him, it keeps the always present temptation to despair at bay. For, no matter what else happens at Mescalero, the reality of the limits of their world and the seeming finality that they will live out their lives in the dome in this way is an undercurrent that grieves the spirit of everyone.

Until they had worked out a way to resolve disputes, the men inevitably looked to James to mediate their complaints. He did not want this responsibility as disagreements were almost constant, and used his sway to call assemblies where decisions would be made by consensus. Gradually, the men came to appreciate this way of doing things, as James lay the groundwork for an infant democracy to evolve.

It had been agreed in the first meeting that all the men should know how to do the different tasks necessary to their survival in the dome, in case someone got hurt or sick. Also, the ones who couldn't work because of age or a handicap would be expected to help wherever they were able. They could do the lighter jobs: pouring beeswax or beef tallow into molds or breaking them out, wrapping candles or soap bars in corn husks for storage, bottling olive oil, or keeping the oil lamps filled throughout the common areas of the building. As far as was possible, everyone had something to do.

The population since the Time of Terror ended is one hundred and sixty-five out of the original two hundred. Twenty-five of the men are unable to work in the fields because of injuries sustained during that time, or disabilities or illnesses they had when they arrived. The remaining one hundred and forty able men rotate, working in the fields, the laundry or rendering vats, the kitchen. Or, they might be in the sugarhouse, the livestock pens or seedling beds, on the olive press or the tunneling crew.

It is easy to spot James in the fields unless he's working in high-standing crops like corn or Pax. Briscoe picks out the tall figure in cloak and hood among the others cultivating the sugar beets.

"James!" he calls from the edge of the field.

James recognizes Briscoe's bright red hair. He waves to him as he sets the hoe on his shoulder and walks to the end of the row.

"Morning, Vince."

"James," Vince replies, looking down at the ground. He has always been uncomfortable looking James in the eye, whose brilliant blue eyes can penetrate like javelins. Even more so since James saved his life. But since the visitations, whether it is real or just his imagination, Briscoe sees an aura around James's face.

"You seem a little agitated, Vince."

Vince is reluctant to speak at first, then he lets it out:

"We need a meeting, James. Everybody. There's too many fuckin' slackers, and Manning's—"

"No need to curse, Vince."

"Yeah, well…anyway, Manning's the worst one. And don't say it's because I got it in for him, tryin' to kill me an' all. That ain't it, James. But he knows I gave my word I wouldn't touch him, and he's playin' that card for all it's worth. It's pissin' me off—us off—James, a lot of us, and he ain't the only one. There's a bunch of guys figurin' if he and his guys don't have to work, neither do they."

"Why do you come to me, Vince? Why don't you call for a meeting yourself—"

"Aw, c'mon, James. You know goddamn well—"

"No need to talk that way, Vi—"

"Yeah, yeah," Vince says, annoyed at James always reminding him about his language. "You know they only show up when you call one, James. You know that."

James looks at the ground, reflecting on the comment.

"So...will you call a meeting?" Vince says, looking at James intently now.

James nods, then turns and walks back up the row he had been cultivating. He knows Briscoe is right. There are a lot of guys slacking, and he spends the rest of the day cultivating the sugar beets with a dozen other men, thinking of how to solve the problem.

That night sleep comes easily for James, from the good weariness of laboring in the fields. He dreams about what Smalley said, his insistence from the outset:

If you don't work, you don't eat.

In the morning, during his meditations he sees that Smalley's policy is part of the solution to the problem of slackers, but it would require enforcement. Here, that can only lead back to violence. Then, in his mind, as clearly as if someone was standing next to him, a voice says:

To each man a portion.

At breakfast, James asks Chico and Joey the Gimp to find out if everyone would be agreeable to a meeting the following morning. Chico is always happy to do anything James asks of him, and Joey the Gimp, knowing that this is a meeting Vince has asked for, is glad to oblige, too.

Briscoe catches up with James on the way to the tunnel excavation site. It is their turn, along with eight other men, to spend the day trying to dig under the foundation of the dome. As they walk, James motions to Briscoe to slow down so that they fall back, out of earshot of the others.

"I have asked for a meeting, Vince, for tomorrow morning, right after breakfast. We will find out tonight at supper if everyone is agreeable."

"Aw shit, James, you know they will be."

"I don't like to assume anything...and speaking like that isn't necessary. Just an old habit, Vince. You can break it if you try."

Briscoe looks over at James and sees that he's smiling, and half-smiles himself.

"I thought about this problem of slackers all night, Vince, and I think there is a way to solve it."

"Yeah, I know, snuff the bastards, right?"

"That's not an option, Vince, and you need to get that idea out of your mind once and for all. No, I'm talking about drawing lots."

"For what, James," Briscoe says, snickering, "a piece of each other's ass?"

"Land…and crops."

"I don't follow."

"Just the way we drew names for the work rotation, we do the same with the land. We divide all the tillable land into roughly equal parcels, one for every man, and draw names for each plot. Every man takes care of his own piece of ground."

"I don't get it. How does that get rid of the slackers?"

"Patience, Vince," James says, then excuses himself and steps off the path into a stand of Pax to piss. Briscoe looks away.

James adjusts his mantle as he steps back on the path, and continues:

"Then we draw lots for what crop each man will grow on his plot, and the order of crop rotation. Now, if a man draws the lot for tomatoes, say, he couldn't and wouldn't want to live on tomatoes alone, would he? So, if he wants some soybeans or corn or squash to go with his tomatoes, he takes a bushel to the man growing those and trades some of his tomatoes for what he wants. The food he grows is his currency. It is known as barter."

Briscoe thinks about this for a moment, then shakes his head. "I still don't see how—"

"If you're growing tomatoes, Vince, and you're a slacker, chances are you're not going to grow many tomatoes, or good ones, either. And if you don't have many tomatoes, and they're poor quality, nobody will want to trade for your tomatoes, especially if some other guy who isn't a slacker grows lots of beautiful tomatoes. So, you'd better not be a slacker. You'd better work hard at growing the most and the nicest tomatoes you can, right?"

Briscoe doesn't say anything, but glances at James, amazed by the simple wisdom. James, unable to see Briscoe because his cowl blocks his peripheral vision, asks again, "Right?"

"Yeah, James…sure," he says, wondering why he hadn't thought of it, "makes a lotta sense."

Throughout the day, James and Briscoe and the others struggle to shore up the tunnel as they dig deeper and deeper, until the lead man, Mickey the Mole, cries out, "Water in the hole!" from the bottom of the excavation, and everyone scrambles for the surface. Just as Mickey makes daylight, a now familiar sound comes from the tunnel: sand and gravel and timbers caving in, splashing into the water.

There are about three hours of useful daylight left out in the dome. The men all look at James, their discouragement obvious, wondering if they have to start again today—or ever. James turns to Briscoe.

"What do you think, Vince? Start again? Now?"

Briscoe is surprised at James consulting him, but he has no hesitation.

"Nah, not for me. That's the fourth time. We ain't ever gonna get under that foundation, for Chris— cryin' out loud. Too much groundwater down that deep."

The others are as surprised as Briscoe that James consulted him, but relieved at his response. James looks around. They're all in agreement. They gather their tools and head back to the cellblocks.

On the way, Briscoe and James again drop behind. James talks about the concepts of property and barter they spoke of earlier, its soundness and simplicity, how it should work, in a subtle way tutoring Briscoe on the subject.

"The bulls and boars and rams could be kept for breeding everybody's stock," James says, in answer to Briscoe's question about the livestock. "The teams of steers trained to harness would be for all of us to use."

"What about the guys who can't work?" Briscoe wants to know.

"They wouldn't have a plot of land," James says. "We'd each give them a little of what we produce to take care of them."

"Ah, bullshit!" Briscoe says. "If I'm gonna bust my balls growin' the stuff, why should I give any of it away?"

"Even if you're the guy growing tomatoes, and they're going to spoil?"

"Hell, I ain't stupid, James. If I was growin' tomatoes, you can bet your ass I'd have 'em all traded before they ever spoiled."

"Ah," James says softly, lifting his chin in an upward nod.

They walk along for a time without speaking. Then, as they come up to the toolshed, James stops and looks at Briscoe with those piercing blue eyes.

"Let's suppose for a moment, Vince, that things are going well for you. You have a choice plot of land. Your crops are doing well. Everyone loves to trade for your tomatoes, so you're well-fed, and so on."

Briscoe is uncomfortable again, antsy. He hates when James starts in like this because he knows it's going to be some sermon or lesson, and like it always happens, James will be right and he'll look stupid.

"Yeah, so what're you gettin' at, James?"

"Well, one day you wake up in your bunk and your right cheek feels funny, numb. You can't speak right because your lips and your tongue won't cooperate. You try to get up out of your bunk and realize that your right arm is limp, and your right leg is almost as bad."

Briscoe has stopped being antsy, his gaze riveted on James's cloaked face.

"You've had a stroke, Vince, and suddenly you're helpless when it comes to plowing and planting and cultivating your land. You're one of those men now, who aren't able to take care of themselves."

Briscoe is motionless, still staring at James.

"Think about it, Vince."

Briscoe snaps out of his astonishment and goes in the shed to put his tools away. When he comes back out he looks long again at James, an indignant look on his face, and without waiting for James, heads for the building alone.

At supper James gets the word from Chico: Everyone is agreeable to the meeting the next morning.

James does not go to breakfast, but meditates longer than usual in his cell. He has learned not to arrive at assemblies too soon. So often someone wants to get him aside before the meeting, seeking some special consideration they think James can get for them. He finds it best to stay away until they are all there. And when he does arrive, the chatter always fades to silence.

"Thank you for agreeing to meet this morning. Before we get into the main reason for it, I suggest we decide about the escape tunnel. As I'm sure you know by now, it caved in again yesterday. That's the fourth time, and it nearly got Mickey this time."

Everyone turns to the back of the room to look at Mickey the Mole, who is embarrassed by the sudden attention.

"I think we're wasting our time on it. There's too much groundwater at the depth we need to get under the foundation. Personally, I think we should give it up. The manpower on that detail would be much more help somewhere else."

The chow hall is silent. He looks around the room at the faces. It is fear mostly that he sees, in its many variations. That's what it always comes down to, James thinks. And reality. They don't want to face it, but it's time. We are not going to get out of here, not on our own anyway.

"So, please think about it. Now, Vince is the one who called this meeting, so I will turn it over to him."

A groan from the men spreads around the room as Briscoe looks over at James, stunned. He seems frozen in place, his gaze locked on James, who motions to him to come over to where he is. Briscoe scurries over in a half-crouch.

"What the hell you doin', James?" he whispers out of the corner of his mouth.

"Go ahead, Vincent," James says quietly, "tell them what's on your mind, and how we could correct the problem."

"But I can't. I don't know how to talk like—"

"Go ahead, Vincent," James says again, "you know what to say. Just speak slowly...and don't get angry."

After a long moment of hesitation, James again motions to him to go on, and Briscoe moves to the center of the chow hall and begins his complaint. The men are quiet, paying attention. This surprises him, and the nervous tic in his left cheek slows. He is surprised, too, as he starts naming those he thinks are slackers, that many of the men agree with him. His confidence bolstered, he introduces the idea James had described on the way back from the tunnel the day before. He glances at James who is nodding almost imperceptibly from under his hood, encouraging him to continue.

When the meeting breaks up, there has been a vote: There will be a drawing for plots of land as soon as approximately equal parcels are stepped off, followed by a drawing for crops. Briscoe looks for James as he leaves the chow hall but he has already left. Heading out into the dome on his way to work at the livestock pens, several men tell him they like his idea, and they're glad he brought it up. Briscoe walks on toward the pens with a vitality he hasn't felt since his warlord days in the Time of Terror.

At the cattle pens, Joey the Gimp harnesses a pair of steers to the manure spreader. He's the only one at Mescalero who has had any experience with large animals. He was a jockey when he was young. Since the servomules are useless now, it takes eight to ten man teams to pull the disk harrow or manure spreader, the seed drill or the sickle bar or the hayfork. Joey was the one who suggested training steers to harness. No one ever thought he'd be the one to save them from such backbreaking work.

When Briscoe gets to the pens he calls Joey aside.

"Who else knows how to drive a team besides you, Joey?"

Joey still gets nervous when Briscoe singles him out, no matter what it's for.

"Well, I, uh, just started showin' a couple guys—"

"Nah, nah, Joey," he says, shaking his head. "We don't wanna do that. We wanna have them hire you out to—"

"But Vince, James—"

"Now, since when do you worry about...." He stops, looks away for a second, then looks back at Joey, frustrated. "Since when do you do what James says, huh? I'm still the boss, right? Didn't I just come up with an idea everybody likes, to put the squeeze on Manning and those guys for slackin'?"

Joey just nods while he continues buckling the halter on one of the steers. He knows there's no point in arguing with Briscoe.

"See, what I got in mind, Joey...the reason I don't want you teachin' anybody else, is then they gotta come to us." He grins at the little man. "Then, when they do, we charge 'em a tomato here, a bushel 'a soybeans there, 'n like that, see?"

Joey nods again as Necco the Turk comes around the corner of the hay barn next to the cattle pens. Briscoe motions for the Turk to come over where they are.

"Is she ready?" Briscoe says.

Necco nods.

"Come with me, Necco," Briscoe tells him, "and stand guard outside. And Joey, remember what I said. No showin' anybody how to work the teams."

Briscoe and the Turk walk to the sheep pens on the other side of the hay barn, and Necco takes a position outside the sheep shed as Briscoe enters.

The ewe is jumpy, pressed inside the squeeze chute. She squirms, turns her head what little it can move from side to side, the whites of her eyes vivid in the poor light. Briscoe steps inside and closes the door behind him, comes up behind the sheep and undoes the zipper of his jumpsuit. A few minutes later, he steps back out of the shed.

"Okay," he tells Necco, "let her back out with the others."

The word spreads quickly that night: James is pissed. He has heard about how Briscoe plans to use Joey and the team. He calls for a meeting. Even before the night rain starts, Chico informs James it's on for the following morning.

James and Briscoe enter the chow hall at the same time. Briscoe nods in a jovial manner while talking with Necco and Joey the Gimp, who accompany him. James returns the casual, almost sardonic greeting with his own measured nod and stare. Necco waits for James to look his way as they all find a place to sit. When he does, the giant half-smiles with a slight lift of his hand, which James returns in kind.

No one moves to begin the meeting, so James reluctantly asks the men to come to order. They know by the tone of his voice and the way he is acting, that he has something on his mind.

"I think we need to decide what belongs to each of us...and what belongs to all of us."

The men look at one another, then at James who pauses to let them mull this over, then around again, not sure what he is getting at.

"What do you mean, James?" Joey the Gimp says, standing up, looking around for approval from the others—especially Briscoe—sitting next to him.

"Well, let me give you what's called a hypothetical, a story that's made up to make a point. Now, if you lived in the woods with—"

"Is this the story now?" Necco interrupts.

"Yes, friend, it is." James replies slowly and clearly to the Turk, then continues, "...with other people, and you found out there was a plant in the woods that was bad for you, could even kill you, would you tell everyone about that plant, or just keep it to yourself?"

Murmuring spreads through the crowd as the men consider the question.

"C'mon, James," Briscoe yells out, "of course you'd make sure everyone knew. Anybody who didn't would have to be a real scumbag." He looks around as always for agreement from the others, annoyed by the elementary question.

James smiles. Briscoe has stepped right into the snare he'd set for him.

"Well, then, let's use a different example: Suppose you were all thrown into a situation you'd never been in before, and to survive you had to learn a lot of new skills. And suppose there was only one guy who knew how to do the most important one of all, but he wouldn't show you how to do it. How would you feel about him?"

Joey the Gimp looks straight at James. He sees where he is going with this little story, and he's uncomfortable.

But Briscoe isn't getting it.

"I'd tell him I was going to cut his balls off, if he didn't show the rest of us how to do it," Briscoe yells out with bravado.

Again, Briscoe looks around the room, nodding and grinning, seeking the others' agreement with his sentiment.

"I see," James says, ready to spring his trap. "Well, yesterday, Carelli made a mess trying to plow his field because he didn't know how. I understand you offered to plow it for him, Joey, for a small percentage of his crop. True?"

Joey looks nervously at Briscoe for direction, then back at James.

"James, I—"

"It's okay, Joey, nobody here is looking at you. We want to hear from the guy who'd cut my balls off if I didn't show him how to do whatever. Vince?"

Joey the Gimp is relieved not to have to say anything against Briscoe, who is looking at James with a sheepish grin. He checks around the room for support, but finds only faces fixed on him.

"Well, I, uh—" Vince begins, the tic of his left cheek causing his eye to wink frequently now.

"By your own words, Vince, you're the guy."

James sits quietly until the grumbling and banter falls off, then gets up and moves to the middle of the room.

"Now, Vince, I don't want you to cut your balls off," James says, his smile hidden by his hood, "but I think if Carelli had to plow his own field, you should have to do the same, no Joey to do it for you, but you by yourself."

There is broad agreement among the men, as they nod to one another and the noise builds in the room. When it is suggested that they ought to all be there to watch him hitch up that team and drive it around, Joey the Gimp jumps up, trying to yell above the din. He warns that they have to be careful with the team, in how they hitch up the harness, how they drive them, how hard they work them. No one but James is listening, and he stands up again, holding his hand high signaling the men to quiet down.

"Joey's right. We don't know what we're doing with these animals and we could hurt them," James says. "We do that, we hurt ourselves. Takes a long time to replace one. Carelli could have hurt one of them. He didn't know what he was doing, trying to plow. And Vince could hurt them, too. But, if Joey teaches us—"

The room fills with boisterous shouts of agreement, and the men start calling for a vote.

Briscoe stands up just then and raises his hand, signaling for quiet as he moves to the center.

"Awright, awright," he says, seeing that the overwhelming majority is with James on the issue, "so Joey teaches everybody how to work a team. That don't mean there ain't gonna come a time when some of you ain't gonna want to plow, or maybe can't for some reason, right?"

The mumblings begin again among the men.

"Hell, maybe some 'a you don't even want to farm. I know I don't, and I don't give a shit if Joey teaches me how to work a team. I'd much rather pay him to do it."

The look on their faces tells James that Briscoe has made a point that he hadn't thought about, as he looks around the room with a critical eye.

"So, here's what I say. Okay, let's have Joey teach everybody how to plow with a team, and all the other stuff you need a team for. And, yeah, let's decide what belongs to everybody and what belongs to each of us, only let's also decide that we can do whatever we want to do with that stuff after that. Right?"

Carelli's booming voice comes from the back of the room near the serving line steam tables, wanting to know what Briscoe means by that. Briscoe goes into a long discourse on the benefits of trading for land or livestock or labor, or anything else, if the parties are agreeable. James continues to watch the men as they listen to Briscoe, realizing this is an argument he should stay out of, one he probably won't win if he gets in the middle of it.

"I mean, take Joey here for example," Briscoe says, putting his hand on Joey the Gimp's shoulder. "He's still got a pretty tight little ass, and if you'd like a piece of it, Carelli, and he's willing to bend over for you for so much of your crop or whatever, then you and he oughtta be able to do that. And if a bunch of us wanna bet on cards or chess or who comes first in a circle jerk, we oughtta be able to."

The vote is taken. James gets what he had argued for. Everybody will be able to learn how to use the team, and the team belongs to everyone. But he gets far more than he had argued for as well.

CHAPTER NINE

Vincent seemed able to see quite well as they started down the tunnel. When Moss, who was helpless without his calcion torch in such darkness commented on it, Vincent remarked that he didn't know why he had such good vision in the dark, but then so much of each day was that way living inside the dome.

The old man's apprehension was evident. He hummed a meditative mantra softly as they made their way toward the office complex. Moss remarked that the answer to why Vincent and the others had been left sealed in the dome might well be found in the warden's office. When they got there they began scavenging the remains of burnt files and disks, but Primary would not recognize Moss's voice or corneal print, so he couldn't play any of the disks or wafers he'd found. He asked Vincent to stay there while he went to his truck to get his portable cipherboard, a retrieval device designed to accept almost any mode of stored information. It had been invaluable in his work at the library sorting many different types of files, from the modern data wafers all the way back to celluloid film and tapes. He assured him he would only be gone a few minutes. Vincent hunkered down in a corner near the door as Moss stepped out of the office, and began to hum his mantra again.

Moss returned with the cipherboard and a small toolbox, much to the old man's relief who, as he stood up, held out a plasticene card on a chain.

"What's this?" Moss said, taking it from his hand.

"While I sat in the corner I noticed it under the Primary console. I've seen it before, Jake, but I don't remember where."

Moss knew immediately that it was a stripe-swipe key. What he didn't know was what it went to. He set it on the desk next to the cipherboard and turned the unit on. For some reason, most likely a security veil, it was unable to decipher the information on the small plasticene card.

He asked Vincent if he would look through any readable paper files while he started through the disks and wafers they'd retrieved from the ashes. He was not much help, however, ill at ease outside the dome, and impatient to return to it.

Moss began with the compact discs, which were the latest technology at the time the facility opened. One after another, he scanned volumes of memos, correspondence, bills of lading, personnel rosters and assignments, all of it having to do with the day-to-day operation of Mescalero. The process was reminiscent of his work at the library the past several years. He was barely interested as the hours wore on, and disappointed not to have come across anything that might explain what had happened here twenty years before he was born.

Near midday the power cell on the cipherboard failed. Moss slumped in his chair when he heard the unit beep and saw the tiny red light flashing. He looked over at Vincent, who was sitting on the floor examining the contents of a plastic file bin.

"The power cell is down," he said, annoyed, "needs to be recharged."

"Ah," Vincent replied, nodding, and setting the box down.

"What's that you've got?"

"It is what's left of the box James spoke of once," Vincent said, "all the letters he'd received from his mother over the years when he was at Carbondale Prison. The warden confiscated them when he arrived here. It hurt James deeply not to have them, but of course he would never let the guards or the warden know that."

"I'd like to look through them," Moss said philosophically, as he looked around the room for an unoccupied power outlet, "when I get a chance to—"

He got up and crossed the room, and knelt down at the far wall.

"Something wrong, Jake?"

"Well, I was going to plug into an outlet to recharge the power cell," he said, disgusted, "but the plugs don't match. These outlets are the old type they did away with decades ago."

"Ah," Vincent said again, nodding.

They were silent for a minute, looking around, at the wall socket, at each other, at the mess all over the floor. Then Vincent spoke.

"Have you noticed the stain on the floor, Jake?"

"Yes, I saw it when I first got in here a week ago. Why?"

"What do you think it is?"

"I don't know...paint maybe?"

"It's blood, Jake...lots of it. Someone died here—was killed here."

Moss stood up, studying Vincent's face. He looked at the stain then sat down at the desk, and lifted his boot to look at the sole.

"You're certain?"

Vincent nodded, smiling to himself at Moss's needless inspection of the bottom of his boot.

"One of the two at the bulkhead?" Moss said. "The stain tracks that way, down the hall."

"Perhaps," Vincent said. "Who can say?"

"Yes, well, it's another puzzle for another time. Right now, I have to figure out how to get this unit recharged."

"And right now, Jake, I must return to the dome for midday meditation. Will you walk back to the bulkhead with me? There is the problem of latching the outer door."

Jake did not want to drop what he was doing right then, but he could hardly say no to the old man. He left everything as it was and escorted him back to the bulkhead. He told Vincent he was going back to the warden's office, and that he would be back at dark or thereabouts. Vincent wished him good hunting.

"Will you be okay?" he asked as Vincent started through the inner door into the dome.

"I will be fine, thank you, Jake. After devotions I'm going to visit my friends on the hill."

Vincent was not sure which meant more to him, not wanting to embarrass Jake by reminding him that he had been okay for many years before he came along, or the genuine pleasure of knowing someone was once again concerned for his welfare. That had not been the case since James died eight years ago.

Moss jury-rigged the latch on the outer door with the pry bar and chain to hold it snug to the jamb. On the way back to the warden's office he thought of a way to solve the problem of charging the cipherboard. When he got there, he went straight to the breaker panel and cut the power to the wall outlets. He grabbed a screwdriver, a pair of wire cutters, and several heat shrink sleeves he discovered underneath everything else in the toolbox he'd found in the maintenance room. He cut off the plug to the cipherboard, then split and stripped the wire ends bare. Then he knelt down at the outlet and removed the screw and cover plate. After he freed the wire clamps inside the wall box, he pulled the excess wire stuffed inside so he could strip them as well, and was surprised to see a couple of data storage wafers fall out onto the floor.

His breathing quickened and he felt a buzz race up his spine, watching the two wafers roll across the room. He knew instantly this had to be something big. No one keeps data wafers behind wall outlet covers unless they don't want them found. Whatever was on them was not meant to be seen by anyone but the one who put them there—and that had to be the warden. He hurried to splice the wires, insulating each splice by heating the heat shrink sleeves with his incendium until they shrank, forming tightly around the wires.

He scrambled up off the floor, went to the breaker panel and flipped the switch, then grinned, hearing the familiar sounds of the start up procedure coming from the cipherboard. His hands shook as he picked up the wafers. He switched the cipherboard power source switch from power cell to outlet source, checked that the cipherboard program was ready to read data in that mode, and inserted one of the wafers into the adapter.

He could get nothing to come up on the screen except the phrase: *Access Denied.* Using the keyboard, he attempted every override strategy he knew. Same message each time. He tried the second wafer. Same problem. Then, in one last try, a small icon appeared in the lower right corner of the screen, which hadn't appeared on any of the previous refusals. He voice-clicked it. For just a moment he thought he'd opened the data as text appeared, and he was elated. But, as he began to read, he realized it was a text message denying access again, explaining the data could only be opened by Primary and only with proper authorization.

Frustrated, Moss removed the wafer from the cipherboard and put both of them in a side pocket on his knapsack, carefully wrapped in a piece of plasticene. He switched the cipherboard power cell to the charge position and sat down on the couch. The box Vincent had been rummaging through was within arm's reach, so Moss pulled it closer to him. There must have been hundreds of letters in the box, though many of them were now just blackened crisps. He thought about Stryker, trying to picture the man who saved them for so long, what they must have meant to him.

At the bottom of the half-melted box were letters that had survived the fire intact. They were stacked in order of receipt and appeared to have been sent weekly. He picked one of them up, dated April 10th 2021, and began to read:

Dear James,
How are you since that whole court mess and Billy being beeten so badly? I've wurried about you ever since you know about your safety and what you might do when you heard what they did to him to get at you. I had a little problem with my hart last week but no need to wurry I'm fine now. The doctor gave me some pills for high blood pressure. Bobby's real busy these days since he took on those electric cars everybody is talking about out here on the coast. I don't know how he does it he always seems to know just the right things to do to make the deelership bigger. He says they are the wave of the future. We think and talk about you every day James and pray that St Mary will watch over you. I have to say one more thing before I finish. James, you don't have to wurry about keeping the money you won from the guvermint. You know they can keep you there as long as they want just by making you mad, like they did by beating your little brother up. Sign the waver or releese form or whatever it is, please. Bobby takes good care of me. I have everything I need—except all my children being out of jail and here with me. Let them have the money, Jamesey. I just want to have my boy back. The minute you sign, you'll be free. You know that's what will happen. Please sign, Jamesey. I have to get supper started now. I miss cooking for you.
I love you,
Mom

P. S. I continue to pray that God will help you learn how to control your tempur, James. You are such a good boy. If it wernt for that, you wouldn't still be in prisun today.

He scanned through previous letters to find out more about the money and the court and James's brother, but since he only had replies from Stryker's mother to whatever he wrote, they revealed little more. So engrossed in trying to get into the files of the hidden wafers, and reading Stryker's letters, he had forgotten the time. The afternoon was spent. It would be dark in the dome now. He gathered his things, all but the cipherboard that he would leave on charge overnight, and left the warden's office, following the drag marks of the bloodstain on the floor as he walked toward the tunnel.

The dome was dark when he stepped inside. He didn't know why, but it had a sinister feel to it, despite knowing he and Vincent were the only ones in there. Moss walked the unfamiliar ground carefully, looking for landmarks as he went, the light of the lantern dissipating into nothingness a few meters out into the dark. Vincent stood at the railing of the landing and watched the eerie glow of the lantern move through the overgrown vegetation toward him.

"I was beginning to wonder if you were coming back," Vincent said when Moss reached the foot of the stairs. "Did you find anything?"

"I think so, but I was unable to open the files."

"Ah," Vincent remarked, nodding in his customary fashion. "You have not eaten since breakfast. May I fix you something, Jake? An omelet?"

"Oh, I can just break open a container of brown bread or something. I don't want to put you—"

"It is no bother, Jake. I returned from Vespers not long ago, just before dark, and wish to eat something myself."

"That would be nice, Vincent. Thank you."

Soon after, Moss caught the intoxicating aroma from the kitchen: eggs and scallions in olive oil. Vincent served mango brandy with the omelets, bowing his head for a moment when he sat down. Moss watched as the old man ate his food. Most of his teeth were missing. He said he was grateful to have eight that still met when he bit down on something. And it was rare, he said, for him to eat foods much more solid than an omelet anymore. The fish fillet they'd had the night before or the dates he sucked on for breakfast was about as solid as he would bother with.

"What did you do for the infection or the pain when you were losing these teeth, Vincent?"

"Ah," he said, nodding, and smiling. "Taste your brandy, Jake."

Moss lifted the cup and took a swallow, and his throat went numb from the burning sensation as it went down, all the way to his stomach.

"A lot of men were sick before they got here, or soon after, because of the experiments. And during the Time of Terror, it wasn't long before what drugs we had were gone. We came to depend on brandy and mead as an anesthetic and an antiseptic, too."

"But after a while you'd be getting drunk on this stuff, wouldn't you?"

"It is true. There were times when many of us were useless, staggering around in the fields or the kitchen, trying to do our job. But, I must say," he said with a great toothless grin, "we were often happy in our sufferings."

Moss had moved the chessboard from his room to the chow hall earlier that day, so they could play there in the evenings after supper. When they finished eating, they moved to the table where the game was set up. He was constantly impressed by Vincent's acumen and physical abilities given his age. He watched as the frail-looking old man would make a move, his hand darting here and there with the precision and speed of a robotic arm. And Moss had not yet beaten Vincent in a single game.

Vincent was unusually talkative as they played into the night. Why did the warden seal them in the dome? He couldn't say, but he and James and the others knew it had to do with the rape and murder of Smalley's daughter. How did they manage without electricity? They learned to do what had to be done in daylight first, using candles and later ceramic oil lamps at night, seeing well enough to tan hides or make bean curd, or patch their garments. Why was the vegetation so lush and successful? As ignorant as they were at first, they eventually learned how to produce hybrids of many crops better suited for the environment in the dome.

"What happened to the livestock, Vincent?"

"I still have some chickens, as you can tell, but over the years the livestock dwindled because of our ignorance. There was not a one of us who had grown up on a farm, though Joey the Gimp had been a jockey and knew something about the livestock. The bull became sterile, we don't know why, and we didn't realize it until after we had already castrated all the bull calves that year. And during the Time of Terror several of the milk cows developed a hardening of the udder—"

"Mastitis," Moss pointed out.

"— because they weren't getting milked regularly, and eventually died. As for the sheep, they are so fragile to begin with—"

"Yes," Moss agreed, recalling summers as a boy, when he worked on a farm. "There's an old saying, 'Sheep are born lookin' for a place to die.'"

Vincent grinned at the apparent wisdom of the simple down home saying, as he reached for his queen's knight, making what many would call an aggressive, and therefore, a risky move as far as his queen was concerned. Watching Vincent pursue this course of action brought to mind the veracity of the maxim: *You can learn a great deal about a man in observing how he plays Chess.* He couldn't help but think, though, that one could learn even more about a man, observing how he plays Chess in prison.

"As for the hogs," Vincent went on, "they were all killed in the first weeks of the Time of Terror." He lowered his head at saying it, recalling his part in those events.

Moss had been studying Vincent's face underneath his scruffy beard while he talked. Deep lines like gullies in eroded fields, followed the curve of the cheek from the corners of his eyes to the corners of his mouth. They would flex, bending and stretching when he squinted or spoke, a living testimony of his journey etched in his face.

Moss matched Vincent's move.

"It must have been hard all these years," Moss said, "not knowing what happened, or if you would ever be in contact with the outside world again."

Vincent became quiet. He studied the board longer than usual. Moss watched his face for some hint of what he was thinking. The game, what his next move might be? Or was it what Moss had said a moment before? Vincent's left cheek began to quiver slightly.

"If I allowed myself to dwell on it, to get caught up in the question of why," he began, then stopped, bowing his head. Moss waited. After several moments Vincent looked up at him.

"It is something that's hard to describe. You have to go through it yourself to understand."

Moss thought back to that first morning in the dome, when he woke up in his bivouac bag on the landing, recalling the troubling sense of loneliness, and the claustrophobic paranoia he'd felt, and wondered if this was what Vincent was trying to explain.

"...something every one of us lived with every day. It was easier for some than for others, the ones who were already dying when they came to Mescalero. They just gave up and waited." The tic had become more pronounced as he studied Moss's move, then took one of his knights. "Then, James taught us how to overcome the crippling feeling of despair."

"What did James teach you, Vincent?"

"Checkmate."

Moss shook his head, and smiled. Vincent had outmaneuvered him once again. For whatever reason, Vincent had avoided the question and he decided not to press it, at least not then. The rain started to fall on the skylight above where they sat. Moss looked at his watch. It was midnight. He looked at Vincent and realized the old man was tired. They said good night and went to their bunks.

As Moss lay on the bed waiting for sleep to come, his mind replayed the day. He reached in his knapsack and pulled out the stack of letters from Stryker's mother he'd taken with him from the office. One was on business stationery from *Robert Stryker Luxury Vehicles*. It was dated May 15th, 2021:

Dear James,
I don't know how to tell you this, but Billy died on the 30th of April at Bennington Penitentiary. I'm sorry to have taken so long to write with this news, but Mom has been so distraught and there's been so much to take care of, going after his body and making funeral plans and all, I couldn't get to it any sooner. I wasn't looking forward to having to be the one to tell you, either. I wish I could have told you face-to-face.
They had shipped him out from Carbondale to Bennington in the middle of the night. He arrived late Friday afternoon, too late to get in on meds call. He told them he was diabetic and out of insulin, and they said that was too bad. He'd have to wait until Monday. He went into a diabetic coma in his cell Sunday afternoon, and died.
They said an investigation for negligence was in the works, but you know how that goes with these motherfuckers. I'm going to sue. If I had my old platoon from the Colombian Conflict of '64, I'd walk right in and clean house.
Don't worry about Mom. She's tough. Still, we're keeping a close eye on her. She's under my doctor's care. She just couldn't write right now, but she will. She says to tell you she loves you. Me too, Jamesey. We miss you. Hang in there and don't let the bastards get you down, as they say.
Bobby

Moss carefully folded the letter and put it back in its charred envelope. He stared at the wall, trying to imagine what kind of person endures one bitter tragedy after another horrific event after another heartless manipulation or cruel punishment. He couldn't. As he began to fall asleep, he wished he had known James Stryker.

He awoke in the morning to Vincent's prodding finger in his shoulder. "Huh? Wha?" he said, dazed from sleep.

"I remember where I saw it," Vincent said with a broad, toothless grin.

Moss sat up rubbing his eyes, as the old man stood above him next to the bed.

"Saw what?" he said, yawning.

"The card...on the chain, remember? The one I found in the warden's office."

"Oh, right. Where?"

"It belonged to Caldwell, the captain of the guard. It was an emergency override for Primary, I think, in case anything happened to the warden. He wore it around his neck. He always had it around his neck."

"You're sure?" Moss said, jumping up out of bed and pulling his pants on.

"I am certain, Jake. I watched them do a practice situation once, in the Command Center. They had me in the trap as part of the exercise."

Moss grabbed his knapsack as soon as he'd laced his boots up and started out the door.

"Are you coming with me, Vincent?" Moss shouted from down the hall, walking almost at a run toward the trap.

"It is time for matins, Jake. I'm sorry."

CHAPTER TEN

2030 AD

Necco the Turk is a giant, fearsome looking man. Swarthy and hairy, built like a great cedar, he looks as though he is a direct descendant of the man of Gath: a twenty-first century Goliath. Watching him and Joey the Gimp walk the corridor together, given their circumstances, is comic relief to the others.

Not long after arriving at Mescalero, when they became part of Briscoe's gang, they formed a mutually beneficial relationship. Joey the Gimp had Vince's ear, and to some degree his authority by association, and made sure Necco was always taken care of. And Necco protected the little man with the floppy foot, particularly since the night in the Time of Terror. Joey saved his life that night, by alerting him to a scheme Bruno and his men had concocted to assassinate him.

The Turk met his "David" in the encounter with Stryker in the chow hall, right after they were abandoned by the warden, a lesson no one else would have dared to give him and one he has never forgotten. But after that confrontation, the giant regarded James Stryker with respect and even a degree of friendship, though he kept this to himself because of Briscoe's dislike of Stryker.

These days, he has become popular because of his strength. Some of the men have never learned how to drive a team, or they have to wait too long for their turn to use one of them to work their fields. It was a welcome surprise the day Necco tried to pull the disk harrow by himself and discovered that he could. Since then, if someone doesn't want to wait for a team, they ask him. Briscoe, of course, had hoped to capitalize on his soldier being in such great demand, but Necco has become more and more independent, accepted for who he is in his own right. And he likes it. He tells everyone he plows for that they don't have to pay him anything, and usually gets paid more than even he thinks his efforts are worth.

Necco is plowing his own plot of land today. The other teams are spoken for already, so he will pull the disk harrow himself. Joey the Gimp is breaking a new team of steers to harness, and thinks this could be a good way to teach them. He tells Necco that by following along beside him, they will learn and help him plow his ground at the same time. Necco is happy to oblige, and starts to pull the harrow through the rich black soil.

As the disks churn and fold and stir the earth, sweat breaks out on his skin, gleaming where the traces looped over his shoulders ride. Joey staggers his team to the right and just behind the swath Necco is making, shouting commands as he pulls this way and that on the halters he's rigged to bridle the steers. Necco slows to begin a turn at the end of the field. Joey jerks the reins too hard. The steer on Necco's right comes alongside the Turk's harrow and steps inside its frame, then bellows in pain as the metal frame pins and nearly breaks the animal's left front leg. Necco looks back to see what's wrong. Joey, standing up on the frame of his harrow, tries to keep the team in check, but falls forward to the ground in front of it. The giant casts the traces from his shoulders and leaps over his rig, throwing himself on top of little Joey as the harrow is about to roll over him. A roar of defiance from the Turk, then silence as the team bolts away, off across the field, dragging the harrow behind.

Joey the Gimp tries to lift his face up out of the dirt, but he is smothered by the great weight of his friend. Necco's blood, slick and warm, spreads over his head and face as he digs frantically to burrow out from under the huge body lying motionless on top of him. Several men working nearby rush over, struggling to pull Joey free and to stop the bleeding all across the giant's lacerated back.

James hears about the accident from Carelli moments later. The two race out to the fields to where a man with a seasoned team is cultivating garlic. They unhook his team and drive it to the shop to get a rubbish skiff. Then they drive as fast as they can to where Necco and Joey are. Four men roll Necco on his side and push the skiff in close so they can roll him onto it belly down. James strips off his mantle and throws it over Necco.

Then, as they head for the building, James and Carelli lie on top of him trying to suppress the bleeding, pressing with the weight of their bodies.

A couple of the men help Joey the Gimp up. He wipes the blood from his face with the hem of his mantle, then tight-lipped, with his gaze to the ground, he hurries to catch up with James and Carelli and the giant. He stumbles and falls, his lame foot unable to support him as he runs. One of the men running up ahead stops and goes back for him.

"Joey, get up on my back. It'll be faster."

He agrees. Under ordinary circumstances he would not.

They crowd into the infirmary with the others. Necco lies face down on the rubbish skiff, unconscious. The room looks like the kill floor in a slaughterhouse.

Angel Fuentes is the closest they have to a doctor, trained as a medic in the army. He and Chico move frantically from wound to wound, one trying to clean the neatly spaced lacerations across his neck and back and legs with homegrown distilled alcohol, while the other applies Pax leaves to stem the bleeding.

Throughout the rest of the day and into the night Angel stays with Necco, trying to keep him from slipping into a coma. He is frustrated. Necco has lost so much blood but he has no way to do a transfusion or even to find out his blood type. If he could keep him awake, he could at least get liquids in him to restore some of the volume of blood he's lost. But the Turk keeps drifting off.

Joey the Gimp takes up a vigil through the night so Angel can sleep.

Toward morning, as the rain ends, Joey glances over at the enormous man lying there on his stomach, his head turned toward him. Necco blinks. Joey comes closer. He blinks again.

"Necco, you're awake. I'll be right back. Gotta get Angel."

Necco grabs the hem of Joey's mantle with his huge hand. Joey stops and leans down close to his face.

"Joey...okay? I...."

Necco's hand falls limp releasing the garment, as his eyes close and the sound of his breathing stops.

A palpable sadness permeates the dome at the news of Necco's death, but there is no time to waste. Corruption of the body is rapid inside Mescalero. The men learned that lesson quickly in the Time of Terror. Extra men help dig a grave big enough to take the Turk's immense body. Angel strips him bare. Cloth is too precious to be buried. He wraps him in banana fronds for the sake of his modesty. Joey the Gimp doubles up harness anticipating he will have to use a team of four steers to pull Necco up the hill, where he will sleep under the Joshua Tree.

It is dusk when everyone gathers for the processional to the gravesite. The men walk in a column of twos, half in front of the makeshift hearse, their candles lighting the way, the rest following. The corpse, wrapped in the wide green fronds tied with Pax hemp and a pillowslip over his head, rocks from side-to-side as the rubbish skiff, with Joey the Gimp at the reins of the straining team, scuffs over the uneven ground.

Joey pulls alongside the gravesite, halting the team when the skiff is even with it. There is no tasteful way to lower Necco into the grave. He is too big and too heavy. Six men stand at the away side of the skiff and lift. As the hulk starts to roll into the excavation, they hold their breath, hoping the corpse will land in some decent repose, not bent awkwardly or jackknifed in some rude manner that requires someone to climb down to straighten him out. They are relieved to see the Turk land straight, though mostly on his left side.

James reads from his Bible:
"There is an appointed time for everything. And there is a time
for every event under Heaven:
A time to give birth, and a time to die;
A time to plant, and a time to uproot...
...A time to weep...
...A time to mourn...."

He reads on, other passages he's chosen. Then James closes his Bible and invites all who would like to, to say a word. No one, not even Joey the Gimp, speaks. All of them are shaken. They don't know what to say, and so they pass by silently, some dropping a handful of dirt into the grave. The men descend the hill single file, giving the surreal appearance of a great serpent in the darkened dome, illuminated by the candles they carry.

James is last to pass before the burial detail starts backfilling the grave. He stops where Joey sits silent on the rubbish skiff, staring at the grave.

"Why did he do it, James?" Joey says, looking up at him.

"Maybe he thought he could get away with it. Maybe he overestimated himself, Joey. People do that sometimes."

Joey looks back down at the body as the men begin to shovel in earnest.

"Yeah, that's probably it," Joey says, nodding.

This seems to help, to ease something somewhere deep in Joey's gut. He casts a fleeting hint of a smile at James, a thanks for his words.

"Or maybe he loved you," James says, looking intently at Joey.

Joey gazes back, motionless, seeming stunned as James turns and follows the line down the hill.

The rain has begun to fall. Joey does not notice, sitting at the foot of the grave, alone. He is trying to think if there was ever anything he did for Necco that even came close to what the giant did for him. This haunts him as he takes up the reins and turns the team to start down the hill.

***

Bruno has begun slipping up to DSU in the evenings to see James. He says he wants to learn how to play chess. James agrees to teach him, but with a catch: The first time he beats James, he has to go and teach someone else. What Bruno really wants, though, is to learn how to read and write. But at fifty and locked in a bubble, probably for the rest of his life, what would be the point? Nevertheless, each time he comes to play, James, who has a sense of what he wants, manages to get him involved in one exercise or other and Bruno realizes one day what has happened. He is reading.

This particular night, returning to continue their chess match and another reading lesson, Bruno finds the door to James's cell ajar. He approaches quietly, listening for the sound of his voice or some movement or activity that lets him know he won't be disturbing him, but there is only silence and the dim light of an oil lamp. Bruno opens the door a bit wider. James is kneeling on the floor with his head and hands lifted toward the ceiling. His eyes are open wide and he is shaking, as if he were cold, his breath coming quickly, almost imperceptibly.

"James?" Bruno says tentatively.

James does not acknowledge him, but continues as though frozen in the rigorous position.

"James?" Bruno says more forcefully. There is no response. He steps into the cell and waves a hand in front of his eyes. Not even a blink. Bruno is afraid to touch him but afraid to leave him, either. He steps by him carefully and sits down on the commode to wait and see. He studies the chessboard on the little table next to the bunk, glancing often at James, thinking about his next move and what move James might make. He moves one of his pawns to back up another .

The Bible James is always studying lies open to the beginning of the book of Ezekiel. Bruno picks it up and reads:

> *Now it came about in the thirtieth year...while I was by the river...among the exiles, the heavens were opened and I saw visions of God.*

He puts the Bible back on the bunk and looks again at James.

"James? Are you seein' God?"

The man he sneaks up to visit at night still does not move, though he continues to shake, taking short, quick breaths.

"Is God talkin' to you, James?"

No response. Bruno continues to wait and watch.

When the oil lamp flickers and goes out, Bruno decides something must be wrong with James. He has been like this for a long time. Too long. He pulls a candle from his pocket, lights it and sets it next to the empty lamp, then leaves to look for

Fuentes. He finds him in the kitchen cooking up more of the wound salve he makes from Pax. Fuentes knows by the way Bruno is acting that he'd better drop whatever he is doing and go with him.

When they get to the cell, James is lying on his bunk reading his Bible. He sits up and smiles as the two men enter.

"Hello, Nicholas, bring Angel along to learn the game?"

Bruno is dumbfounded, shrugs his shoulders looking at Fuentes.

"James, you...you okay? I mean—"

"Yes, fine, Nicholas. Ready to continue our match?"

Bruno nods, taking his seat opposite James, looking back and forth between Angel and James. Bruno won't let it go, if for no other reason than he doesn't want Fuentes telling everybody that he is losing touch with reality.

"James, do you remember I was here earlier tonight?"

"Not tonight, Nicholas," he says emphatically. He knows Bruno often enjoys more mango brandy than he should. "No one has been here tonight."

Fuentes looks at Bruno as if to say, *Well, Nick, is that true?*

"James, look at the board. I ain't been near it since Angel and me got here just now, right?"

James nods in agreement.

"Well, look at my queen's pawn. It's been moved to back up my king's pawn, right? You didn't do that, right?"

James says in a soft, contemplative voice that he can't explain that. Bruno tells him again that he was there earlier. He holds up the pitcher of oil he brought back with him to refill the empty lamp, though James had already refilled it. How would he have known about the lamp if he hadn't been there earlier, Bruno argues. And what about the candle set on his lamp? Again, James does not refute what Bruno is saying. He is willing to consider it, though he is clearly puzzled.

Fuentes excuses himself, saying James seems fine to him. He's got to get back to his Pax on the stove. James looks at Bruno.

"What did Angel mean, I look fine to him?"

"James, I'm tellin' ya', I was here and you was in a trance or something. I went and got Fuentes in case you was really sick."

"And it came about when I was in Jerusalem and praying in the temple, that I fell into a trance.... The apostle Paul in the Book of Acts," James says, "chapter twenty-two, verse seventeen."

Bruno looks at James, bewildered.

James is quiet again for a moment, then looks at the board. He praises his student on a very good move, and the game resumes.

"James," Bruno says after a while, "did you see God?"

James stops in the middle of a move, holding his knight suspended above the board.

"No man has seen God at any time.... The Gospel of John, chapter one, verse eighteen." He completes the move, placing the knight at queen's bishop four.

"Well, did he talk to you?"

James looks steady and straight and deep into Bruno's eyes, holding his gaze until it becomes uncomfortable.

"Somebody talks to me, Nicholas. Maybe it's God," he says, releasing Bruno's eyes from his mesmerizing stare.

All at once, Bruno is ill at ease, and with no explanation, excuses himself.

By the end of breakfast the next morning, the story has already been well circulated:

God talks to James.

2032 AD

It is Sunday according to the Mescalero calendar. The true day and date is not certain. That information became suspect during the weeks of chaos following The Abandonment, when no one was keeping track of anything except whether they were still alive. Futile arguments about it would erupt, until the men realized that what the actual day and date was out in the world had no significance inside the dome. And so, a calendar was established arbitrarily, an agreed upon day, month, and year, designated for the occupants of Mescalero.

The men do not work on Sunday, a habit begun by agreement in 2023 a year after the Time of the Person began. During that year, after the land division, James was not seen at all on Sundays unless it was his turn to work. He would remain cloistered in his cell, meditating, often fasting as well, and working on his project of memorizing the Bible.

Bruno eventually beat his teacher in a game of chess, and kept his promise to teach someone else to play, though his victory always remained suspect in his own mind. He couldn't be sure whether James lost, or let him win. Joey the Gimp was his student, who taught Mickey the Mole, who taught Carelli, who showed Manning, and so it went.

At first, the popularity of the game created a problem because there was only one set of chess pieces. There were times when the men became frustrated or angry, having to wait for long periods before they could use the set. But Carelli had acted quickly, whittling crude chess pieces from lumber he found out at the cattle pens, so more could play at one time. As time passed, he replaced those sets with some from a plaster he had created, cast in wax and then baked in the kitchen ovens, or whittled from branches of the Joshua Tree up on the hill where Necco was buried. And some were chiseled from the deep red stone of the ledge on the backside of cemetery hill.

Sunday, then, evolved into more than a day of rest. It first became a day of leisure pursuits, particularly chess. Those things that could not be overlooked, such as tending the livestock or preparing meals, were set in a rotation, so everyone did these chores in turn. Gradually, the day became one of learning and creativity beyond the intellectual stimulation chess produced. The library would be filled not only with men playing chess, but also the ones James was teaching to read and write.

Near the end of that year, the men had agreed that a coin should be created to replace bartering. Briscoe suggested it despite strong objections by James, who did not attend the meeting—a silent protest—regretting once again ever having allowed Briscoe any assumption of leadership. James could see the problems introducing a form of currency might lead to and, as always, Briscoe could see no farther than the end of his arm.

Necco produced the coins shortly before his death, cutting bars from cell doors with a *Permanente* steel-cutting saw, then slicing across the round bars in quarter-inch increments. But questions arose: How many should be produced? How much would each coin be worth? How should they be distributed initially? They looked to Briscoe for answers since it was his idea. He cleverly avoided the expectation by calling a meeting. The fact was he had never thought about any of those things when he suggested it, he'd just been looking for a way to overcome the perishable nature of wealth in Mescalero, which was primarily farm produce. Truth be known, he had no idea what to do about such issues.

One hundred coins all having the same value, was agreed upon by a vote and distributed to each man. By the end of the decade Briscoe had accumulated many of them, however, as well as several parcels of land. Some he acquired by default on debts, some by casting lots when the owner died, or when someone sold at auction.

2040 AD

Bernie Pelletier has died. He left his field, bordered on all sides by land Briscoe has acquired over the years, to his friend, Ike Tremblay. But the field is up for bid today, Tremblay is too old and feeble to work it. Jack Manning and Nick Bruno, who have developed an agreeable relationship, are interested in it and are present to bid. So is Briscoe, who has made it clear all week that he wants the field, the field that's right in the middle of his property.

When the auction is over, Briscoe walks past Manning and Bruno, a subtle but obviously triumphant smirk on his face, having outbid everyone once again.

"No one's ever got enough money to outbid him," Manning says, disgusted. "It's like there's no end to his coin."

Bruno nods as the two start toward the building for supper, sloughing off any lingering disappointment by imagining all the aggravation they would have with Briscoe as a neighbor, if either of them had won.

Jack Manning is a tall, rangy man, who has lost his hair except for a wide ring of it from ear to ear. He is intelligent, and sometimes, thoughtful. Temper and competitiveness had been his obstruction, until he slipped into his fifties and found himself working at something surprisingly satisfying: Farming.

As he sits eating supper with the others in the chow hall, thinking about the auction and listening to Bruno rehash his complaints about Briscoe, a pain in his back begins to radiate down his right leg. Digging spuds is work for a short man, he thinks, wincing as he lifts his leg over the bench seat to leave. That night he is unable to sleep and wakes Fuentes to find out what he can do to ease the discomfort. Angel gives him a small container of jam he makes from Pax. He tells him to go out and pick four or five large Pax leaves, the tough ones at the bottom of the plant. Heat them in water, he says, then rub the jam on the sore muscles and lie down with the hot leaves over the jam for half an hour at a time. Do this three times a day for a few days, and take it easy.

There is a patch of Pax growing just around the south end of the building where the junk heap is. Manning covers himself with his piece of plasticene and heads out into the light, steady night rain. As he picks half a dozen of the thick rubbery Pax leaves at the bottom of the stems, he hears a noise. It is difficult to tell just where it is coming from because of the sound of the rain, but his guess is the junk heap. He starts in that direction but the pain in his back gets worse. He dismisses the sound as nothing, and goes back inside with the leaves, heading for the kitchen.

It is possible to see all the way through the chow hall out into the corridor from where Manning stands stirring the Pax leaves in the heating water. Someone slips by the entrance in the shadows. Manning walks out to look. No mistaking the gait. It is Joey the Gimp turning into A Wing. He goes back to the kitchen to get the kettle and heads for his cell. He notices Joey's trail of wet footprints as he walks along, and wonders what he was doing out in the rain at this time of night.

Manning doesn't mention this to anyone, but watches for Joey from the kitchen the next several nights while heating his Pax pack as he's come to call it, but Joey doesn't appear. It is not until a week later, when he is picking leaves for a new heating pack because he is again unable to sleep, that Manning spots Joey coming out into the dome and follows him.

Joey, despite his floppy foot and weak right leg, steps his way through the junk heap nimbly. He stops where barred doors and windows, taken out of the lab when they converted it into a lounge, are stacked. Just to the right of them Joey leans down and pulls something out from under a small piece of plasticene. Manning cannot make out what it is and moves closer, still hidden by a stand of Pax. He watches for a few minutes before he realizes what Joey is doing. Moving in a slow, steady rhythm, Joey is cutting coins from the bars with the Permanente steel-cutting blade saw, and putting them in a sack he has under the tarp. Manning slowly withdraws until he's out of sight, gathers his Pax leaves, and heads inside to the kitchen.

At breakfast, Briscoe is moving from table to table, obviously perturbed, asking if anyone has seen Joey the Gimp. He has errands he wants him to do. But it's not until midday, when Chico takes a wheelbarrow load of busted concrete out to the junk heap, that Joey is found, face down, his skull crushed under a stack of doors and windows that have fallen on him. As soon as Manning hears, he races out there. They have already taken the body away, and no one is around. He spots a corner of the plasticene tarp crudely buried next to the doors and lifts it up. There is nothing under it.

As is the custom, all able-bodied men gather to draw for a grave-digging detail. Single file, they step up to the great urn on the landing to reach inside for a stone. Most of the small, smooth stones inside are white quartz or red sandstone. But there are black stones too, black and shiny as raw silver ore. The men pass by the urn silently until six black stones have been picked.

Manning hasn't gotten a black stone for years until today, and he falls in with the others in the detail as they head for the hill. On the way, they stop at the toolshed for their shovels, and as he steps inside to grab one, he is surprised when he notices the Permanente saw hanging in its place above the workbench.

Six men working in teams of two and relieving one another often can dig a proper grave in a couple of hours if the spot they have chosen is clear of the sandstone ledge that runs beneath areas of the hill. Manning spends the time silently, preoccupied. He barely responds to the others who chide him for this unusual silence, behavior they are not used to from him. The spot they have chosen is, most appropriately, next to Necco. And they have been fortunate not to run into any ledge. When the grave is ready the men return to the building to take up their responsibility as pallbearers. All during the procession back up the hill, then through the service and backfilling the grave, Manning's mind churns.

The week following Joey the Gimp's death, Briscoe produces a statement signed by Joey, willing his field to Briscoe. This is not a surprise given the little man's unerring loyalty to him, but it is enough to start Manning thinking. He decides to find out how much coinage there is in in Mescalero, and how much of it is Briscoe's. After a couple weeks of polling everyone, he's sure that what he suspected is correct: There's more in circulation than the original distribution of a hundred coins per man. Uncertain how to handle this revelation on top of what he already knows, he takes it to James.

"The first thing I'd do is get the Permanente saw out of the toolshed," James advises, sitting cross-legged on the floor of his cell. "Put it someplace where everyone can see it, maybe hanging on the chow hall wall."

Manning nods, grasping the wisdom in this: it is the only tool in the dome that can cut those bars the way Necco did, to produce coinage. It's good for lots of other things, too. But, if it's where everyone can see it, everyone will know who's using it, and for what.

"But what about Briscoe, James? The coinage, I mean. Who knows how much more Joey might've cut for him?"

James nods.

"This is an issue for the whole assembly to consider, Jack. I think you should call for a meeting."

"And what about Joey? Honest, James, his death was no accident. I'm sure of it."

"Can you prove it, Jack?" James says, his eyes fixed firmly on Manning.

"No."

The Assembly, as Manning refers to it opening the meeting the following day, is so he can declare what he saw out in the dome, and they can decide what to do about it. Briscoe sits at the back of the chow hall on the steam table, surrounded by what were called soldiers years ago. Briscoe considers nearly a third of the men in Mescalero still loyal to him to one degree or another, having nurtured, coerced, or extorted obligations from them.

James watches from a corner of the hall as Manning presents his case.

"Joey was cutting coins for Briscoe." Everybody knows what a "kiss ass" he was to Vince, always looking for ways to curry favor with him. And it was a clever idea. "So," Manning asks, "how much land did Briscoe acquire with the coins Joey cut for him? And how did the Permanente saw I watched Joey hide in the junk heap get back in the tool shed where it's supposed to be? And, oh yeah, where's the money bag I saw Joey bury out there, under the plasticene?"

Briscoe objects strenuously, his raspy voice hissing like a serpent from the back of the room. They all know Manning tried to kill him years ago, he argues. James was witness to it, he says pointing at James. And he's still trying, Briscoe insists.

Others ask to speak. One after another, they recount their experience with Briscoe, a chiseler who's bilked them out of land and money and labor, and who has reneged on debts and promises over the years. They cannot prove he killed Joey, most likely to keep him from talking, but they don't care anymore. They've all had enough of him.

Sandoval Hunsinger, a powerfully built man, stands with his arm raised.

"I think we oughtta kick his ass out into the dome."

The room is silent. Faces turn toward where James is sitting.

"The term is banishment," James says, answering their unspoken question.

A new order of business is called for: Request for a vote to banish. If Necco were alive, just his standing there with Briscoe would have had a decided impact on the vote. But he's not, they all know very well, and the ones who had always claimed to be Briscoe's supporters begin to distance themselves from him, from the man who it appears is about to be cast out into the dome.

James is astonished at how quickly it happens. He stands and asks to speak.

"I urge you to reconsider, to give Vince a chance to change his ways. You could use this vote today as a warning to him, place him on parole, so to speak."

The grumbling is so loud throughout the room, a vote on his suggestion isn't even called for.

"How do we enforce it?" Chico asks.

"Simple, just man the trap," Hunsinger says, "it's the only way in."

James, watching what was inevitable unfold, gets up to leave, disheartened that this is all the farther they've gotten since they were left on their own. But as he starts for the door, he sees that several of the men have begun moving toward Briscoe, like hyenas getting up the nerve to pounce on wounded prey. He walks to the back where Briscoe is sitting.

"I will help you get your things, Vincent," he tells him in a loud voice, to be sure everyone hears him, "and walk with you out to the landing."

They won't touch him as long as James is with him, and so they withdraw, and the two walk the corridor, turning in at A Wing. Briscoe gathers what he can carry in a gunnysack. As he picks up the mattress of his bunk, pulling out the leather pouch filled with his coins, he looks at James.

"What're you thinkin', James?"

" '...*and the deeds of a man's hands will return to him,*' Proverbs, chapter twelve, verse fourteen."

CHAPTER ELEVEN

Moss nearly sprinted the full length of the tunnel with the card when Vincent told him what it was. In the warden's office he switched Primary from standby to active, and inserted the card into the verification slot on the front panel.

"State your name and authority," she said in the same sultry voice that had denied him access a few days ago.

"Jack Caldwell, Captain of the Guard," he said clearly, careful to speak in a normal tone he could duplicate easily.

Primary was silent but Moss saw this as reason to be hopeful. She hadn't rejected him out of hand. He was sure she would require a reason for the override, but in his excitement and haste had forgotten to prepare one he thought she would accept.

Hoping there wasn't some code or password required he tried to think of a response that would make sense to her. He wasn't going to be able to charm her into giving him what he wanted. He was also aware from his research work in the capital, that this class of computer was capable of sophisticated logic and problem solving. As he stood in front of the screen, he noticed the digital date sequence in the lower left corner, and couldn't believe it.

It's current for God's sake!

"Please state the purpose for override of present authority," Primary announced.

Moss was taking too long trying to think of a reason acceptable to her logic program. She announced a second request. He knew if he didn't respond by the third request the sequence would be aborted, and initiating a new one would in all likelihood be more difficult. He looked again at the date and time sequence.

"Third req—"

"Warden Smalley is dead!"

Primary stopped. Moss waited, watching the silent reasoning process proceed rapidly around the panel and the screen, as tiny indicators flashed on, then off, and on again.

Then, the digital date sequence became illuminated, and the search stalled. He waited for more than a minute, though it seemed much longer, staring at the illuminated DDS, wondering if *Primary* had aborted the request. Just then, all the indicators on both the panel and the screen flashed at once, then off, then on again.

"Authority approved. Access granted," Primary announced.

Moss kissed his fingers and touched them to the screen. He could only assume that, although she had been shut down for fifty years, the calcion batteries continued to count time, and with her database on personnel, she deduced that the warden probably wouldn't be alive in 2071. Whatever the reasoning process, Moss didn't care, he was in. He placed the first of the two wafers he'd found in the vector slot on the front panel of the computer.

The wafer was a visual recording, and from what he could make out, it appeared to originate in the Command Center in the dome. The date and time was displayed in the upper right corner of the screen: January 12, 2022, just after nine in the morning. Initially, the subject appeared to be routine movements of security personnel, then various locations: cellblocks, corridors, common areas, then the laboratory, where an attractive woman was taking an inmate's blood pressure while three others stood by. Another woman was setting up an intravenous drip at a contoured recliner, while an armed guard stood at one wall, watching.

The screen went black. Moss realized that that must have been the now infamous blackout caused by the solares. After about thirty seconds, the screen flashed on and off and on again, and a visual jumped up, then off, then on and steady. The inmates had disarmed and shot the guard. In the following minutes Moss was horrified, as he watched both women being stripped and then raped by each of the inmates. Then the screen went blank again.

He shook his head to clear the awful images from his head, then stood up, sick to his stomach. The nausea passed after a few minutes of taking deep breaths, and splashing his face with cold water from the tap in the lavatory across the hall. Still, he didn't go back right away, but walked out into the big office, then to the dormitory, then to the shop and the receiving area where his pickup was parked, trying to rid his mind of the violence he'd just witnessed. When he finally felt as if he could, he went back to the warden's office and inserted the other wafer.

Moss gave a sigh of relief to find the second wafer was not a visual, but an accounting journal listing credits, debits, receipts of expenditures, bank deposits and withdrawals of considerable sums of money. At first he thought this might have been the routine bookkeeping for Mescalero. It did seem to be tied to the budget funding for the prison. But then he noticed that it had not been initiated until near the end of the first quarter of 2022, so it had to be something else. Why, after all, would someone have gone to such trouble to hide normal, everyday records?

Late in the afternoon, Moss had skimmed most of the information on the wafer, and was beginning to postulate possible explanations for the various types of entries and how they were related. One piece of data was especially intriguing: a contax number followed by a five-digit number, letter, and symbol combination. He knew immediately that the contax number was out of country. Thinking about what the curious number represented, it occurred to him that he had never tried the contax since he'd entered Mescalero. If the power was still working, why not the conny?

He pressed the call switch on the contax on Smalley's desk and there was indeed an active tone. He was elated, but felt stupid at the same time. That was the sloppy investigation undergraduates did, not someone about to receive their Ph.D. He entered the number from the accounting journal, and listened while it queried several times. Then, someone answered.

"First Depository of the Grenadines, Ms. George speaking. How may I—"

Moss switched the contax off. An offshore account. Had to be. This was something big, he was sure, and he was energized. It was late. He needed to get back to the dome. There was a lot he wanted to ask Vincent about, and a lot to tell.

With Moss off at the warden's office, Vincent had spent the day in his usual way: Matins, then breakfast, then seeing to his chickens and gathering the eggs. A little time at the shrine of James the Wise, pruning the gardenias that formed a semi-circular hedge around the back of it, or edging the stone terrace floor in front. After midday meditations, tending his vegetable garden, picking Pax for his afternoon snack. Tending his bees. Fishing for their dinner. At dusk, Vespers.

He thought about how nice it was having someone to play chess with, or just to talk to after such a long time alone. But then, a troubling thought. What would happen when Jake was finished there? He would have to tell—would want to tell—what he had found. What would happen to him, then? They would take him away from there, put him in some terrible place with other men, men who did not appreciate the way of The Assembly.

They'll take me away from my paradise…my solitude…my chess…my friends. They'll take me away from my Pax!

It was dusk when Moss reentered the dome. He knew where he would find Vincent, and headed for the shrine. As he got closer, the sound became clearer and stronger. Vincent was singing in plainsong:

> *Abide with me, fast falls the eventide;*
> *the darkness deepens: Lord with me abide.*
> *When other helpers fail, and comforts flee,*
> *help of the helpless, O abide with me.*

Moss sat beneath a tree in the olive grove, at the edge of the garden, waiting for Vincent to finish. When he stood, so did Moss. Vincent acknowledged him and Moss approached the shrine, eager to tell him what he had discovered on the wafers. As they left the garden and the heavenly fragrance of gardenias that enveloped them, Moss picked up the pail with the fish Vincent had speared, and they started back to the building in the deepening darkness.

"Vincent, you seem rather serious this evening. I thought you'd be a bit more excited to hear what I'd found out."

"Ah," he said, looking at the ground as he walked. "Surely, I would have been so fifty years ago, Jake. But what does it matter now? Can it change anything? Would I want to at this late date?"

Moss had no response, surprised by Vincent's subdued reaction.

At supper, Vincent ate his fish with bean curd and spinach quietly. He seemed distant and contemplative. Moss felt as though he were talking to himself at times, watching the little man patiently manipulate food in his mouth so eventually it would get at least partially chewed by the teeth that still met when he bit down.

Moss agreed with what James and Vincent and the others had concluded. The warden had sealed them in the dome. And it seemed obvious to him that one of the skeletons in the tunnel was Eddie the Tin Man. He was a welder, last seen leaving his cell with a guard. And when he found them, the remains of the man with the hoses underneath had been welding when he died. The other skeleton had to be Caldwell.

There was only one explanation in Moss's mind that might explain why Smalley left all the cells unlocked—a hope that the inmates would kill one another off. Vincent thought about this for a moment, then nodded.

"It makes sense, Jake, a perverse kind of revenge, though I must say, that idea never occurred to us."

"Well, I have to say, in reading James's early journals, it looked like that's just what was going to happen, didn't it?"

Vincent nodded again, reminded, too, by Moss's comment, how large a part he had played in all the killing.

"I keep meaning to ask you why you chose to bury everyone, Vincent. I noticed the other day, the plans show a crematory in the physical plant."

"Without power for the exhaust system, we were afraid the atmospheric balance in the dome would be thrown too far off to recover, especially at first, in the Time of Terror. It was James who warned us about that. Of course, when it came to Necco," he said, "it was simple: He wouldn't fit in the chamber."

Moss nodded, smiling, noting again Stryker's impact on life inside Mescalero.

As for the revelation about Smalley's fraud in diverting the prison budget to an offshore depository, Vincent showed no interest at all. Moss recounted to him all the documents of transfer and falsified receipts for goods and services he'd found, as well as the contax call to the depository. Vincent did not care.

After supper, Vincent peeled a mango, watching Moss set up the chess pieces to begin a new game.

"I do intend to beat you at least once before I'm through here, Vincent." he said, smiling. Vincent grinned, shrugging his shoulders apologetically.

"And when will that be, Jake?"

Moss stopped and looked at Vincent, noting the odd tone of his question.

"Well, I don't know, I guess. I hadn't given it much thought. I'm due back at school the end of August, and—"

"And what will you tell people?"

Moss thought for a minute, wondering what he was driving at. Judging from the look on his face, Vincent had something on his mind.

"Well, Vincent, whether you know it or not, this place—and you—are a treasure trove of immensely valuable data. The whole world will be eager to know what I've found here. This place is a veritable gold mine."

"Ah," Vincent said at Moss's jubilant declaration, lifting his head, and nodding.

He looked at the chessboard and made his opening move. Moss followed suit and the new game was under way. There were several opportunities for Moss to have checked his King, Vincent observed, but in his exuberance over what the Mescalero Project represented for him, he had overlooked them.

Moss chattered on, explaining that his findings concerning Mescalero would establish his career. They would be sure to be published. He would be a sought-after lecturer. His future would be secure. Vincent listened politely, until the wear of the day came over him. He got up and excused himself and turned to go to his cell, and Moss finally stopped talking.

"Jake," Vincent said with an anxious look, "I am happy that what you want will come to pass for you, but what about me? What will happen to me?"

Moss was unprepared for the question and flushed red with embarrassment for having been so thoughtless. He watched as Vincent started down the corridor to his cell, unable to think of what to say. When he realized that this was what had been bothering Vincent all evening, he went after him. Vincent was sitting on his bunk with his legs folded, meditating silently when Moss came to the door of his cell. He waited, watching Vincent's shadow, magnified by the candlelight, dancing on the wall.

"I can do this later if you like," Vincent said, looking up at Moss. "I can see that you have something you want to say to me."

"Yes. I'm sorry, Vincent, I hadn't given a thought to what happens to you. I've only been thinking of me. I'm sorry. Really."

Vincent didn't speak, certain Moss had more to say.

"Knowing the government, they would most likely want to move you to another prison, but if they did it would only be for a short time, because I would insist that I need you for all the studies that must be done. I'll make sure you live with me. I promise."

Vincent smiled. He slipped the hood of his mantle down to his shoulders, and let his long, silvery hair loose.

"You are a nice young man, Jacob Moss, and I believe you mean well, but if you can...well, you must try...to understand what this place is for me."

Jake stepped into the cell and sat down on the floor, with his back against the wall opposite Vincent's bunk.

"Please tell me, Vincent. I want to know."

"When we first came here," he began, "we were angry men, but that was nothing new. We had always been angry men. We were incorrigibles. And in the first year, after we were left alone, we were even angrier, because we had been left alone with no explanation. Even if you're the lowest, filthiest, most horrible human being on the planet, to be left the way the warden did us, takes its toll. The men wouldn't admit it, tried not to show it. First rule in *slam*: Don't ever show any emotion or tell anyone anything about yourself that they can use to push your buttons. Doing what Smalley did, had a powerful effect on all of us.

"We were scared—scared of each other—old grudges from long before Mescalero, or since coming here. Cons never forget, Jake, too much time to do nothing but think. Most of us didn't sleep for more than a few minutes at a time for weeks, always watching for the ones who had it in for us. And we were scared that maybe something terrible had happened outside, that we were the only ones left anywhere, that no one was ever going to let us out of here.

"This does something to a man, Jacob. You get this terrifying feeling of loneliness, you know, that feeling I was not able to describe? I suppose it's how you might feel to find out you were the only person left alive on earth. Your reasons to live are gone. You can't see why you should continue to live. What would be the point? What would you do? And with whom? You would spend all your energy surviving. Hard work, Jake, surviving, and for what? So, one day you can die? Who would know? Who would care?"

"When did the fear go away, Vincent?" he said, seeing that Vincent was upsetting himself by explaining this, and wanting to change the direction of the narrative somehow.

"It has never left altogether, but after The Visitor, you know, Melchior, began to visit James, it started to change. It was gradual, but when we saw that James was right, that we did need one another and therefore we did need to be concerned about each other. That's when the fear began to subside, to become something we could live with, get used to just like getting used to being locked in a cage."

It was near midnight, Moss realized, hearing the rain begin to tap on the skylights overhead.

"But Vincent, it seems to me that wanting to stay here is the same as what you've been describing. What's the difference between being the only person left in the world, or being left alone here, in this world?"

Vincent smiled in a kind, fatherly way, a way that said he knew something his bright young friend did not.

"I am an old man, Jake. You believe you can insure my well-being out there," he said, waving his arm in an arc signifying the world outside the dome, "but I tell you, they never forget. Even if all the people I hurt or stole from or killed, and all the people who caught me and tried me and sentenced me and said, good riddance; if all the people whoever heard of me were dead and gone, the ones who took their place would never let me go free, either."

"But Vincent, for Heaven's sake, you've served any ordinary man's lifetime already. Surely that's enough for—"

Vincent shook his head.

"It is never enough, Jake, especially when lives have been taken. Only your life, forfeit, whether by execution or locked away until you die will satisfy the debt. They will not let me go free, I assure you, and I will die in their cust—"

"—I don't believe it, Vin—"

"—ody, and it is not the dying that matters. It is that I would rather die here where my friends are buried, than leave."

They were both quiet, Vincent with a smile on his face, and Moss looking at him, his brow creased in bewilderment.

The candles were nearly spent. Jake got up off the floor, stretching and rubbing his butt that had gone numb. The rain pelted the skylights steadily now as he said good night to Vincent, ducking his head to step out of the cell.

"I never had a friend until the day James saved my life, Jake. Not one. The people in my life had just been people I used to get what I wanted. In The Assembly, I had a hundred friends and more."

Moss gave a tentative smile, turned, and went to his room in the infirmary.

He had taken to writing in his own journal each night before going to sleep. As he sat at the little table in the inadequate candlelight, he wrestled with what he wanted to write because of Vincent's revelations after supper.

A fly landed on the edge of the table. Without thinking, Moss took a swing at it and missed, and it disappeared out into the hall.

***

Ketchum slipped out of town in his battered old wrecker well before daylight, so no one would notice he'd gone south into the desert. It would surely be a topic of discussion at the café when he got back it was so rare to see anyone head into that Godforsaken country. He nearly missed the turnoff to the prison, it had been so long since he'd been there. The sun was well into the sky, searing in through the window from above his left ear. He adjusted the wide-brimmed hat he wore to shade that side of his head, as he started up the gravel road.

By mid-morning, a wind had come up strong out of the southwest. Sand swirled across the front of the vehicle obscuring his vision, as he picked his way along the indistinct access road. He cursed the sand stinging his neck as the wind whipped it through the break in the rear window. He stopped frequently, visibility often going to zero, for losing sight of the road. He came to the ivory white sea of sand that marked the start of the desert in earnest. The dunes, like great surging, frothing waves frozen in space and time, stretched to what could just as well have been the end of the world. He stopped altogether, tired of straining to see his way, and afraid the blowing sand would eat up the charging magnetos at each wheel. He reached for his canteen, and waited in the stifling, furnace-like heat of the cab for the storm to pass.

At noon, the sky cleared as quickly as it had become obscured. Ketchum got out and checked the condition of the magneto rotors while the scorching sun regained dominance as the primary threat to life. He continued south. Stretches of the road were clear now, the wind having swept the roadbed bare where it was higher than the lay of the ground.

Early in the afternoon, Ketchum reached the escarpment that hid the dome at Mescalero. He rounded the western end and turned east, driving along the base of its cliffs in welcome shadow. He recalled how he and two of his buddies nearly died of exposure the only other time he'd been there, back when he was a kid. If it weren't for the money Schilling paid, he thought, no one could ever have talked him into coming to the place again.

He drove slowly, watching for a vehicle or tracks the wind might not have erased as he approached where he recalled the entrance should be. A glint of sun off the steel door of the pedestrian entrance caught his eye and he stopped. He reached for his binoculars and studied it for a minute, wiping beads of sweat from his brow now and then with the sleeve of his shirt. He scanned the landscape for a vehicle, but didn't see one. He looked again at the entrance: a recent excavation.

Where are they? How'd they get here?

Ketchum got out of the old wrecker and walked cautiously to the entrance. Glancing to the east, the tip of the dome was practically invisible, engulfed in the shadow of the canyon. The door had been pulled open somehow. He stepped inside the stairwell and looked down into the pitch black, as cool, dank air wafted up to him. Basking in it for a minute, he checked the time. Mid-afternoon. He had four, maybe five hours of daylight, so he returned to the truck for a calcion torch and his Lukens Magnum.

He strapped on his holster, checking his cartridge belt to see that it was full. Then he grabbed his torch and went back to the entrance, releasing the safety strap on his holster as he walked. He started down the stairwell with the torch set on broad beam, noticing tracks in the dust and broken cobwebs hanging to each side. At the bottom of the stairwell the tracks headed in both directions several times. He looked left toward the dome. There was only blackness. But looking to his right, toward the office complex, he saw a thin blade of light. He quickly switched the beam of the torch to narrow distance focus and shined it in that direction. The light was coming from beneath the door to the offices. He walked toward the door, drawing his pistol from the holster as he approached.

CHAPTER TWELVE

2062 AD

Mickey the Mole plucks the strings of the harp cradled in his arm as they sing:

> *Swift to its close ebbs out life's little day;*
> *earth's joys grow dim, its glories pass away;*
> *change and decay in all around I see:*
> *O thou who changest not, abide with me.*

The sound of harp and voices resounds through the library. Candles and oil lamps cast shadows that dance on the walls and ceiling, lighting the room that has served as the sanctuary of The Assembly for three decades now.

Vespers. Eventide, as Nicholas prefers to call it. It is his turn this evening to offer the message. Picking up James's Bible, frayed and loose-bound with pages nearly blank from wear, he turns to the fifth chapter of Matthew and begins:

> *"Blessed are the poor in spirit,*
> *for theirs is the kingdom of heaven.*
> *Blessed are those who mourn,*
> *for they shall be comforted.*
> *Blessed are the meek,*
> *for they shall inherit...."*

James sits cross-legged beneath the magnificent podium Carelli carved years ago from a beam that collapsed in the hay barn, watching Nicholas with the others. How confidently he reads, James thinks, smiling, recalling the first time Bruno came so secretly to see him in the night. And now, so articulate and with such richness of voice.

At the conclusion of his homily, Nicholas hands the dilapidated old Bible back to James and resumes his seat in the circle of men on the floor. Mickey picks up his armharp again and plays the melody of a new hymn he's composed, and Nicholas recites the lyrics he has written for it. Each time they repeat it, the others heartily approve, trying to pick up the words and melody a little more. After a while, they adjourn to the chow hall where Vincent, whose turn it is today, is in charge of the supper preparation.

Walking the corridor to the chow hall, James passes the trap, and an image from long ago flashes across his mind: Putting a tray of food out on the landing for Vincent every night, after he was banished.

***

Briscoe lives in one of the huts Bruno and his men built at the north end of the dome, way back in the Time of Terror. He filched plasticene from the pump house to patch the roof and sides. He is seen in the undergrowth at the edge of the cultivated land occasionally, watching everyone work in the fields that used to be his. Now, they belong to no one person—but are shared by all the men. He no longer approaches, trying to talk to the men the way he did at first, because as it was agreed among all the men—except, of course, for James—they ignore him.

Even though he is banished, Vincent still must work. His job is to pick the tree fruits, the bananas and oranges, mangoes and dates, and the avocados when they are ripe, and leave them on the landing in front of the building. He catches and cleans gourami, too, saving the innards for Angel, who extracts the oil for use in poultice preparations, then gives what's left to Chico to use in the compost. At first Briscoe refused to do anything he was told to do, but that didn't last long when he was told—no work, no hot meals.

How long Briscoe would be expelled was never settled at the time of his banishment. It has been two years. The men have been meeting in the library for meditation and singing hymns before supper for some time now. Every night after Vespers, before he sits down to eat, James first takes a meal tray from the kitchen and puts it out on the landing for Vincent.

Chico spots it at first light, returning from cutting flowers for the dining hall tables and the sanctuary vases. Sitting there on the landing just outside the door to the trap, Briscoe's tray from the night before has not been touched. James isn't surprised by the report. He has been getting more and more concerned about Vincent in recent months, since he began moving about the dome naked.

Out in the fields, James watches for Vincent, working his way along a row of strawberries, hoping to have a chance to speak to him, to see how he is, why he didn't touch his supper last night. At the end of the row he gently sets his last full basket into the wheelbarrow sitting there. It is the last row, he is done for the day, and his back is weary from bending over the plants. He has watched for him since he began, just after breakfast. That night at supper, Hunsinger tells James he saw Briscoe in the olive grove.

"How did he seem, Sandy?" James says.

"You mean, beside being filthy and naked and looking like a wild man?"

"Yes," James says, impatient with Hunsinger's sarcasm. "Did you talk to him? Did he say anything?"

"Yes and no. He talked. I ignored him," Hunsinger says coldly. "That's what we agreed to do, right? Ignore him. Not speak to him. Right, James?"

"Tell me what he said, Sandy. How did he act?"

"He started talking, that's all, asking about how it was 'inside' and stuff. When I wouldn't look at him, wouldn't answer him, he started pleading with me, asking me to say something, anything. Then he grabbed my arm and fell to his knees. He was bawlin', James. Briscoe was bawlin' like a little kid."

"What did you do?"

"Do? Me?" Hunsinger says, surprised at the question. "Nuthin'. I pulled my arm free and walked away."

James looks long at Hunsinger with icy eyes.

"He who shows no mercy, shall receive no mercy," he says in almost a hiss of a whisper, and gets up from the table with his tray.

In the morning, as he steps out onto the landing from the trap, James meets Chico coming in from his flowerbeds. He is impatient to see for himself if the tray was taken last night. This one, too, hasn't been touched. He asks Chico to take his place on the kitchen crew, for the morning at least, so he can go look for Vincent. Chico is agreeable, as he always is with James.
The morning shadow of the canyon wall outside the dome is receding to the east as the sun climbs higher in the sky. James walks first to the huts at the north end of the biosphere. If he does not find Vincent there, he will go to the banana grove, then the orange grove, the olive garden, then the pond. He does not find him anywhere. On his way back to the building for lunch James sees a flash of sunlight reflect off something across the dome, near the Joshua tree at the top of the cemetery hill. It has to be Vincent, James realizes, and he turns and heads in that direction.
James naturally moves as silently as a shadow, and when he reaches the crest of the hill, Briscoe is sitting under the Joshua tree next to Necco's grave. He is as Hunsinger said, filthy and naked, sitting in a forlorn posture, his head low. As James comes closer, he sees the noose of the rope hanging from a thick branch of the tree. Just then, still unaware of James, Vincent gets up and starts to climb the tree. James springs forward and is at the tree in an instant, reaching up to grab Vincent around the waist pulling him down. Vincent struggles to hold on but loses his grip on the flaky bark of the tree, collapsing into James's arms. He hugs James tightly, his head tucked into his neck, and begins to sob.
"Don't leave me, James," he begs. "Don't leave me."

***

Late in the evening, still haunted by memories of those days so long ago, James sits in the solitude of his cell, in the flickering lamplight, writing in his journal:

May 24, 2063—Most of us have gone on now. Only half a dozen left. Jack and Vincent and Nicholas, Mickey the Mole, Tito, and me. We do not farm any longer. The livestock have been gone for some time. We tend a garden sufficient for our needs, and there are chickens, and so eggs, for which we are grateful, none of us having many teeth left.

We spend the days in prayerful meditation, and in pursuit of our passions. Mickey the Mole is designing yet another of his curious but delightful musical instruments. Vincent putters in the old laboratory, nurturing his hybrids and grafting experiments. Carelli, of course, will keep on until he can no longer hold a chisel and hammer, sculpting creations in what red sandstone he is still able to cut from the ledge behind the cemetery and carry in a wheelbarrow. He has asked me to pose for a bust.

Nicholas continues to pen his never-ending epic poem on whatever material he can find that will hold the ink he makes from charcoal and rendered fish oil. And Jack brightens our quarters with landscapes of places out in the dome, and portraits from memory—of Necco, Joey the Gimp, Chico, Angel—on plasticene canvases he hangs in the dining hall or lab, in our cells or on the walls along the main corridor. And of course, we are all still avid chess players.

Over the past thirty-odd years we call the Time of the Assembly, *we have learned much, not the least of which was our need of one another, but most of all—and most surprising— that we were capable of far more and far better than we'd ever imagined or been led to believe....*

James puts away his journal. On his knees, a short prayer of thanksgiving for the day, and a request for another one tomorrow, then climbs into his bunk. He slips into slumber, well enough content now, in his mid-eighties, having long ago become resigned to the vagaries of life that had come upon him.

Vincent and me sitting across from each other at a long table, eating. We are alone, but where? Where are we? It is bright, sunny, a bucolic landscape around us, great boulders, old, smooth, bleached and weathered, in a grassy field. Scrub pine and live oak here and there, and buttercups and columbine dance among the clover and timothy in the soft breeze. I do not know the place.

I want to speak to him. I try. He smiles at first, but becomes pensive in his countenance, making no effort to speak. And then, the long table splitting in half down the middle, from end to end, he is pushed farther and farther away from me. I reach for his hand but cannot reach it. He is too far away now.

James awakes with a momentary sense of panic, but is relieved. Only a dream. He turns over, adjusts his pillow, and falls back to sleep.

A rutted old road, Vincent and me, walking. We come to a fork, and he starts to take the fork to the right. I stop and yell to him, "Vincent! This way!" He keeps getting farther and farther away. I try to go after him but the road becomes muddled, and now I can't make it out clearly.

James coughs, to clear his throat of night phlegm, and he is awake again.

Today the men are devoting their time to finishing an altar of sorts they'd started a while back in the olive grove. The Patriarchs in the Bible were always stopping to build altars along their way, more as markers of events and encounters than something on which a sacrifice was performed. James thought it a good idea for them to do the same, and everyone agreed. When it is complete, he thinks, it will be a lovely grotto where they can pray and meditate. Gardenia bushes Chico planted and groomed into a hedge extend out from both ends of the stone altar in a semi-circle. When someone comes to the garden, they are met by the fragrance of the delicate, cream white blossoms.

Vincent is by far the most active—and productive—in this project, as he is always more energetic, stronger, possessing far greater stamina than any of them, even James. Why this is has often been a topic of discussion in the evenings when they play chess, and a consensus was reached some time ago: Vincent is the only one who has Pax as a regular part of his diet. It must be why, they've decided. No one can remember him ever being sick.

But many others have suffered through the years. Internal ailments: blood disorders that manifested themselves in great boils or skin that turned purple at the touch of a blade of grass. Cancers they suspected were of the lung or prostate, the kidney or liver, disorders Fuentes was not trained or equipped to handle. He thought most of the illnesses had developed since they entered Mescalero, but he did not know to what degree Pax was the cause, or at least involved.

Although he had discovered characteristics of Pax that had remarkable healing qualities in topical applications such as for a rash or joint swelling, he had also found that it could be a ruthless killer. Only weeks after the killing stopped in the Time of Terror, three men who had dried Pax and crushed it up like tobacco to smoke it, died of asphyxiation. Fuentes cut them open and found the nodules of their lungs were hard as pebbles, paralyzed, apparently from something in the Pax smoke.

On the other hand, if as Vincent has always done, the tiny top leaves of the plant were sautéed in olive oil and eaten like spinach or any other leafy vegetable, they were not only harmless, they were delicious. If the same was done with the great leathery leaves from the bottom of the stalk, it was a cruel poison that threw its victim into agony, twisting the intestine into knots and causing the spleen to explode.

Mickey the Mole is not with them today. He has been feeling poorly. All through the day, while they are out in the dome, the men take turns checking on him in his bunk. They are afraid his symptoms may be what has taken so many lives at Mescalero: Specious Salient Mycosis. SSM, as Fuentes would say. He said it was a fungus that eats the body from the inside out, according to notes he found when he began treating casualties in the lab during the Time of Terror. Worse than the global AIDS virus epidemic back in the 'teens, the notes said. Clearly from the Pax extracts, he said. Unexpected by the research scientists and the doctors.

"How does he seem?" James asks, when Bruno returns from checking on Mickey.

Nicholas, who has become close to Mickey over the past ten or so years, does not reply.

"Nicholas," James persists, "how is he? Please, tell me."

Bruno looks at James, his head cocked a little to one side, looking into those stunning blue eyes as if hoping somehow they can cauterize what is about to bleed unchecked.

"I think he's dying, James. Remember how fast they all went once the SSM got to a certain point? I think he's there."

James nods, assuring Nicholas his spirit and that of the others aches as his does, and begins to chant a mantra as he works. The others join in, Bruno first, then Manning and Carelli, then Vincent. They lay the stones, Manning passing them to Bruno, who must then pass them on to Carelli. This, so he cannot think about much beyond the task at hand for a time.

It is going through all of their minds, how helpless they feel. There is nothing they can do. Even Fuentes couldn't do anything. It used to drive him half mad he would say, the sameness in the dome, the rain every night, the work every day, the waiting to find out if you had the fungus or not. And if you did, just the waiting for the end because there was nothing anyone could do. Now, whether they will admit it or not, the six of them, in their eighties, are at that point, that place, at the edge of a season of dying—their dying.

At what point, James ponders fitting stones in place, when or how does a man begin to think about how much time he has left, or say to himself, my time has come? How does he feel, the utter certainty of it? What does that make him do?

It is Vincent who brings him to the garden, to Chico's lovely garden. It was his turn to check on Mickey. They all know, seeing Vincent coming toward them from a distance. Nicholas and James, Jack and Tito, stop what they're doing and stand up as Vincent approaches. Little Mickey the Mole is dead, slumped in Vincent's arms.

***

By spring, though marking the passage of time in the dome by seasons is a guess more than anything, only three men are left. In the Fall of '63, Carelli was crushed by a great piece of ledge. It collapsed on him while cutting stone for a new sculpture, a bust of Bruno, who had agreed to sit for him. They all surmised that their friend had died instantly, no one having been with him at the time, and considered it a blessing, so few over the years had died quickly.

Shortly after the first of the year, Bruno died choking on a bone in a piece of gourami he had filleted. The way he died had not been what anyone would call merciful, convulsing furiously for several minutes as James and Vincent tried desperately to dislodge the obstruction in his throat. Still, it was only minutes, not months as it had been for so many others. And now Jack Manning has been bedridden for three days, and has become so weak, it is all James or Vincent can do to get even a bit of liquid into him.

They have taken a bed out of the old lab and set it out on the landing for Jack. It is so cool inside the building, Vincent thought it might be good to put him out there at midday, to warm his bones, he had said.

"Thank you, James," Manning says in a whisper, as James props another pillow behind him, settling him into the bed.

"You're welcome, Jack, but it was Vincent's idea."

Manning nods then lets his head droop, exhausted from trying to hold it up.

"Now, Jack, let's try to eat a little something."

James sips the broth, stirs to cool it a little more, then patiently brings the spoon to Manning's lips. After a while, Manning takes hold of James's wrist.

"James…could you…go get Vincent?"

James nods and puts down the bowl and spoon, then goes to the lab where he knows he will find Vincent puttering with his hybrid plant projects.

When Vincent steps out of the trap and sees Jack across the landing, he is afraid he has died while they were inside. But, when he gets closer and touches his shoulder, Jack turns his head and reaches for Vincent's hand.
"How you doing, Jack?" Vincent asks, leaning down close to his face.
"Never mind that, Vince," he says impatiently, "I'm going."
Vincent starts to disagree emphatically, but Manning cuts him short.
"Vince...I need to...I want to ask you...." He stops to catch his breath.
"Take it easy, Jack, take it easy," Vincent coaxes, suddenly aware of a foul odor wafting up from under Manning's bedclothes. "I'll be right back," Vincent says as he gets up and starts to leave.
"No, Vince, don't bother about that." Manning pleads to no avail.
Vincent returns a few minutes later with a basket, a bucket of warm water, and a bundle of wide strips of cloth. He folds the bedclothes down and starts to turn Manning onto his side.
"No, Vince," he whispers, tears of embarrassment wetting his eyes, "don't bother with—"
"Oh, quiet, Jack," Vincent says, in a lighthearted way, "you'd do the same for me, wouldn't you?"
"I tried to kill you, Vince," he says so softly, struggling so hard for breath Vincent can hardly hear him.
"What's that, Jack?" he says, as he wipes Manning's emaciated buttocks and genitals with one piece of cloth after another, patiently turning him from side to side, then throwing the soiled strips into the basket.
"I said...I tried to kill you...I'm sorry. Please, Vince, forgive me."

Vincent bathes him with warm water. Then, after he dries him, he dabs Pax ointment on the raw sores around the anus and under the testicles with the skill of a mother.

But Vincent is silent regarding Manning's request.

James returns just as Vincent finishes and folds the bedclothes back over Jack.

"What happened?" James says, looking at the basket of soiled cloths.

"A little accident," Vincent says.

"That little bit of soup I managed to get into his stomach ran right through, didn't it?"

Vincent nods.

Jack is so easily exhausted he drifts off to sleep often.

"Will you watch him, James? I have to wash my hands and soak these cloths."

It is obvious to James that Vincent is troubled as he gathers his belongings, and assumes it is Jack's condition that's bothering him. He sits down in the chair next to the bed, and begins to hum a mantra softly, watching Jack Manning for any sign of change.

At dusk James and Vincent cover the bed on the landing with plasticene in anticipation of the always nightly rain, and take Jack back to his cell. They had wanted to set a bed up for him in the chow hall, so they would not have to walk all the way to C Wing to bring him his meal or hot towels and such. But Jack would not hear of it. "My own bed," he kept insisting, "my own bed."

Vincent hardly touches his supper, and seems preoccupied to James during their chess game after Vespers.

"What's troubling you, Vincent?" James says quietly as he moves his pawn to king's bishop three.

"Jack asked me to forgive him for trying to kill me," Vincent says straight out.

"But that's a good thing, Vincent, isn't it?" James says, waiting for Vincent to make a move. "Why does that trouble you?"

"I couldn't do it, James," he says, looking down. "I couldn't do it."

As he thinks of what to say to this, James finds his gaze focused on the healthy shine of Vincent's scalp where it is exposed at the crown of his skull.

"You have done it already, Vincent."

Vincent's head springs up.

"What are you saying, James? I'm telling you, I couldn't do it. I couldn't say, 'I forgive you, Jack.' "

"Vincent, let me ask you: Do you think a man who has not forgiven his enemy could wipe the filth from between his legs, and wash him like a baby as you did today?"

Vincent is silent and staring at James, then looks to the game again.

"I will tell him in the morning," he says decisively, moving his rook to queen's knight four. "I will go to him and say the words."

"It's late," James says, getting up. He is first as they begin alternating night watches now. "Time to check on Jack."

In the morning, before they begin matins, Vincent tells James he's going to look in on Jack. James waits in the library until it seems Vincent has been gone too long a time. With a sense of foreboding he walks to Jack's cell in C Wing, and finds Vincent kneeling at the bunk where Jack lies covered. He looks at James as he kneels beside him.

"It was too late. He was gone."

James doesn't speak, and puts his arm around Vincent.

All morning, James and Vincent work at digging Jack's grave. They don't stop for lunch, mindful of the need to get the body in the ground right away. They are grateful for the labor. It is somehow a salve for the ache and raw sorrow they are feeling. And though neither speaks of it, they are acutely aware that one of them will, soon enough, be left alone in this place.

***

Vincent thought he'd noticed it back in April, the day they buried Jack. James wasn't himself. Seemed out of shape. Had to stop so often, digging the grave. Very unusual for James, Vincent had thought at the time. Now, it seems evident to him. James is failing. Much of the time he just sits on the landing, in the rocker Mickey the Mole made for him as a birthday gift one year. He faces the muted mid-day sun, lower now in the September sky, and warms himself, writing in his journal or trying to memorize passages of Scripture, dozing in and out of sleep.

Oddly now, the last two souls in this forgotten world have little to say to each other. They simply are not inclined to talk. James has never cared much to speak preferring silence and solitude, writing down his thoughts instead. And this is what he continues to do, or tries at least, his writing hand more feeble by the day. And Vincent is content to muddle the mysteries of nature in the laboratory where, curiously, he has much more to say to his plants than to James.

Even when there is good reason to speak, in the evenings during a game of chess or at a meal, Vincent resists, saying only what is necessary. It is not that he doesn't wish to talk to James, it is that he must get ready. He knows he is going to be the last one, and unlike James, he has never been at ease with solitude.

But tonight, at the conclusion of Vespers, as they sit down at the table to resume their chess match, Vincent has decided there are some things that need to be said.

"James, why didn't you ever call in the favor I promised you?"

"Favor?" James asks, not sure what Vincent is referring to.

"When you saved my life...the first time. I promised, 'Ask anything, James,' I said. Remember?"

James shakes his head, astonished by the question, and tries to steady his hand enough to place his queen on her king's bishop three.

"Well?" Vincent persists, centering James's chess piece in the square on the board after he lets go of it. "How come?"

James is annoyed that in all these years Vincent has never been able to rid himself of thinking like this.

"Well, I guess there was never a time of equal importance where you could have changed the outcome."

Vincent is still, staring at James, who looks squarely back.

"What was there that I couldn't do...me or my men, that is? Tell me."

"You couldn't open the bulkhead and set us free."

At this, Vincent squirms in his chair and looks away. James considers Vincent's profile: the leathery face and neck, hair and beard nearly as white as his, as he waits patiently for him to digest what he can of the remark. Once or twice he thinks he sees the old tic twitch slightly in Vincent's cheek, something he has not seen for years.

"Shall we continue?" he asks after several minutes.

Vincent nods, then sits up, turns to face James, and makes a move.

After a while, his eyes fixed on the chessboard and unable to look James in the eye, Vincent confesses how he intended to kill him that night they met in the trap, after James had humiliated Necco in the chow hall. But James makes no response. He looks up. James is rigid, his teeth bared and clenched. He's drenched with sweat, and the tendons of his neck are flexed taut. His breathing is rapid and short, and blood is dripping from his nose and mouth, standing out in stark contrast to the white of his beard.

"James," Vincent shouts, scrambling out of his chair and around the table.

"My belly...lungs...on fire."

Vincent is panicky, not knowing what he should do. He races to the kitchen for water, and cloths for compresses. When he gets back, James is slumped over on the table, not moving.

"Aw, James," Vincent pleads, as he straightens him up in the chair, "don't die, James. Please!"

He wipes the blood from James's face and begins putting wet cloths on his forehead and the back of his neck, and against his chest and stomach. James moans softly at the relief the cold spring water gives. Seeing this, Vincent gathers him in his arms and heads for the trap as quickly as he can, and out into the dome.

In the deep darkness of night in the dome, always an obstacle for the other men, he hurries along. James groans from the jostling as Vincent shifts him in his arms along the way. His arms and legs threaten to give out, and his breathing is heavy and labored as he comes to the bank of the pond. He wades out to his waist and immerses James in the cold water. James stiffens for a moment, then gives an unmistakable sigh of relief, and looking up at Vincent, tries to smile. Vincent holds him there, cradled in his arms, until James nods that it's enough, the pain and bleeding have subsided.

Vincent slowly makes his way back to the building, James being heavier now, just as the night rain begins. He takes him to his cell where he dries him and wraps him in the bedclothes. For the rest of the night Vincent sits on the hard steel floor of the cell, talking while James sleeps.

"James, I'm sorry I wanted to kill you back then, especially with you saving my life not long after that. Forgive me, James?"

"James, I'm scared," he confesses, looking to see if James is awake and relieved to see that he's not. "I'm scared to be alone. Can't stand to be alone. My mother used to leave me alone, James, in the basement, for days sometimes. I'd go crazy down there, in the dark. I was only four then, James.

"Prison isn't so bad, James. At least you're never alone, right? And I had a knack for being able to make things happen, get what I wanted...or what someone else wanted, you know? Nah, it isn't so bad.

"Wish I had a stronger faith, James...like you. I mean, my faith is never strong except when you're around, you know? What am I going to do when you're not around, James?"

Over the next two weeks James has several more episodes of excruciating pain and bleeding. Vincent keeps a wheelbarrow at the bottom of the landing now, so he can wheel James to the pond and back more easily. He has taken to giving James Pax broth like he drinks. Surely, if it keeps him so healthy, he thinks, it will make James well again.

Then, during an especially brutal attack, as Vincent strains to get James out of the wheelbarrow and into the water, James says he wants to die. Vincent will not hear of it, cradling him in the water, but James reaches up and grabs Vincent's cloak at the neck, pleading. Vincent shakes his head vehemently. James pulls Vincent's head down close with his last ounce of strength.

"Put my head under the water, Vincent, please. Push me under the water."

"No, James, I can't! You'll be fine, James, you'll see. The Pax will make you better. Try, James! Try!"

"Vincent," James hisses in agony, coughing blood into the water, "you owe me a favor. Anything, you said. Remember?"

Vincent is shuddering, sobbing, shaking his head.

James turns his head to the side, coughing more blood into the water. He lets go of Vincent's cloak, and in a whisper muffled by the gurgling of blood in his throat, asks again.

"Hold me under the water. Please."

CHAPTER THIRTEEN

It was in the morning, at breakfast, when Vincent commented on it. Whether it was the same fly Moss had seen in his room the night before was anyone's guess, but there it was buzzing around the oatmeal and the honey on the table. It was what Vincent said, though, that it was the first one he had seen in fifty years that stuck in the back of Moss's mind.

After breakfast he asked to borrow Moss's roll of toilet paper, then excused himself. When he returned he thanked Moss again and again for the use of it.

"Nicer than corn husks, eh, Vincent?" Moss said, grinning.

"Yes, Jake, it's little things like that, and salt—and coffee—that are often the hardest to do without. Though, I must admit a tea made from Pax has been an adequate substitute."

Vincent liked to pick the eggs then tend his garden after breakfast. Moss went along to continue interviewing him while he worked.

Pearls of moisture from the night's rain sat on the tomatoes and cucumbers and squash and peppers, as Vincent dug carefully in around the plants and vines, loosening the rich, black soil. He had stripped to a loincloth which he explained, was the way they always dressed during the day out in the dome. Cloth was precious and reserved for use from the end of the workday, after washing up, he emphasized, through breakfast the following morning. Of course, since well before James died reserves of cloth from those who had passed on had been accumulating. But, he had done it this way for so long, it was just habit. Jake had not seen him without his cloak before, and noticed the raised scars around his wrists and ankles.

Moving at a brisk pace along the rows in the garden, which was probably an acre in area, he bent down and picked a yellow wax bean and handed it to Moss. The snap and crunch of the crisp bean, and its earthy scent and flavor, were delightful, as good as any he'd ever tasted, and he picked another.

The morning shadow from the east wall of the canyon had crept back toward the northeast as the sun moved higher in the sky, and the atmosphere in the dome had become sultry once again. A shine came on Vincent's skin as the first coat of sweat broke out on him, moving along the rows, swinging his hoe deftly so as not to chop into the roots, but to aerate the soil. Moss watched the old man work with the vigor of an Olympian. The mass and texture of muscles in his back and belly, shoulders and arms went against any knowledge he had of the potential for the physical conditioning of elderly men.

"Vincent, you would put me to shame if we were working together. How is it possible to be in such condition at your age?"

"I think it is because of the Pax," he said, standing up and leaning on the handle of the hoe, "the broth and the greens of it. I have both every day."

"But the experiments. Didn't you say they made many of you deathly sick?"

"Ah," he said, nodding, "but that was different."

"How do you know?"

"We didn't know," he said, starting in on a row of soybeans, "until long after we'd been abandoned. It was James who found out…in the lab…whole piles of notes by the scientists running the experiments."

"What did James find out?"

"They had no experience with Pax. We were guinea pigs. And they were not using the plant. They were trying different combinations and amounts of extracts from the plant. Highly toxic, James discovered."

"But you've outlived James by—"

"They had it in for James. They used him much more than anyone else. I didn't know for years what he was forced to suffer because of that poison. And me," he said, looking away from Moss, "well, I worked a deal. I'd get out of the experiments if I'd keep them informed of the kinds of reactions different guys were having, how bad they were, and how often. It was between them and me. Nobody in population knew."

A fly landed on his chest, on his left nipple. With the speed of a cobra's strike he caught it with a cupped hand and a split second later held his closed fist out in front of him. He opened it and the fly flew away.

"A few years ago I tried to make friends with a honeybee," he said with a grin, "but it was always too busy. I wonder if I could make friends with a fly."

There was a compost pile at the far end of the garden. Vincent would spread a little of it each time he worked the soil of a section. Moving closer to it as Vincent progressed along the rows he was working, Moss noticed an odd movement out of the corner of his eye. He stepped closer to the small whitish mass that seemed to undulate, yet was not.

"Vincent," he called out, "what did you do with the innards of the fish?"

"In the compost," he yelled back.

Moss nodded his head more vigorously the closer he got to it. He had seen this before, as a boy on the farm: Maggots. They writhed over the offal of the fish as though they were one creature engulfing it, consuming it.

Vincent reached the end of the row and walked over to see what Moss was looking at.

"Maggots?" he said, surprised. "We've never had them before. I've always thrown the offal in the compost. Excellent fertilizer, you know."

"It's the outer bulkhead door," Moss said. "Can't close it fast enough, or tight enough. And the cleansing chamber isn't working, either. Can't use the cleansing modulator without power. I let them in, I guess."

Vincent pulled a couple scoops of the rich compost over the maggots with his hoe to bury them, and the two men started back along the edge of the garden, toward the building. As they went, Vincent took great pride in pointing out some of his horticultural successes creating hybrids, explaining how he never thought he would've liked gardening. Moss was impressed, not only with the size and shape and color of the vegetables, but that he had arranged things in the garden so something was almost always ready to pick.

They picked tomatoes and cucumbers and went back to the cool interior of the building to have lunch. While they ate,

Vincent answered more of Moss's questions. How long was the Time of Terror? The worst of it, the chaos went on for two weeks, he explained, until James got the men to realize what they were doing. It was a couple more weeks before the killing stopped. That was when James first saw The Visitor.

"What about the Time of the Person?" Moss said, as Vincent nimbly peeled his second cucumber, explaining that eating it with the peel gave him gas.

"Well, that went on for quite a while...I suppose eight or ten years," he said, "until it got out of hand."

"Out of hand?" Moss's curiosity was piqued by the remark.

Vincent excused himself for a moment and walked behind the serving counter. He had put on a large pot of Pax leaves in water to simmer before dawn, to make a broth. He was checking to see if it had cooled and reduced enough since shutting it off midmorning. When he came back to the table his mood had changed.

"If you don't mind, Jake, I must tend my bees. The new queens. It's time to get rid of most of them, before they swarm. And, of course, the honey must be gathered."

"Oh, yes, Vincent. Sorry. I'm always asking too many questions," Moss said, aware of Vincent's sudden unwillingness to look at him. The old man smiled halfheartedly, looking down at the floor, almost bowing as he backed away from Moss, turned and walked back to the stove.

Vincent acquiesced when Moss asked to come along. With the pot of Pax broth in hand, Vincent and Jake went out through the trap into the sultry midday atmosphere of the dome. After stopping at the toolshed for a wheelbarrow and his honey collecting paraphernalia, Vincent led Moss out across the neglected hay and soybean fields in the center of the dome. About ten yards from the first hive, he set the wheelbarrow down under what Moss believed must be the largest tree in the dome, a huge avocado tree. He stripped to his loincloth again, and taking a ladle from the pot of Pax broth, began to pour the odd-scented liquid over his body, using the large, rubbery leaves in the pot like a washcloth.

Moss took notes as he watched the curious process.

"What are you doing, Vincent?"

"You will see in a minute," Vincent replied, smiling at Moss. He was clearly more like himself again, Moss thought, than after he had mentioned the Time of the Person. "Stay here, Jake, and stay still," he said, walking toward the hive with a leather sack of hand tools and what he called his honey pot. "Don't make any sound, either."

The bees began to swarm as soon as he disturbed the stack of white wooden boxes, in ever-widening circles, searching for the intruder. Then, just as quickly, they returned to the hive. It was as though Vincent was invisible while he removed the caps of the honeycombs, collecting them in one pot, and the honey in another. Throughout the afternoon, he repeated the process, at one after another of the dozen hives in the dome.

Having watched him do this for a while, Moss left him to his labor of love and went back to the building. He wanted to read more of Stryker's journals, as well as write more in his own. It was when Moss began reading journal entries from the Time of the Person that Vincent's reticence to speak about it and his odd mood change earlier in the day became clear.

Stryker commented often on his frustration with Vince Briscoe, who was, it seemed, unable to break out of his lifelong pattern of behavior:

May 7, 2022–Carelli tells me Briscoe wants fifty pounds of potatoes to have Joey the Gimp plow his ground. I will have to speak to him....

May 8, 2022–Held an assembly to vote on what things belong to each man, and what belongs to everybody. It was decided that plows and farm tools and the team of steers are for everyone to use. Briscoe can't charge to have Joey the Gimp plow for anyone....

May 15, 2022–Carelli is complaining that Briscoe won't let Joey the Gimp drive the team to plow. No one else knows how. Carelli made a mess of his field trying. Unable to plant yet because of it....

Although the men had voted to divide the land equally and draw lots for each year's crop, Moss could see that Briscoe was always looking to capitalize on a situation, or someone's misfortune. If he wasn't trying to hire Joey out to plow, he was undercutting someone on their price for the same crop he was raising. He was careful to watch for those who couldn't work their ground, Stryker noted, because they were sick or had been injured, and would offer to do it for a portion of their crop. In short, Vince Briscoe was a prick. Moss was bewildered trying to imagine the Vincent he was with every day, the Vincent who meditated, prayed, tended his garden; who created hybrid plants of remarkable quality, as being the same man described by Stryker page after page.

Moss stopped reading. He had been engrossed in the journals as always, but now flies were disrupting his concentration, annoying him, landing on his forehead or his hand, or crawling over his bare ankles. He thought of that farm again where he'd worked as a boy, mucking out the horse stalls and cow troughs. Flies were filthy. They thrived on filth. And merciless, pestering the horses into a momentary madness, sometimes.

He put down the journal and walked to the trap and out onto the landing, to see what had become of Vincent. The atmosphere in the midafternoon heat was heavy and close on his skin in the ghostly white light of the dome. He sat on the top step scanning the fields, and a lush laziness that makes eyelids heavy on hot summer afternoons came over him. He lay back on the landing, breathing slow and deep, and dozed off.

Vincent set the almost full honey pot back in the wheelbarrow, checking to see that everything about the hive was as it should be. The shadow of the west wall of the canyon outside, crept imperceptibly across the fields as the late afternoon sun slipped lower in the western sky.

He was uneasy with the disturbing ideas that had come to mind concerning Moss. He knew he could never get him to stay.

He was an ambitious young man, too ambitious, he thought. He could not make him. Even if he weren't, why would he ever choose to stay there, to give up everything, to be alone, cut off from the rest of the world. Only someone who has an investment here would want to stay.

What to do? Lock him up? How? There is no place in here that I can lock. What, then?

It was his habit to visit the cemetery each day, and as he had to pass it on the walk back to the building, he decided this was something he must discuss with James and the others. He set the wheelbarrow with the honeypot and the Pax lotion down at the base of the hill, and climbed to where Bruno and Manning and Joey, Mickey the Mole and Carelli were, and yet close enough to where James was so he could be involved, and began explaining his predicament. When he had finished, he waited, listening. After a while, he got up, and after straightening Bruno's marker and tidying up a bit around one or two of the graves, he left unsatisfied. He felt little had been achieved in the way of a solution.

When Vincent reached the base of the stairs to the building, he saw Moss lying on the landing above him and became frightened. *Is he hurt? Did he fall, have a seizure, or something?*

As he started up the stairs with the honey pot, for a split second he realized he was hoping maybe something had happened. He shook his head to dispel such a shameful thought from his mind. When he got to him, Vincent saw that he was asleep, and realized how vulnerable Moss was.

Moss awoke with a start when a fly crawled in one of his nostrils. He thought Vincent was looking at him in an odd way, as he stood there over him. He pressed his right nostril with his thumb, blowing hard to clear the other one.

"Damn, I hate that!" he said. "Must've dozed off."

"Ah," Vincent replied, nodding, then kneeling down and picking up the honey pot.

"How'd you do?" Moss asked.

"Oh, fine, as always." Vincent said, starting toward the trap. "I must put this away now and get ready for Vespers meditation, Jake. Please excuse me."

Moss nodded, stretching vigorously. He got up off the landing, sweeping the dirt and dust off his pants, and followed Vincent in through the trap. Vincent headed for the kitchen with the honey pot and Moss went to the library.

He had laid out Stryker's journals on a drafting table, in chronological order. For the past few days he had been searching for mention of or descriptions of the experiments James underwent. He wanted to find out how much a part of the operation at Mescalero they were, and how they affected the men from James's perspective. One entry he came across was especially troubling in the callousness of the technicians and scientists toward their inmate subjects:

October 1, 2021–(Written December 11, 2021) I went blind this date. They implanted an inch square lozenge under the skin on my left upper chest, at the top of the pectoral muscle, the day before. I overheard the doctor refer to it as Myacin. He was saying it was a combination of three extracts of Pax. Within twelve hours I noticed everything getting fuzzy. When I woke up the next morning, everything was dark. I could not see.

They did not remove the implant for two full weeks, hoping the blindness was temporary. I couldn't do anything except grope my way around my cell, to find the crapper or my food tray, so I lay on my bunk and stayed still.

Another side effect of the lozenge was profuse, uncontrollable salivating, as well as loss of control of my tongue. The scar tissue from biting it trying to eat or to speak is still sore, and has been slow healing. Also, because of the constant salivating, I was experiencing significant dehydration.

A month after removing the lozenge my vision was nearly normal again. Chico told me this morning that they implanted lozenges in six other guys yesterday, to see if the reaction was just me or if it happened to everyone. What I wouldn't give to be able to do the same to them....

Moss sat back in the chair trying to imagine what it would be like to lose his sight. Even more, he wondered about the sense of panic it would create, and how he would handle it, waking up one morning to find that he was blind. He panned around the room a few times, wanting to set a picture of it in his memory. Then, keeping his eyes closed, he got up and began moving around the room.

He walked straight to the door leading into the library, recalling in his mind's eye that there was no obstacle between it and where he had been sitting. At the door he turned around, then moved to his right, toward the bookshelves beyond the drafting table, with arms outstretched, reaching lower, in a sweeping motion like a cricket's antennae, feeling for the table. Just then, his eyes bulged open as he crumpled over at the abdomen, having walked straight into the corner of the table at his groin.

Moss sat back down in his chair to wait for the ache in his testicles and the accompanying nausea in his belly to subside, feeling a bit foolish about the predictable outcome of his experiment. But, beyond his mild embarrassment, it didn't take much to transpose the make-believe blindness into reality in his mind, and in doing so, to find it frightening.

That evening, after supper and a game of chess with Vincent, who spoke little, Moss sat at his little table writing in his journal, wondering as he wrote what was troubling Vincent, that would make him so reticent. Now and then something caught his attention out of the corner of his eye, moving along the base of the door to the small closet in the room. When he looked in there, he didn't see anything unusual. Then, again occupied with his writing, it would happen again.

He got up, and holding his calcion torch high, walked over to the closet. Opening the door slowly, he shined his torchlight inside, and there in the back corner of the closet, was a nest made of shredded paper and cornhusks woven loosely together. Stooping down, he poked the fluffy construction. There was a squeak and the occupant darted from the nest, between his legs, and out of the room. He carefully pulled the nest apart, and knew at once who the occupant was. A packrat.

***

L'Oiseau watched the man cast for a while from the other side of the public pier. He was almost certain it was the man he wanted: Travis Collier.

It was evening, dark, and the heat of the day was more manageable as an onshore wind moved through the palm trees along the beach. The surface of the water shimmered, reflecting the lights of Port du Poisson behind them, as the slightest of waves made their way to the beach. An elderly black couple came near to L'Oiseau to set up to fish, putting down their bait bucket and cooler, rods and tackle box, but quickly retreated when he cast his line. Red snapper were still running, though the run was tapering off, and the steady crowds of the last several days had dwindled as well, to only half a dozen or so.

L'Oiseau asked the couple if they would watch his gear while he went to the men's room. They smiled and nodded and he walked the hundred fifty meters to shore. At the admission and tackle rental office, he asked the dark-skinned boy if he would page someone to the contax in about fifteen minutes. The boy looked at him, poker-faced. When L'Oiseau pulled out a large silver coin and placed it on the counter, the boy smiled broadly and nodded. L'Oiseau wrote the name on a slip of paper and handed it to him, and told him that if he did well, there would be another coin just like it later.

The page came over the loudspeaker not long after he'd gotten back out to the end of the pier, and he watched his reaction. The man hurried to reel in his line and set the rod against the railing, asking the two fishing next to him if they would watch his gear while he was gone. L'Oiseau waited so as not to be obvious, then followed him to the office. Moments after the man went into the office, he came back out, slamming the door and cursing the boy inside, and walked back out to resume fishing. L'Oiseau entered the office and handed the boy another coin, smiled, his gold canine tooth glinting in the harsh overhead light, and left. It was the man he wanted he had no doubt. Again, he waited a bit, then went back out and gathered his fishing gear. As he was leaving, he offered the old black couple the two red snapper he'd caught just before they arrived. They thanked him with broad smiles and many thanks in the island patois, and he walked off. He stowed the fishing gear in his antique Champion electropod parked on the street, then walked over to La Granouille, the little café across from the pier, and took a seat at a sidewalk table.

Amadoux's instructions were explicit: Agree with Collier on the terms he has set, but be sure to obtain all the implicating documents. The waiter brought his demitasse and he handed the young man a bill, signaling for him to keep the change. With cold gray eyes fixed on the pier exit, L'Oiseau patiently waited for Collier to emerge. The string of overhead lights illuminating the pier flicked off and on three times. Closing time. The fishermen filed out the exit gate struggling to various degrees with their gear, and there was Collier, next to last, behind the old black couple. L'Oiseau went across the street and met Collier at his transport.

"Do any good?" L'Oiseau said, as though he was interested in Collier's catch.

"Three good-sized red snapper," he said. "Not bad."

L'Oiseau raised his eyebrows, tilting his head left and right, and shrugging his shoulders in agreement.

"Mr. Schilling would like to buy you a drink, Mr. Collier," L'Oiseau said politely, looking into Collier's large, sad brown eyes.

L'Oiseau could see that Collier was taken by surprise. He tried to cover it and this stranger's distinct advantage with bravado.

"I wondered when he'd be contacting me. Where is he?"

"He regrets he could not be here. I am his representative. He has given me authority to make an agreement on his behalf. My name is L'Oiseau."

L'Oiseau gestured toward the café with a sweep of his arm, inviting the tall, broad-shouldered Collier to accompany him. As they crossed the street, each man sized the other up. Collier was a head taller, in his late fifties, according to Amadoux. He was a man who, like his father, Big Red Collier, before him, could have been a formidable foe at one time. But it was apparent he had not taken care of himself over the years, with a large belly that hung over his belt, and his stride giving away a problem with his back.

L'Oiseau, on the other hand, though only a half dozen years younger, had always taken care of himself. A foot shorter and nearly seventy pounds lighter, he moved with grace and precision and quickness, like an Egret fishing the shallows of an inlet.

The waiter brought their drinks: rum and soda for Collier. Sweet vermouth on the rocks with a twist of lemon for L'Oiseau.

"Mr. Schilling is agreeable to the amount you have set as your selling price for the merchandise," L'Oiseau began, looking around casually to see if anyone was interested in their conversation. "Of course, as you would expect, he would want assurance that he was buying all the documents, that this was a one-time transaction."

Collier sipped his drink, his eyes fixed on the tanned and slender man sitting opposite him.

"Of course," Collier said, deciding Schilling's representative was thoroughly unimpressive. "When and where?"

"On the pier? Tomorrow night after closing, say midnight?"

Collier thought about L'Oiseau's suggestion for a moment, then agreed, knowing there would be no surprises out in the open at the end of the pier. They finished their drinks quickly and left, L'Oiseau tucking cash for the drinks under his glass and bidding Collier au revoir.

The following night, with a clear starlit sky and a nearly full moon shining on the water, Collier did not see anyone as he approached the end of the pier, but there was a tackle box and a bait bucket and fishing rod on the bench underneath one of the now-darkened overhead lights. He set the scuffed black attaché case he was carrying on the bench at the end railing and sat down facing the shore, watching for L'Oiseau. At quarter after the hour he got up and paced the width of the pier for a minute, squinting as he looked toward shore, then sat again next to the attaché case. There was no sound at all, no warning, as the monofilament looped over his head and around his neck, and his head was pulled back against the railing behind him with a thud.

That evening's newspaper, *The Island Sentinel*, described how a tourist had evidently jumped over the turnstile to go fishing illegally after hours at the pier. He was found in the morning, hanging halfway down to the water from the railing at the end of the pier, apparently having become tangled in his fishing tackle and fallen over the edge.

CHAPTER FOURTEEN

It had only taken sixty seconds at the time, but the image of James looking at him from under the water—smiling even, Vincent was never sure—had been with him for seven years. And now, he was thinking about doing it again. He sat under the Joshua tree, discussing it with Necco and the others buried nearby: Joey the Gimp, Manning, Bruno.

Moss was a big man. Young. Strong. Perhaps he should kill him while he sleeps, just to be safe. What do you think, Necco? Vincent wondered, but Necco was silent on the question. Vincent felt that Joey the Gimp was in agreement with him: kill Moss while he sleeps, but then Joey would, being so small. He sensed Bruno would insist Vincent had to face Moss and say he was going to kill him. It was the honorable thing to do. Vincent laughed out loud, wondering if Nicholas thought he'd lost his mind. "I am an old man," he reminded him, "remember?"

Moss had been insistent when Vincent came up to him earlier in the day. *Yes, Vincent, we are leaving*, he recalled him saying as he was gathering his gear and packing. *Yes, you are going with me.* Vincent felt Moss had spoken to him as if he were a child. This only added to Vincent's resolve, making it easier to go through with it, to do what he had to.

At the other end of the tunnel, Ketchum had relaxed finding no one in the offices or dormitory, but when he came across Moss's pickup in the receiving area, he recognized it and went back on his guard.

He made his way up the tunnel to the bulkhead, balking when he came upon the two skeletons. Picking up the crowbar Moss had left there, he pried the outer door open enough to get inside the cleansing chamber. The inner door was much easier to open, and he stepped into the dome which even for him, was an incredible sight. He took the path toward the building, and as he got closer he saw two men descend from the landing, and head out across the fields. He squatted in the undergrowth to keep from being seen, as the two passed the sewage pools on the way to the pond.

Vincent was trying to carry on a casual conversation with Moss, to cover his preoccupation with how he would kill him, when he would kill him, why he had to kill him. Jake was agreeing with Vincent that Gourami and scallions, with boiled potatoes, would be a fitting last meal before leaving. They stopped for a moment in the late afternoon swelter, on the bank above the pools, amazed to see them blanketed from end to end in a writhing coat of maggots.

"Mescalero has been corrupted, I'm afraid," Moss said dispassionately.

Vincent just stared at the animated bog of human waste, until they started again toward the pond.

"People will be so excited to meet you, Vincent, when they hear. You will be a celebrity!"

Vincent made no noticeable reaction. Being a celebrity had little appeal for him.

"Jake, you are a fine young man, someone I might've wanted to be like when I was young...."

Moss found the compliment satisfying and told him as much, thanking Vincent for saying so.

"...but you don't understand the things that are important to an old man, an old man who has spent most of his life in prison—in this prison."

"What do you mean, Vincent?" Moss said, bewildered. "This is your freedom. What could be better than that?"

"Being with my friends."

He was certain Jake never heard his response, but there it was: He didn't care about freedom. He would not leave.

When they got to the pond, Vincent excused himself saying he had to "take a dump." A few meters into the dense stand of Pax growing along the pond through there, he watched Moss as he sat there, waiting. *Do it now. Hit him over the head, then hold him under the water.*

He uncovered Carelli's sculpting mallet that he had hidden there the night before. He turned to start back when a man appeared on the bank, at the edge of the thicket, not ten meters away. The man had a pistol in his hand and was sneaking toward Jake, who hadn't seen him yet. Vincent crept toward him, low in the cover of the Pax. Just as Vincent got to where the man stood, the gun went off and he saw Jake fall into the water. In that instant he launched the mallet, hitting the man squarely in the side of his head. The weapon fired again then fell from his hand as the man crumpled to the ground, the sound of the shot echoing throughout the dome.

Vincent sprang from the Pax as the stranger struggled to shake off the stunning blow from the mallet, picked it up, and hit the man again with all his strength. The contents of his skull spattered out onto the mud of the bank. Vincent scrambled to his feet, looking to where Jake had fallen into the water. Jake was standing up, sopping wet in waist-deep water, waving to Vincent.

As Jake walked over, Vincent picked up the pistol and flung it into the underbrush in a moment of temper he had not felt in years. Jake looked down at the dead man lying with the side of his head bashed in, and recognized him instantly. It was Ketchum. But why? he thought, looking around quickly.

"You okay, Jake? I thought sure he'd shot you."

"Nah, I'm fine. Slipped on the bank just when he fired. What about you?"

"Oh, I'm all right. Just shaken a bit, killing a ma—"

"We have to get out of here, Vincent, right now!"

Jake had to make a third trip out to the tunnel because of the journals and letters and other items he had accumulated on top of the gear he'd come in with, and because Vincent didn't offer to help. He had insisted on burying the intruder, though not in the cemetery with the others. When Moss finished he went to where Ketchum had been killed to find Vincent chanting an appeal for mercy for him as he was covering him up.

"We have to go, Vincent. There's no time to waste."

Vincent did not respond, but continued the liturgy as though it must not be interrupted to have its full potency, shoveling in time with the rhythm.

"May the Lord, mighty God, be merciful to you…"

"Vincent, we gotta go."

He finished mounding the earth neatly on the grave.

"…gracious He, Who can know His ways…"

"Why do you do this, Vincent? The man would've killed you if he'd had the chance."

"Every man deserves someone to make one more appeal for mercy on their behalf, wouldn't you say?"

Jake made no reply to the question, intent on leaving as quickly as possible.

"Vincent, come on, we—"

"I'm not going with you, Jake. I told you."

"Oh please, Vincent, let's don't go through that again. You have to go with me, even more reason now. It's not safe here. Now, let's go."

Jake reached for his arm to usher him toward the bulkhead, but Vincent pulled it away in a single, powerful jerk. Jake was astonished not only that he would do that, but that he could do it so easily. Vincent reached down under his cloak where it lay at the end of the grave, and stood back up with Ketchum's pistol, the one he had thrown into the thicket, in his hand.

"I had decided to kill you myself, Jake," he said, a mixture of shame and resolve in his voice. "I was going to drown you."

Jake looked at Vincent, then down at the weapon, steady in his hand. He was stunned by the words coming from the old man's mouth.

"Yes, in fact I was just about to do it. I didn't have to shit, as I said. That mallet I threw at him was meant for you, Jake." Vincent's skin glistened with sweat, standing there steady as a tree in his loincloth.

Jake was reeling, trying to take it in.

"Why didn't you just let him kill me, Vincent?"

"Dunno. Instinctive reaction? I can't explain it, Jake. Maybe it's because he wanted to kill you. Me? I didn't want to, but I figured I'd have to unless you let me be."

They stood there looking at each other, neither of them sure what to do next, when Vincent motioned toward the bulkhead.

"I'm serious, Jacob. I'm not going with you. If you try to make me, I will kill you. Now, daylight's gone. The road out to the paved road will be treacherous in the dark. You'd better get going."

"Okay, but like I said, I have to tell what I found here. They will come after you, Vincent. They will."

"This is where I belong. This is where I want to be. I will not leave. That's all."

It was not how Moss imagined things would've ended at Mescalero. And as he made his way to the bulkhead, the certain sense of how much he had grown to care for Vincent gripped him unexpectedly. In the tunnel, he stacked everything on the hand truck carrying the calcion torch and whatever wouldn't stay put on it, and made for the receiving dock.

When he got there he switched on the servomotors to begin opening the hydraulic platform while he packed everything in the pickup, and as soon as there was clearance he drove up onto the desert surface. He saw Ketchum's vehicle parked near the pedestrian entrance. He needed to get it underground, then close the platform.

He walked as quickly as he could in the soft sand over to Ketchum's old wrecker. It was an old hybrid "gasser," and there were no keys in the ignition.

Shit! I'll bet they're in his pocket.

His first thought was to race back to the dome and dig up those keys.

As he started back to his truck, he realized that would take too long. Then, he thought he'd try to "hot-wire" the rig, but as he made his way across the sand, he changed his mind. It occurred to him that there was no longer any point in trying to keep things out of sight. His incredible project had been found out. And, since he'd begun packing to leave the dome, a gnawing sense of urgency to get out of there had been building in him, as though the timer on a bomb were ticking.

To hell with the platform.

Driving away in the brilliant moonlight, he had less difficulty making out the roadway than when he had first arrived, able to see occasional stretches where Ketchum's tracks had not yet been obscured by the wind. Bats flew in and out of his lights feasting on katydids and mosquitoes as he picked his way through the sagebrush and mescal cactus. Just as he reached the two lane he was startled by a Kit fox sprinting through the beams of his headlights, and he hit the brakes hard. He took a deep breath, aware that he was still a bit jumpy, more so than he would like, and turned onto the paved road heading north.

He got to Felicity around midnight. The town was dark. He continued north out of town. Through the night, the only lights he saw anywhere were brilliant stars, and he wondered how Vincent would've felt seeing them for the first time in half a century. Then, just before daybreak he grew sleepy and pulled off the road to nap.

It was his own crying out that woke him, just as Vincent, standing above him at the edge of the pond with the mallet high above his head, brought it down. He sat up on the seat breathing hard, disoriented, sweating, the sun now high up in the northern sky, burning in through the windshield. He felt almost sick to his stomach as he thought about the reality that Vincent had been planning to kill him.

How could he?

He drove ahead several yards to where the cab of the truck was in the shade of a stand of cottonwoods along a dry creek bed. He took a swig from his canteen and broke open a new container of beef jerky, trying desperately not to recall the image of Stryker lying in his bunk as he had struggled to cut off a piece of the deltoid muscle.

Late in the day, in the still belching July heat, the pickup began to lose power. He looked for a decent place to pull off to see what was wrong. Up ahead, the road cut through a canyon, and when he started into it he pulled off into the shade of the leeward side.

While crawling around under the vehicle, inspecting the magnetos at each wheel, he heard heavy steps crunching in the gravel close by. Moss crawled out from under to find a half dozen curious cows sniffing up close to him, but then backing off quickly as he stood up. There were maybe thirty head in all, Santa Gertrudis if he was not mistaken, and not looking all that bad considering the Godforsaken range they were grazing in. The joke and the moment came gushing up from memory:

"Out west, son, they raise a special breed of cow. They call 'em 10/80 cows," Clint said, all serious like, as they hefted bale after bale of horse hay onto the wagon.

"How come they call 'em 10/80 cows?" Jake asked, just as Clint hoped he would.

"Well, I'll tell ya," he said, still serious as could be, "they got a mouth ten feet wide, and they gotta run eighty miles an hour to get enough to eat in a day."

Jake chuckled. Fooled again with another one of his boss's corny jokes.

The memory was interrupted by the sound of a rotorcraft. It broke over the canyon, whapping and whacking the air as it passed, disappearing over the next butte. The cattle seemed to understand that this had to do with them and hurriedly headed off to the north.

Moss thought the immediate problem was the capacitors. They weren't holding the charge from the magnetos. He knew this was serious.

Won't get far. If I start walking, do I have enough water? And where is the nearest place to get help? Can't take a chance going back to Felicity. Ketchum's from there. Day's almost over. Foolhardy to start out now. In the morning, early, I'll have to start walking north.

In the dusky light just before dark, as he sat there still considering his options, he saw headlights up ahead coming toward him. A pickup pulled in alongside and a tall, stately man stepped out.

"Ortega," he said, extending his hand. "Fernando Ortega. I saw you from the air. Transport trouble?"

"Oh, that was you in the chopper," Moss said, extending his hand as well. "Jake Moss. Yeah, my capacitors aren't holding the charge from the magnetos. Practically a brand-new vehicle, too, you know?"

Ortega nodded. He could tell Moss was annoyed. He explained that he lived not far from there and asked if the vehicle ran. Moss said yes, though it wouldn't for much longer. Ortega assured him they had a good shop there. They could fix most anything. Moss was grateful for the offer of help, and they set out with Ortega leading.

They wound along the dry creek bed through the canyon for half an hour before breaking out into open range again. Moss stayed close behind Ortega, running without headlights to conserve what charge he had left in the storage batteries. They came to a turnoff, a gravel road heading east. As they crossed over the cattle guard, they passed under an impressive arch above the entrance. In large wrought iron letters, the words, *Sunburst Hacienda*, were set in a frame.

They followed the gravel road for another half hour. Moss was getting anxious as the pickup became more and more sluggish, wondering how much farther they had to go. Coming around a butte just then, he saw the lights of the hacienda, less than a kilometer ahead. The pickup was down to a groaning crawl as he crossed the bridge over a dry wash gully, and climbed the grade up to where the house and barns were. Ortega was at the barn, waving him over. Moss turned in that direction, but there was a series of loud clicks under the floorboard and the pickup stopped.

Ortega walked back.

"Leave it here, Mr. Moss. It will be all right," he assured him. "We'll see to it in the morning. It's late. Why don't you get what personal things you need for tonight, and we'll go inside."

Stepping up onto the colorful mosaic tile floor under the portico, Ortega opened the door and motioned to Moss to step inside. As Ortega closed the door behind them, a stocky, pigeon-toed man came toward them, down a long hallway that skirted one side of a lush tropical atrium.

"Ah, Ortega," the man said pleasantly, still some distance away. "What have we here? A visitor?"

"This is Mr. Moss, Sir. He was having transport trouble. I spotted him flying back from Cow Camp. I drove out and escorted him here. I thought perhaps Manuel could have a look at his vehicle in the morning, then send him on his way. I hope that was all right, Mr. Schilling."

"Of course, Ortega," he said, coming up and extending his hand to Moss. "Seth Schilling. Of course it's all right. This is rough country to break down in."

"Jake Moss. I'm grateful for the help, Mr. Schilling."

"Please, don't mention it. But you must be hungry. Probably could stand a shower, too, eh? See to it, will you, Fernando," he said, apologizing that he was expecting an important contax conference, but would see him at breakfast, when they could chat.

The house was immense, all on one floor, in a great square surrounding the sunken garden. As he followed Ortega to his room, he noticed the fifty meter pool in the center of the atrium.

Ortega opened the thick wood door. It had a rich, dark lustre of rubbed oil in its grain, and swung on its hinges without a sound. The room held the scents of polished wood and potpourri, and a slight mustiness revealing that it had not been occupied for a while. The furnishings and appointments were of rare kinds of wood as well: a cherry wood desk, two mahogany wing chairs, a tea table made of apple wood. A cedar chest of drawers. A teak vanity. And the bed, chestnut, its mattress nearly as high as Moss's waist, the posts as thick as a jack oak and intricately carved.

Something Carelli would appreciate, I'll bet, Moss thought, setting his pack on the wing chair.

Ortega asked if there was anything Moss did not like to eat, and on hearing his enthusiastic "No!" excused himself. Moss dug out the cleanest of his dirty clothes and immediately climbed into the shower. When he came out of the bathroom there was a silver tray on the tea table. On it was a crystal decanter of red wine and a goblet, and under a glass cover ornately trimmed in silver, a bowl of gazpacho, thick slices of bread and a wedge of sharp cheddar, and a bowl of fresh strawberries accompanied by brown sugar and sour cream. A cigar was wrapped in the scarlet cloth napkin, an ash tray and an incendium alongside, and a note saying breakfast was at seven, in the atrium by the pool.

When he had finished eating, Moss sat in the wing chair, clean and cool under the gentle breeze of the fan overhead, delirious with the moment, and fell into a restless sleep. Images of Vincent swept through his dreams: praying, at the water's edge spearing fish, in his garden, playing chess. After some time, he stirred awake, got up from the chair and crawled into the bed.

At breakfast, they sat at a glass-topped table at the pool's edge. His host was wearing a robe, a towel around his neck, his hair slicked back, still dripping from his swim. As impressed as Moss was by the decor and conventions of the wealthy, there was an atmosphere of informality that kept him from feeling ill at ease. He was sure it was Ortega who brought this about by allowing latitude to the uninitiated guest, graciously overlooking the blunders in aristocratic protocol.

Pepito, a dark-skinned young man with thick, straight, coal-black hair, served orange juice, crepes and chorizo, and a fresh fruit compote. Ortega looked on, seeing to the coffee refills and anything else required, careful not to intrude.

"How is your breakfast, Jake? Do you go by Jake?" Schilling asked, patting his neck with the towel.

"Yes, sir," he said, swallowing hard so as not to speak with his mouth full, "and the breakfast is delicious."

Schilling watched Moss when he wasn't looking, sizing him up.

"What brings you to these parts, Jake. Where are you from?"

Moss had practiced the answer to this question a hundred times on the drive out, at the beginning of the summer.

"Ph.D. candidate," he gulped, the chorizo giving his throat a respectable burn. "I'm starting my last year this fall. Cultural anthropology. I'm doing my thesis on ancient cultures in the region."

"Oh, I see. So you've been visiting the sites, the cave dwellings and such?"

"Yes, sir."

"Where were you headed when Fernando found you?"

"Back to the capital, to my job at the national library. Start transposing my notes…you know…getting ready for classes."

Schilling nodded, insisting Moss finish the last crepe.

Moss wanted to know what he did for a living but decided it would be rude to ask him. He thought maybe Ortega would impart this information at some point. Schilling excused himself as he had to get ready to fly to Urbana for the day, expressing his hope that Manuel could fix Moss's transport, and assuring him he was welcome to stay as long as he needed. As he was leaving the room, Schilling took Ortega aside.

"Have we heard anything from Ketchum? he said in a near whisper.

"No sir, not yet."

"It's been too long. Call Amadoux and tell him I want L'Oiseau to look into Mescalero."

Ortega nodded, and out of habit, gave the slightest bow. Schilling started out of the room, then stopped.

"And, Fernando, make sure he knows not to show up here."

By mid-morning, Manuel had determined the problem with Moss's pickup, informing Ortega he didn't have the parts he needed and would have to send for them from Urbana. Ortega was able to reach Schilling by contax later in the day. After reporting he had conveyed Schilling's wishes to Amadoux, and that it was being taken care of, he explained the situation concerning their guest's vehicle. When Schilling flew back that evening, he brought the parts Manuel needed with him.

Moss stood in front of the hearth in the study, admiring Schilling's display of antique weapons mounted on the wall above the mantel.

"I am grateful for your help, Mr. Schilling,"

"It was a simple thing, Jake," he said with feigned graciousness. "Think nothing of it. And please, call me Seth."

Schilling offered him brandy. Moss declined. A cigar? Thank you, no, Moss's reply.

Jake reached for the .44 Magnum and removed it from its cradle as his host, with his back to him, was pouring another snifter.

"Nicely balanced," he said looking the magnificent antique revolver over, and hefting it in his hand.

The etching in the chrome plate and the carving in the pearl handles were striking. And something else. Engraved along the barrel, on the side that had faced the wall, was an inscription: *To Warden Samuel Smalley for valor in the line of duty*. Moss was stunned.

Smalley!

Schilling had picked up his snifter and turned around.

"Put that back!" he shouted, with a menacing look.

Moss was embarrassed at his apparent impropriety, and confused. What had he done to justify his host's fierce reaction? But even more, he was reeling at the words engraved on the weapon, wondering what the connection was between Schilling and Smalley.

Schilling moved swiftly across the room as Moss was trying to reset the revolver on its mounts, took it from him, and saw to it himself.

There was a long, uncomfortable silence.

Moss began to stutter an apology even before he had thought of what to say when Schilling stopped him.

"No, young man," he said in a tone of sincerity Moss didn't quite believe, "do not apologize. It is I who must apologize."

The awkwardness subsided, Schilling working to regain his composure as the wealthy, unflappable patron and defender of the common man. But Moss was on his guard. As much as he detested any kind of pretense, he made sure to agree or laugh or sigh with concern at appropriate moments in conversation, so as not to give his host the slightest sense that what he had just seen meant anything to him.

He asked Schilling if it would be all right to place a call to the capital, as what had been a tense and awkward evening drew to a close. He wanted to try to get in touch with one of his professors, he explained. By all means, his host had replied. Feel free. But as he started to engage the number on the contax in his room, he stopped.

Schilling might listen in, or even trace the call.

He wasn't sure why, but he decided right then that he didn't want him to be able to do that. He wouldn't place any calls until after he left.

At breakfast, his host asked about his call. Was he successful in reaching his friend? Was he well? Looking forward to seeing him? Moss told him he had not been able to reach him, that there was no answer.

It took every bit of Moss's concentration to keep from seeming hurried through breakfast, from being anxious, nervous, from wanting to sprint to the truck and leave. He thanked Ortega and Manuel for their help and his host for his generosity. Once he cleared the great standard at the entrance to the hacienda, turning north, he could not help watching his side mirrors almost constantly, and looking up in the sky behind, for a rotorcraft coming after him.

It was almost a week before Schilling heard from Amadoux. L'Oiseau was dead, strangled during sex with a young black male prostitute. There was no one else he knew of that could be as discreet or as thorough. Schilling sat in his study, fuming at the unexpected turn of events. He snickered at the thought of L'Oiseau taking it in the ass from this guy while he strangles him. He was always told that L'Oiseau was too smart, too cunning. Invincible. Every man has his blind spot, he reminded himself.

Ortega served Schilling one of his famous rum drinks, the full contents of which he would never divulge to anyone, and left. Schilling sat in his luxurious leather chair, and voice-clicked the telescreen to watch the news. Representatives from all four parties were speaking about the funding abuses uncovered recently in various government agencies. The rhetoric was as predictable and therefore as boring as ever, and he was about to click it off, when a tall, good-looking young man came on screen. He recognized him immediately: Moss.

He leaned forward in the great leather chair as Moss began telling what he had discovered at Mescalero, detailing the sabotage, the double murder made to look like a murder/suicide, the records of fraud. While he spoke, the images on the wafers he'd found were being projected on screen: The guards rushing to the lab, his father raging—gone mad. His neck began to tighten as he watched. He was breathing as though he'd just sprinted 50 meters.

And then, there it was—the inmates climbing onto Abby. He tried to turn away but some cruel excitement compelled him to keep looking. He stared at his sister, watching how her head bounced each time one of them pushed himself into her, lying on the examining table, hands pinned above her head by one of them, legs held by the others.

It was an infernal mixture of revulsion, aching to look away from what was happening to the only one he'd ever loved, and at the same instant a riveting compulsion to look, helpless to turn away from witnessing the intoxicating power of life and death. And when one of them approached with a surgical knife, and slipped it across her throat as softly as making a watercolor brush stroke, his testicles pulled up tight to the point of pain, and he had to hold himself to get them to relax.

Moss underestimated the reaction to his findings at Mescalero, and found himself unprepared for the constant din of notoriety. It was bittersweet wanting recognition for his discovery, yet finding it tedious and troublesome being interviewed all the time. It was keeping him from the things he wanted to focus on, the things that would not only assure his future, but might serve justice for Vincent and James and the others he'd come to know.

He descended the stairs to the sub-basement of the library, with familiar, almost welcome smells and sounds now that he was back. Consistent with his nature though, at least until classes began, he was going to be of one mind. He put his backpack and the cipherboard down on the glorified door on sawhorses he called a desk: Who was Seth Schilling, really? This was what he wanted to know, what he intended to find out.

Everything was in order. He settled himself in and went into the verified archives, looking for anything he could find on Samuel Smalley, specifically, had there been other children besides his daughter.

Amadoux came on the contax. Schilling had waited before calling him, composing himself. He did not want to sound shaken by the investigation, though he was sure it would soon point to him.

"Max, please have the staff open the rooms at the compound. I think I'll come down for a vacation. Perhaps we'll have a little party just after I get there, eh?"

He disconnected, then asked Ortega on the intercom to come to his study.

"Fernando, double check the aerofoil and see to my personal things. I will be leaving late this evening."

"A flight plan, sir? Are you piloting?"

"No, don't file a flight plan. I'll take care of that. It's complicated. Oh, and is the rotorcraft fueled?"

"Yes, of course, sir."

"Thank you, Fernando. That will be all."

Mid-morning, Schilling took an electrocart up to the airstrip and took off in the rotorcraft, heading south, Ortega noted, watching from beneath the portico at the front of the main house. He had not mentioned where he was going, or when to expect him back.

Schilling spotted Ketchum's old wrecker near the entrance when he set the little two-seater rotorcraft down nearby. He grabbed the antique Colt .44 Magnum Moss had admired in his study, and headed for the stairs leading down into the tunnel. When he stepped inside the entry and looked into the blackness below, he realized he had forgotten to bring a torch along. He went back to the rotorcraft and rifled through the emergency bin under the seat. He needed something that would produce light or he'd break his neck down there. There was no torch—a matter he would discuss with Manuel when he got back—but there was an emergency beacon. It would have to do.

Back at the stairs, he started down into the pitch dark, the flashing red light rotating around the stairwell walls, creating a dizzying, surreal scape of light reflecting off hanging cobwebs and seeping wet walls. His senses confused by the light, he missstepped several times, nearly losing his balance. At the foot of the stairs he saw the crack of light at the base of the office doors and went toward it, the tunnel now illuminated in time to the rotating strobe of the beacon.

He had never been inside Mescalero, had never even heard of it as a youth. Whenever he had asked his father or sister about where they worked, they would explain they were not allowed to say. It was not until long after moving offshore, when Sam Smalley began preparing him for his inheritance, that he found out all about the place.

All the overhead lights were on as he stepped inside the office complex. There were tracks in the dust everywhere. They couldn't all be Ketchum's, he thought. He checked the lounge and locker room, the toilet, and then went to his father's office. Standing at the door, he surveyed the mess everywhere. He was surprised to see that Primary was on. He noted the stain that led out and down the hall. He kept standing there, looking around the room, waiting to feel something. Anything. It never came. On his way out, he checked the dorm, then headed for the tunnel and the dome.

Vincent applied the syrupy Pax liquid over his body as he always did when he was going to tend the hives. Moss had been gone a week now, and whatever anxiety he had suffered about being forced to leave, about having to kill him maybe, was gone. He had resumed his routine of prayer and devotions, of tending his garden, the chickens, of visiting and chatting with his friends up on the hill. He did not dwell on it, but he was concerned about what was happening in the dome: the weather, the flies, a pack rat. Moss had mentioned it and he had seen it since. Things were changing. Stripped to his loincloth and pushing the wheelbarrow, he headed toward the first hive.

Schilling was at the bulkhead, validating in his mind what he could see of his father's handiwork: the two men he'd murdered. And he could see the door had been unsealed. Somebody was inside, or had been, that was certain. With considerable effort, he got the first door open, then the second, and stepped inside the dome, unprepared for such astonishing beauty, and the silence. It made him uncomfortable. He hadn't walked a hundred meters when he saw the nearly naked old man off to his right, assembling or disassembling a stack of white wooden boxes, he wasn't sure. He moved closer, pulling the Colt from where he'd tucked it in his belt, and cocked the hammer.

Vincent saw him when he was about ten meters away, and the revolver aimed at him. The bees were swarming, looking for the intruder upsetting their hive. Vincent stopped what he was doing and stood there, looking hard and steady into Schilling's eyes, holding a tray of honeycomb. The two stared at each other for only a moment. The tic in Vincent's face that had all but disappeared over the years twitched violently, as it would so many years ago when he was about to snuff out the life of some poor soul.

Then, without a word or hesitation by either, Schilling fired at the same moment Vincent flung the tray. The impact of the magnum slug slammed into Vincent's chest, forcing his body backward onto the stack of trays that formed the hive, his body crumpling and then rolling off to one side and collapsing to the ground. And the bees came upon Schilling with a fury, filling his nostrils and his throat and ears, stinging him until he was blind and fell to the ground, writhing, puffed up by the bees' stings. He screamed until he could no longer, until his throat swelled shut. But they could not find Vincent because of the Pax.

The flies found Schilling's swollen body quickly, and went about laying their eggs in the sores and breaks in the skin even before he was dead.

And it shall come to pass in that day, that the Lord shall hiss for the fly that is in the uttermost part of the rivers of Egypt, and for the bee that is in the land of Assyria.
And they shall come, and shall rest all of them in the desolate valleys, and in the holes of the rocks, and upon all thorns, and upon all bushes. (Isaiah 7: 18-19 KJV)